THE FIRST MADAM PRESIDENT

(and the dirty bombs)

KENNETH J. KERR

Dedicated to Kryl and Kathryn
And, in memory, to my mother, Hilda M. Kerr

Table of Contents

Chapter 1

December 8th

Ann Hunt, the young CIA analyst, was escorted into the Oval Office. It was exactly nine pm. Two men and two women were standing between the two couches in quiet conversation. She walked toward her boss, CIA Director Warren Simpson, and said, "Good evening, sir." Warren greeted her and introduced her to Steve Postles, FBI Director and Jane Evans, Secretary of Homeland Security.

Rebecca Owens, the President's National Security Advisor said, "Hi, Ann. Good to see you again." Then she added to the whole group, "The President should be here in a minute. Let's wait for her so you don't have to go over everything twice."

The mood among the meeting participants was serious. Ann sensed Warren seemed a little tense.

The Oval Office door opened and the President walked in and took control, "Thank you all for coming. Please be seated and let's get started. I understand the CIA wants to pick up a couple suspected terrorists. Walk me through what we know, and what you are proposing."

The President sat in a chair and the others sat on the two off white couches

Warren Simpson began, "Madam President, as you know we believe there is a cell of Al Qaeda terrorists who are in our country with the intention of detonating one or more dirty bombs somewhere in the Washington D.C. area. Members of a prominent family in D.C. are assisting them. Earlier today, two brothers from that family eluded our people who were watching them. One of the brothers was later seen in D.C., with two other men in his car, when he stopped to pick up two additional men we believe are part of the terrorist cell. Late this afternoon, the two suspected terrorists returned to their apartment. One of the men was wearing a backpack, which he didn't have when he left his apartment early this morning. We believe the backpack may contain one of the bombs, and we believe their attack may be imminent.

"We are recommending the FBI and CIA raid the suspects' apartment, take them into custody for interrogation, and confiscate any evidence in the apartment, hopefully one of the dirty bombs."

The President was tired after a long day of meetings, but she had listened carefully to Warren's summary of the situation. She said, "Warren, I understand we arranged for one of the brothers, suspected of involvement, to purchase fake explosives and detonators, and you were monitoring the location of these materials. Where are they now?"

Warren looked at Ann and said, "Ann, why don't you answer that one."

Ann paused for a moment as she looked directly at the President and then began, "Madam President, we arranged the sale to Mohammed, the younger brother. We placed tracking devices in each of the six detonators. Mohammed put the explosives and detonators in the trunk of his car and drove to his apartment in Richmond. A few days later all the signals from the tracking devices stopped transmitting. There are two possibilities. He found the devices and destroyed them, or he is using a blocking device. I might add, if he found the devices, he may have concluded the explosives and detonators are fakes. If he tested the explosive he would know it is fake, and he may have obtained real explosives and detonators."

"Thank you, Ann. Sounds like a lot of unknowns and speculation to me."

Ann replied, "Yes Madam President. I would describe it as a lot of circumstantial evidence and educated opinions."

The President was a little surprised with Ann's passively aggressive response. "And do you think if we go to a judge requesting a search warrant based on this circumstantial evidence and educated opinion, the judge will grant us a search warrant?"

Ann said, "Questionable, Madam President."

The President had only met Ann once before, but her initial impressions of the young lady were quiet positive. She smiled inwardly realizing that the CIA Director had given Ann a more important role in this meeting.

"Ann, you and your Director were here previously on the suspected plot, and I said come back when you have more evidence that will stand up in court. Do you think we are there, yet?"

Ann responded, "Madam President, with all due respect, you may be using the wrong standard. My team is tasked with following Al Qaeda, collecting intelligence, analyzing the intelligence and the situation, and preventing another terrorist attack on the United States. Sometimes we collect intelligence in ways that would not meet the standard required in a court of law. We may have that situation facing us now. It is highly likely that a cell of terrorists plan to attack sites in Washington D.C. soon. It could be tomorrow, or the next day or several days from now. Hopefully, they are using fake explosives and will be unsuccessful. I don't want to take that chance. And Madam President, I don't think you should take that chance either. We have reliable intelligence that indicates an attack is imminent. I don't believe you want to be known as the President who had intel about an attack and did not act. There are times when the standard for evidence useable in a trial, may be too high. This may be one of those times."

The President stared at Ann. Everyone else in the room was dead silent, wondering how the President would respond to Ann's comments.

Finally, the President warmly said, "Ms. Hunt, I like a person who speaks her mind, knowing the risks involved, but believing in herself. I agree with you. Thank you for being so frank. We need more of that in this city."

The President continued, "Anybody else have an opinion on the CIA's recommendation that we raid the apartment and find out what's in the backpack?"

Homeland Security and the FBI both said they support the recommendation. Then Steve Postles added, "Madam President, we have a team standing by once we have the green light. We can implement later tonight. We will take the suspects and the backpack to Quantico where we have bomb experts and interrogation capabilities."

The President said, "You have my approval to proceed. Keep Rebecca informed. Thank you all for coming this evening."

Ann and Director Simpson walked out together. He said, "Well done, Ann. I was a little worried for a moment that you had gone too far, but tonight we learned something good about our first woman President. Thank you."

"Thank you, sir. I'm going to call Meyers at the FBI. I want to be there during the raid, and see what evidence is in the apartment."

* * *

Eleven months earlier

Carolyn Holliday awoke at five am on her first day as President of the United States. She enjoyed the smell of the fresh flowers that had been put in her bedroom, and she was amazed at how quiet the White House residence was. She still could not fully grasp that she was now the first woman president of the United States.

She got out of bed, turned on the TV to watch the news, and walked to the window to see what the weather looked like. To her surprise it had snowed during the night and the ground was covered with a couple inches of snow, and it was still snowing.

Suddenly, the door to her bedroom unexpectedly opened and a Secret Service agent entered. He calmly but firmly said, "Madam President, there has been a security breach, and we need to go to the bunker immediately."

She quickly grabbed a long coat from her closet to cover herself, and as the agent lead her by the arm, she wondered if the security problem was really serious. She decided to wait until they were at their destination before she asked any questions.

When they arrived at the bunker, another Secret Service agent informed her that an individual, across the street from the White House perimeter, had aimed a rifle with a high power scope at the White House and fired two shots. He had been subdued, without any injuries, taken into custody, and was being questioned. The President was escorted back to her residence. She was pleased to realize that she had not been afraid or panicked when the Secret Service agent burst into her bedroom. On the way back to her residence, she asked the agent, "How often does this kind of thing happen?"

He responded, "There is no way to know what the frequency will be, Madam President. During the last year, we only had a few incidents, three or four."

The President sat at her breakfast table enjoying a cup of coffee. She was thinking about the grueling campaign and how happy she was that it was over. She was now presiding over a country where the voters had put the presidency in the hands of a Democrat and both houses of Congress in the control of the Republicans.

The divide in philosophy of government was enormous. She was facing the hardest decisions of her life. She could govern holding to her liberal beliefs and do battle with the Republicans on every important issue facing the country. Or she could try to find common ground with the Congress and avoid four years of a do nothing government.

It would not be easy. If she abandoned her liberal base she would likely be a one-term president, but if she could build the relationships necessary with the Republican leaders in the Senate and the House, she had a chance to break the Washington gridlock, make history, and make the country strong again. She would reach out to the Republicans and begin to mend some fences and unite the country.

Carolyn Holliday had made her reputation as a leader when she was the Governor of California. The state government, like the federal government, was split by strong philosophical differences on priorities and how to solve the problems. She forged alliances with the opposition and found solutions that both sides initially were against, but eventually both sides came to understand that a partial win for each was a better solution than no progress at all.

Carolyn was a very attractive, distinguished woman who had just celebrated her sixtieth birthday. She was almost five feet ten, with black hair that she wore shoulder length. It was beginning to show a little gray, but she didn't bend to the temptation of having it colored. Her wardrobe consisted of almost a dozen business suits, most of them with skirts rather than pants. She always wore a very elegant silk blouse under the suit coat. She had far more blouses than she did suits. For evening activities and more formal events she had many elegant dresses for those occasions.

She grew up in San Francisco and graduated from UC Berkeley in the early eighties. She met John, her future husband, at Berkeley during her senior year. After graduation, she went to law school and he began work in a small technology company just south of San Francisco. He soon left to start his own company with a couple of his friends from Berkeley. When Carolyn finished law school, John convinced her that his company needed help with a variety of legal issues, and she joined the company as chief legal counsel. One year later, they were married. A few years later, John took the company public and suddenly the Hollidays were very wealthy. Carolyn enjoyed the business world, especially the experience of working with Goldman Sachs and JP Morgan during the initial public offering. But she yearned to return to academia and teach law. She remained on the Board of John's company when she joined the faculty at Stanford. While teaching at Stanford, she became involved in the political scene in California, first as an appointed Commissioner on the California Public Utility Commission (CPUC). That was followed by several other committees and boards that were part of the California government system.

John's company continued to grow and expand internationally which required frequent trips to Asia. Occasionally, Carolyn would join him on a trip, especially when his itinerary included meetings with important government leaders.

While teaching at Stanford, Carolyn was impressed by one of her students, Judy Webber. She was small, only five two, and quiet slender, but what she lacked in physical stature she made up for with her intelligence, work ethic, and her confident attitude. Carolyn became Judy's unofficial mentor and they developed a very close friendship. After law school, Judy became her administrative assistant, and theirs became a lifelong relationship.

Carolyn and John, with their new wealth, became active in the San Francisco social scene. Eventually, she was persuaded to take a step into politics and run for Mayor of San Francisco. She lost the election, but learned a lot about politics. Some of it she liked and some she did not. She definitely was attracted to the power, but she detested the shady deals that went on behind the scenes.

Later, she ran for Governor of California, won, and served two terms. Judy had been very active behind the scenes in her campaigns, but when Carolyn asked her to be her Chief of Staff, Judy politely declined. After a lengthy discussion, Judy persuaded Carolyn that she could be more effective as a less visible, silent advisor and counselor.

While Carolyn was Governor, John contracted an infectious disease during one of his trips to Thailand, and after a year fighting the disease, he passed away. Carolyn was grief stricken, but poured herself into her job. After John's death, her friendship with Judy became even stronger as she leaned on her for strength.

When John first contracted the disease and was hospitalized, it made headline news because he was the husband of the Governor of California, and the CEO of a very successful technology company. After his death the story was again covered in the press, but little was mentioned about the specifics of the disease. The press generally liked the Governor, and left her alone to grieve her loss.

The Hollidays never had children.

Carolyn, while finishing her breakfast, thought back to her inaugural address. She was pleased with the tone of the speech and the balance between articulating her strong liberal ideals and the need to reach out to the Republican lead Congress to find ways to work together. She knew John would have been proud.

* * *

Paul Marino asked, "What did you think?"

Robert Wolf (R), Speaker of the House, and Paul Marino (R), Senate Majority Leader were having their first regular breakfast meeting since the President took her oath of office. Paul always hosted these meetings in the Senate Dining Room. Robert was from South Carolina. It was easy to tell he was from the south when he opened his mouth and turned on his southern charm, always speaking slowly with an educated, southern accent.

Physically he was a large man, six feet three inches tall and just over two hundred and fifty pounds. He still had a full head of hair although it was now gray, or as Robert insisted, silver. His fellow Republicans in the House had nicknamed him the Silver Fox, both for his physical appearance and his negotiating skills.

Paul was shorter, just less than six feet, and much more physically fit. His fitness routine was to jog three days a week and exercise in the gym three days a week. He rested on Sundays. Unlike Robert, he was nearly bald and wore wire-rimmed glasses.

In his slow, southern drawl, Robert said, "I assume you are referring to Madam President's inaugural address, Paul." He paused and then went on, "I thought she gave a very good speech. Luckily it wasn't too long so we didn't have to worry about freezing to death. Obviously, I disagree with most of her priorities, but she said the right things about wanting to work with Congress to accomplish things for the sake of the country. At least that is a refreshing change. Only time will tell if she was sincere." Robert had serious doubts about the President's sincerity, but he kept his doubts to himself.

"I agree," added Paul. "She is one tough lady, and she is about as liberal as the last guy, maybe even more so, but she is smart enough to know she has to find some things we can all work on together. It will be interesting to see how long before we hear from her and what tack she takes to get things moving forward. I think we should show some initiative and develop our own list of priorities, like she did in her speech. Then we can urge her to work with us on defining one list of priorities that we can work on together."

Robert was worried that Paul was too eager to compromise. He responded, "Don't you think we should just wait awhile and see if she takes the initiative?"

"No, I think we should be proactive so she can't continue to label us as the 'do nothing Congress'. I will have my staff draft a list of priorities and you can have a look at it and make suggestions for minor changes, ok?"

"Deal", commented Robert.

A few days later, Robert Wolf received a "confidential" letter from the Senate Majority Leader. Attached to the brief letter was the following list of priorities:

> Budget
> Health Care Reform (ACA, Medicaid, and Medicare)
> Debt limit
> Corporate income tax reform
> Individual income tax reform
> Business friendly regulatory reform
> Social Security reform
> Immigration reform, both legal and illegal

The Speaker reviewed the list with his staff and his leadership committee. They agreed this was an acceptable starting point.

The same day the Speaker was discussing the priorities with his staff, he received an invitation from the President to visit the White House for an informal meeting with the majority and minority leaders of the Senate and the House of Representatives. She said her objective was to discuss working with Congress to address the problems of the country. She included with the letter an attachment showing her list of major priorities.

> Budget
> Immigration reform
> Debt limit
> Regulatory reform
> Income tax reform
> Health Care Reform

* * *

The President began, "Jim, I thought we should sit together and talk about how things are going to work between us. You know I am going to depend on your help with members of Congress. With your long career in both the House and Senate, and the fact that I have no experience in that area, you can make a major contribution because of your relationships."

The President and the Vice President were having their first working lunch together since being sworn in. The Vice President,

Jim Townsend, had spent his political career first in the House and then moving to the Senate. He was from New York, and was chosen to be the Vice Presidential candidate more to bring a geographical balance to the ticket than for any other specific capability. He was a capable legislator, and had many friends in Washington. He was tall and handsome with greying, thinning hair, and his wife was a high-powered lawyer in one of Washington's leading law firms.

Carolyn knew that Jim, like most Vice Presidents, was concerned about his role in the administration. She wanted to keep him motivated and feeling like he was an important part of her team. She knew she would need his help with Congress.

"Thank you, Madam President. Before I respond I have a serious question. Must I call you Madam President all the time, or can we make an exception when we are having a private meeting, like this?"

Carolyn smiled and said, "Jim, call me Carolyn when it is just us. When others are present, showing respect for the office, address me as Madam President. Likewise, I will address you as Mr. Vice President in front of others."

"I appreciate that very much, Carolyn. Back to your comment, I will be happy to use my personal relationships with members of the House and Senate to help move your agenda through the congressional process. They have some unusual rules and procedures in both the Senate and the House, plus there are many oversized egos to manage. I encourage you to use me when you see a difficult situation developing."

"Jim, beyond your relationship with Congress, I want you to feel like you are free to involve yourself in other areas where you have a strong personal interest. If you want to learn more about a particular issue, or if you feel you can bring some expertise, feel free to jump in and join the fun."

"Thank you, Carolyn."

"One other subject I want to discuss is our selection process for the long list of job openings we have in our new administration. The process is well underway, but I want to explain my philosophy and then hear some thoughts from you. First, I want to find the most qualified candidates for every job. I especially want to give women opportunities in our government, beyond where previous administrations have gone. However, to be considered for a job, their qualification is obviously of the utmost importance."

The President continued, "Let me also comment on cronyism. There is too much of that in our government today. Don't misunderstand me, being a good friend or a generous contributor should not automatically disqualify someone from consideration for an important job, but that person must have all the skills needed for the job and be qualified beyond any doubt.

"Jim, share some of your thoughts on the important criteria needed to work in our administration."

Jim thought for a moment and responded, "Intelligence, good judgment, excellent resume of meaningful experience, no flaws in their personal background, and political philosophy that matches ours. Those are a few that come to mind off the top of my head."

Carolyn said, "I would add a few others like, unquestionable moral character, and willing to say what they believe even if it conflicts with my opinion. They must also be a team player, meaning they can fight for a different position but they must be willing to accept and fully support my final decision. I want to choose people who are willing to do what is best for the country, even if it may not necessarily mesh totally with their political beliefs. I want people who have a strong legal and moral compass, and follow it even when tempted to do something by any means to accomplish the desired end.

"Jim, I also want your help as a sounding board. I am extremely comfortable with my judgment and decision making ability. Having said that, I often look at the problem and ask myself, 'what would a man do?' Because I am the first woman in this job, I want to be able to look back on my decisions and be confident I made the best decisions for the country, based on what we knew at the time. I will always listen to input if you think I am making the wrong decision or a bad decision. I may disagree and go ahead with my decision, but I want people around me who are willing to give me their input, especially you."

The President spent much of her time working with her transition team on hiring people for her administration. She was obsessive about hiring the best person for the job, while giving women every opportunity she could find. In the end, for the first time in history, women filled a majority of the Cabinet level posts.

Martha O'Rourke, an outstanding CEO from private industry became Secretary of State. Linda Bennett, a personal friend and highly successful executive at Goldman Sachs, was persuaded to join the administration as Treasury Secretary. General Jane Evans, from the Pentagon, retired from the U.S. Army and accepted the position of Secretary of Homeland Security. And many other women found themselves serving in significant positions throughout Carolyn Holliday's administration. Judy Webber, after long discussions with her dear friend and boss, agreed to become the President's Chief of Staff.

* * *

Paul Marino and Robert Wolf travelled together to the White House meeting.
Charlie Banfield (D), Senate Minority Leader and Steve Caldwell (D), House Minority Leader, also shared a car. It was a cold and windy winter day when they arrived at the White House. Clouds were forming for another snowstorm. They passed through security and were escorted to the Cabinet Room. Jim Townsend, the Vice President, was waiting to greet them all.

The room itself was impressive. A large rosewood table, large enough to accommodate eight people on each side was centered in the room. At one end of the room was an old fireplace with one of the many historic paintings that adorned the White House. One of the long walls of the room had three large windows, and the opposite wall had more historical paintings displayed. Behind the chair where the President would sit, were the American flag and the Presidential flag. After everyone found their designated seats at the table, the door opened and the President and her Chief of Staff walked in. Everyone stood.

The President walked around the table greeting each participant with a warm smile and a handshake. The four leaders of Congress were seated on one side of the long table and the President, her Chief of Staff, and the Vice President, were seated on the other side of the table. There were bottles of water and glasses placed in front of each participant. Regardless of the size of the meeting, the room and all its history created a powerful environment.

As she returned to her seat and settled herself, she began, "Welcome to the White House. I know this is not your first time visiting, but this is the first time I have invited all of you here. I consider this possibly the most important meeting we will have, because it will set the tone for all things to come. We all have a choice. The government of the United States has gotten progressively more gridlocked over the recent decades. We can continue to perpetuate the gridlock by standing firm on our principles, or we can all work together to unite this great country under our leadership. I am not naïve to think the Republicans will suddenly accept all my liberal ideas, nor should they think I awakened today and realized that I am now a conservative. What I do believe is that we can agree to work together, respecting each other's principles, while looking for ways to find common ground on the important issues.

"When I sent your invitation to 'my party' today, I included a list of my priorities. Senator Marino and Speaker Wolf, you may be surprised to learn that Senator Banfield and Congressman Caldwell were not consulted on that list of priorities. So I don't even have a consensus within my own party yet, but I thought the list was a good starting point to try to reach an agreement on what the legislative priorities should be. Not for the Democrats and not for the Republicans, but for the country. I have heard a rumor that without any prodding from me, the leadership of the Senate and the House has already developed its own list of priorities. Well done. This may give us an alternative starting point. Now all we have to do is find a way to reconcile the lists into one that we can all agree on. Then we can start the process of addressing the top priority and eventually work our way through the list. I think there are enough things on the list to keep us busy for my first term. And when my liberal supporters find out I am working closely with the opposition, I may only have one term. So, let's get to work.

"I would like to go around the room and let each of you express your thoughts on the process. Anyone want to go first?"

Senate Majority Leader Marino took the initiative and said, "Madam President, first let me offer my personal congratulations to you on becoming our President. It is refreshing to hear your comments regarding working with the Congress. I think your approach is a sound one, and I can assure you we look forward to working with you. I acknowledge that there has been and still is, a wide divide between liberals and conservatives, but the country has spoken and it is our responsibility to find solutions to the many problems facing this great nation."

"Thank you, Senator Marino." The President thought Marino had made a good start. It was nice in tone, but short of any real substance, but expected as a starting point.

Speaker Wolf went next, speaking slowly in his southern drawl. "Madam President, I echo all of Senator Marino's comments. I am sure you are aware of the deep distrust that exists in Washington. You have a huge challenge to overcome. We'll give you the benefit of the doubt, and assume, for now, that you are sincere. It is a refreshing change. We don't expect you to agree to everything the Republicans want to do. But we do hope you will listen to our ideas, even though they may be very different from yours, and work with us to find common ground for the good of our country. It is time to break the gridlock."

Again, politically correct, thought the President. I wonder how the Democrats will respond.

"Thank you, Speaker Wolf. I appreciate your forthrightness. I will make the same assumption you made regarding sincerity. I will trust you are sincere, until you give me a reason to think otherwise."

Senator Banfield decided it was his turn. Charlie Banfield was an old fashion Texas Democrat. He was a big man, physically, nearly six feet two with wide shoulders and a big chest. Unfortunately, his stomach was also getting larger. He had a full crop of silver hair, and occasionally wore black-rimmed glasses. He could have passed for Lyndon Johnson's brother or cousin. The similarity was so strong that a few of his closest friends had nicknamed him Lynde. With his best Texas drawl he began, "Well Madam President, it is obvious there is a new sheriff in town. My feelings were a little hurt when you didn't reach out to Congressman Caldwell and me prior to this meeting, but we'll all get to know each other and our styles as we work together. I don't like the gridlock in Washington any more than you do, Madam President. I'm hopeful Senator Marino will allow us to actively participate in the legislative process, even though we are the minority party."

Senator Marino responded, "Senator, your President has reached out to all of us to work together. Let's all start with an optimistic attitude. There will be time for positioning later. You don't have to start it today."

Now it is heating up a little, thought the President. Also predictable from our Senator from Texas.

She added, "Thank you for you comments, Senator Banfield. Congressman Caldwell, would you like to add your thoughts?"

"Thank you, Madam President. I sense we are experiencing a new beginning in Washington, and it is time. I know there are difficult days ahead, and it will not be easy to reconcile our differences, but I can assure you the Democrats in the House will work with you, Madam President, to solve the many problems facing our great country."

"Thank you Congressman Caldwell." President Holliday continued, "Gentlemen, I have a suggestion. The most polarizing issue facing our country is health care. It is very unpopular with a majority in the country and even though the Affordable Care Act (ACA) was the Democrat's crowning achievement, I am willing to put it back on the table. I don't know if repeal and replacement is the right answer or major modifications to the existing law is a better solution, but the status quo is unacceptable to me. I suggest, as a major concession by the Democrats, we put the Affordable Care Act third on the list, just after the budget and debt issues. Additionally, I am willing to include Medicare and Medicaid reform together with the ACA. I do that to show I am serious about working together."

The Senate Minority Leader and the House Minority Leader both winced, but reluctantly agreed. The group spent another hour and a half discussing the list of priorities and left the meeting in agreement. The President thanked them all for their comments and support.

The new, agreed List of Priorities would be used in the President's upcoming State of the Union address.

Agreed List of Priorities

Budget
Debt limit
Health Care Reform
Immigration Reform
Corporate Tax Reform
Individual Tax Reform
Regulatory Reform
Social Security Reform

* * *

When the President didn't have a dinner meeting, she and Judy would frequently dine together, in the President's residence. It was a small dining room that the President had redecorated to make it feel warm and casual. She always had fresh flowers in the room to give it a fresh, pleasant fragrance. Carolyn had convinced Judy to live in the White House in a separate suite that was adjacent to the President's private residence. Judy had never married, and had dated infrequently. Her life, after law school, was primarily devoted to assisting Carolyn.

Judy was clearly Carolyn's closest friend and advisor.

She was born in the Bronx, and came from a large family of six brothers and sisters. She was the youngest. She had gone to public school through high school and graduated from NYU with a degree in Political Science before moving to California to pursue her law degree at Stanford.

She rarely visited her family. On the rare occasion Carolyn questioned her about them, she kept her answers simple, saying she had moved on and didn't have much in common with them any more.

Over dinner one night Carolyn asked Judy why her parents didn't attend the inaugural celebration. Judy responded that they were elderly now and not in very good health. Carolyn said, "You should be sure you stay in touch with your parents and siblings. Anytime you want or need to go see them, please do. Things will always be hectic around here, but family is important."

Carolyn was from a small family, with only one younger sister. Her parents had both died while she was Governor, her father first and her mother one year later, both from cancer. Her younger sister, Julie, lived in Newport Beach, California with her husband and three children, all girls. Carolyn and Julie talked on the phone on a regular basis, but their lives were so different they had little in common.

Carolyn asked Judy, "How do you think the meeting went with the congressional leaders?"

"They all said the right things. I was a little surprised we made as much progress as we did. It was great getting agreement on the list of priorities. Frankly, I think you might have more trouble with your Democrat colleagues than the Republicans. Reading the body language, Senator Banfield and Congressman Caldwell both seemed uncomfortable. Obviously they don't like being in the minority, but I think they may be concerned that you are going to lessen their influence even more by working directly with Senator Marino and Speaker Wolf."

"Interesting, I sensed the same thing. We will need to give Banfield and Caldwell some extra attention to help their egos. Maybe the Vice President can help. I am curious how you read Marino and Wolf? I am walking a delicate line with them, wanting to show them I want to work with them and find solutions we can all live with, but I don't want them to misread my intentions as weakness."

Judy replied, "I am sure they will test you soon to see how 'weak' you are. You established a good beginning today, and you're on the right track."

"Thanks, Judy. I think I am going to do some reading and then try to get comfortable with sleeping in the White House. I wonder if we ever get use to it?"

"I am sure you will, Madam President. Good night."

"Good night, Judy. Let's have breakfast in the morning."

As the President left the room she thought to herself how lucky she was to have Judy as a sounding board for her ideas and her perspective on people. She was pleased she had Judy as a confidant and a friend.

That began a routine of the two having breakfast together almost every morning. Once in a while they would have a visitor join them, but generally it was a private time for the two of them.

Chapter 2

During the U.S. war in Afghanistan, the Taliban and Al Qaeda used villages in the rugged mountainous region of northwestern Pakistan known as Waziristan. The U.S. had used drones to strike repeatedly at human targets within this region with some success. The Pakistan government had no control over the region, but they were offended that the U.S. persisted in continuing the drone strikes over their objections. The Pakistan government walked a delicate line with the U.S. They needed the billions in foreign aid the U.S. provided, but they pushed their objections to the drone attacks as aggressively as they dared.

Akbar Khan, the leader of an Al Qaeda cell, lived in the village of Damadola in the Bajour tribal area of northwest Pakistan. He had been trained in Afghanistan when bin Laden was alive, and he was still in contact with Al Qaeda's Ayman al Zawahiri, bin Laden's successor. Akbar and his cell were in the advanced stages of planning an attack on Washington D.C.

Akbar was in his late thirties, but most of his fighters, numbering only fifteen, were in their twenties. He was a rugged man with little education, but a natural leader. He was tall, nearly six feet, with a full beard and a full head of black hair. He was a fierce fighter, and had demonstrated his courage on many occasions. He was lucky to have survived some of the battles.

His number two, Faisal Uzmani, was traveling by car, with three other fighters, into Afghanistan to the border with Iran. They carried with them two million dollars in U.S currency. Their mission was to buy three packages of uranium yellow cake from a contact in the Republican Guard of Iran. They met in an Afghanistan border town just inside Afghanistan in the middle of the night to make the transfer. The leader of the Pakistanis could tell the Iranians were nervous and at one point he felt like the deal would come apart and they would be killed. But the leader of the Iranian group took control of the situation and sent them on their way. The yellow cake was in lead shielded packages, to protect from radiation, and placed in three backpacks. Two million dollars was given to the Iranians and the Pakistanis drove away with three backpacks filled with enough yellow cake to make three dirty bombs. Now all they had to do was drive back across Afghanistan without being stopped and searched by an Afghan patrol. They were making good time but came around a bend in the road and were facing an Afghan checkpoint. They pulled to a stop, waiting for the Afghans to approach their car and question them. Luckily the Afghans were tired, just looked in the windows, and didn't make them get out of the car or search the backpacks. They were waved through the checkpoint and continued along their route back to Pakistan.

Akbar was excited when the four arrived from their trip across Afghanistan. He complimented them on their success and said, "This is a great day for our cause. We will bring the U.S. to its knees for their brutal killing of our great leader, Osama bin Laden."

A few days later Akbar had arranged the transport of the three backpacks to Karachi where they were packed inside a container of agricultural products that would go on a ship bound for Mexico.

* * *

Ann Hunt had interviewed for a job with the CIA during her senior year of college, and by the time she graduated she had passed all the requirements to work for the spy agency. She was five feet six inches tall, slender and very attractive. Her hair was auburn and shoulder length, but she usually wore it back in a ponytail. She was obsessed with eating the right foods, and exercising to keep herself in good shape.

She had talked to her Dad, Jim, extensively after he informed her on her eighteenth birthday that he was an undercover agent working for the CIA. She thought he had joined Dow Chemical after serving in the Army during the Vietnam War. He explained to her that he had been recruited by the CIA while in college and had worked for them in Vietnam. After serving in the army he had decided to pursue a business career instead of staying with the CIA, but circumstances had caused him to rejoin the CIA while using the cover of working for Dow.

Jim explained that he had not told her earlier because of the risk she might leak the information, but now she was mature enough to keep the confidential side of his life secret. Jim had never liked keeping secrets from Ann, and he was glad the day had come when he could tell her about his secret life.

Ann had three diverse skills. First, she had an almost photographic memory. Second, she had a real talent for learning foreign languages. She learned Mandarin while living with her parents in Hong Kong. She majored in languages in college, and was now proficient in Russian, French, and Arabic. Finally, she was a computer wiz. In addition to her language major, she also majored in computer science.

At the CIA, she had been hired as an analyst and was sent to special training on computers. She was taught by the CIA to become a master hacker.

She now worked as a team leader at CIA headquarters in Langley where the team was tasked with keeping track of Al Qaeda and all its affiliates. Her assignment, in addition to being the team leader, was to follow the money. Her team was in frequent contact with CIA operatives throughout the world who were gathering intelligence on Al Qaeda cells and their activities. Ann spent her time working to understand how Al Qaeda financed their activities. There was not a bank anywhere in the world that she could not penetrate. She looked at the money flowing in and out of accounts.

Her team had recently received intelligence from an agent in Iran that the Republican Guard was rumored to have sold some uranium yellow cake to someone. The intel didn't identify the buyer, but the quantity of yellow cake was reportedly enough to make several dirty bombs.

Ann monitored the bank accounts of the Republican Guard in Iran to see if she could identify money flowing into their accounts. A few days after the intel came from Iran, she saw a deposit of one million eight hundred thousand US dollars into one of the Republican Guard accounts.

There was no evidence that the one million eight hundred thousand dollars was related to a yellow cake sale, but it was suspicious enough to pass the information up the ladder.

Ann's team contacted operatives in several countries as well as the NSA to be on the alert for any activity related to making one or more dirty bombs. Among the list of countries most likely involved were Yemen, Libya, Afghanistan, Syria, and Pakistan.

A few days later, NSA contacted Ann and informed her they had picked up some chatter about yellow cake in Pakistan. They were still working on the specific people involved, but one of them was definitely a senior official in Pakistan's powerful intelligence service, the Inter-Services Intelligence (ISI).

Ann went to work on the known ISI banks and found two accounts controlled by the senior official identified by NSA. Looking at his accounts she noticed a recent withdrawal of two million dollars from one of them. She could not identify who the recipient was because the money was not transferred to another account, but simply withdrawn as cash.

A two million dollar withdrawal by a Pakistani official of the ISI and a one point eight million dollar deposit into a Republican Guard bank account in Iran within several days of each other, was this a coincidence or were they related transactions? Ann discussed it with her team and they decided it was important enough to send the information upstairs.

Warren Simpson, the new Director of the Central Intelligence Agency, had started his career with the Army Military Intelligence and after a few years moved to the CIA. He was tall, with short thinning hair, and carried himself like a military man. He had finally succumbed to wearing horn-rimmed glasses after denying the need for several years. He had spent his time with the CIA working his way up the ladder to become the Director of Clandestine Operations. When the Director of the CIA retired, he was promoted to Director of the CIA. This was somewhat unusual because the Director was usually a political appointment. During his time at the CIA he had developed good working relationships with the Congressional oversight committees and Homeland Security, and one of the first appointments by the new President was to promote him to Director of the CIA. His confirmation through Congress had gone smoothly.

Jack Clark, the new Director of the National Security Agency was meeting in Warren's office.

"Jack, I think we have signs of a potential problem brewing. Our people picked up some intelligence about the Iranians selling yellow cake to someone to make several dirty bombs."

Jack responded, "Yes, our people picked up some chatter in Pakistan that we believe might have been related to the yellow cake. We passed that info on to your analysts."

"I know, and we appreciate the help. Our super hacker saw a deposit into a Republican Guard bank account around the time of the alleged yellow cake sale, and she saw a similar amount withdrawn from a bank account of Pakistan's ISI."

"Warren I don't know how well you know the President, but I suggest you set up a meeting right away and bring her up to speed with what we know. I'll attend if you want, but I don't think it is necessary at this point."

"Thanks, Jack. It sounds like we are on the same page. I'll get to the President as soon as I can arrange it, and I'll let you know what happens at the meeting. Can you put a high priority on signals in and out of the ISI and others in Pakistan to see what else we might pick up?"

"Will do. Keep us in the loop on any operation that may be related to this one, and we will keep all our ears open."

The following morning Warren walked into the White House for a meeting with President Holliday. She had her National Security Advisor, Rebecca Owens, with her for the meeting. The President said, "Warren, you have the floor. Tell us what you have."

Warren told them about the suspected sale of yellow cake by the Iranian Republican Guard to unknown people. He explained that a deposit in the range of two million dollars was observed in a bank account controlled by the Republican Guard, and a few days prior a withdrawal of a similar amount occurred in Pakistan. "Madam President, we believe the money came from a senior official in Pakistan's ISI. We have a lot more work to do, but I thought you needed to know about a potential terrorist plot to make several dirty bombs for use somewhere in the world, possibly the U.S."

The President asked, "At this time you have no information on where or when this plot will take place?"

"No, Madam President, but I thought it was important enough to give you the information we have at this point. The NSA is in the loop, and will pay particular attention to communications into and out of Pakistan to see if we can learn more."

"Do you need anything from me?" asked the President.

"No, Madam President. Not at this time."

Carolyn thanked Warren for the briefing, and asked him to keep Rebecca informed as more information became available.

As the meeting ended, Carolyn was pleased with the way her new CIA Director had handled himself during the briefing. She wanted to build a good relationship with him, because she knew she needed someone in that position she could trust.

* * *

The container ship arrived at the port of Manzanillo in the state of Colima, Mexico. Once it was properly docked and cleared immigration and customs, the dockworkers began off-loading the containers. Manzanillo has one of the largest container ports on the west coast of Mexico.

A Pakistani living in Mexico City had received a message from Pakistan with the name of the ship, the number of the container, and the estimated arrival date. He had a contact in the port at Manzanillo who would contact him when the ship arrived. When he received the call, he immediately contacted his two friends who would ride with him to Manzanillo to pick up the backpacks. He had paid the port employee well, and with his help they would enter the secure storage area where the containers were stacked awaiting pickup for delivery, mostly to Mexico City.

When they arrived in Manzanillo it was late afternoon. It was hot and humid, even with the stiff wind that blew from the west. The Pakistani called the port employee and arranged to meet at a little bar near the waterfront at ten o'clock that night.

The three men from Mexico City were waiting when Ricardo, the port employee, arrived. The bar was one of several frequented by the dockworkers, but at this late hour, it was pretty quiet. It was poorly lit with a long bar and stools along one side and several wooden booths along the other side. The smell of beer and cigarettes and human sweat permeated the atmosphere. Two ceiling fans were moving the air around and helping a little, but it was still hot. The front door was left open and the sounds from the street found their way into the bar. They had a round of drinks while the local explained how he would get them into the storage area. He had checked the computer and knew exactly where the container was stored. He explained, "There are a few security officers that patrol the yard at night, but they are all pretty lazy and should not be a problem. If one sees us in the yard, don't say anything. I will be able to convince him that we are authorized to open a container to retrieve some packages for one of the officials of the port." He assured them it would not be a problem. If necessary he would give the guard a little money for his troubles. His final comment was, "Going in now is better than trying to sneak in at two or three in the morning. That would be more suspicious to the guards if they happen to see us."

The Pakistani drove them to a parking lot near the entrance, following Ricardo's instructions. Everyone except Ricardo was armed, and one of the men carried a pair of heavy bolt cutters stowed in a canvas bag. The storage yard was well lit for security, and looked deserted. Ricardo unlocked the gate and the three men followed him into the storage yard.

He looked at his piece of paper where he had written the container number and location. The containers were stacked three high, in neat rows. He led the others around containers until he found the right container on the ground level near the fence that surrounded the storage yard.

When they were sure they had the right container, the one with the bolt cutters placed them on the lock and squeezed. It cracked after a little exertion. He removed the lock from the container, and put the lock and bolt cutters back in his bag. The Pakistani grabbed the door handle of the container and it gave a loud screech as it opened. He wondered if any of the guards had heard the noise. He knew exactly where to look, and told his two helpers to start unloading the bags along the left side of the container. The bags were fifty-pound bags of rice. They had removed about thirty bags, stacking them outside the container, when they found the three backpacks. The Pakistani lifted the first backpack and placed in carefully on the ground. As he finished removing the second and third backpacks he heard a voice.

A guard came around the corner of the container and exclaimed in Spanish, "What are you guys doing?"

Ricardo looked at the guard and said, "Pedro, it is me, Ricardo. My boss asked me to get some things out of this container for him. These men are helping me."

The Pakistani was standing near the three backpacks and his two men were standing close to him, but a little closer to the guard. They all stood frozen.

Pedro said, "Ricardo, I didn't recognize you at first." He looked on the ground and noticed the backpacks. "What's in the backpacks?"

"I don't know, Pedro. My boss just said to get them out of this container and put them in his office."

Pedro grinned and said, "Let's see what's in them. Maybe I'll take one and you can just tell your boss that there were only two backpacks."

The Pakistani sensed trouble. He quickly reached behind his back and drew his Sig Sauer 9mm and shot the guard in the head. He then aimed at Ricardo and shot him in the head. Luckily, he had a silencer on his Sig so it sounded like someone sneezed twice. Both men dropped to the ground, dead.

The Pakistani said to his two helpers, "Throw those two bodies in the container and get those bags of rice back in the container quickly, so we can get out of here." He knelt down over Ricardo and went through his pockets to retrieve the envelope of money he had given him earlier. He also checked to see what else he might have on him that would be a problem. He took the piece of paper that showed the container number and location and he took his keys. He left his wallet untouched.

They had the two bodies and all the rice back in the container within a few minutes. The Pakistani wiped up most of the blood and threw the rag inside the container. He then closed the door as quietly as he could, quickly wiped the handle with his handkerchief, and said, "Let's get the backpacks and your canvas bag and quietly walk out of here."

As they walked out the gate, the Pakistani stopped to lock it with the extra keys he now carried.

The three walked to their car, placed the backpacks and canvas bag in the trunk, got in the car, drove away, and didn't look back.

The Pakistani was thinking to himself about the whole incident. It didn't bother him killing the guard and Ricardo. But now he realized he had to take care of the two men riding in the back seat. He decided to drive for a while before he addressed his problem.

The drive to Mexico City was quiet with no one wanting to talk about what had happened. They had been driving for a little more than an hour when the Pakistani said, "I think I might stop somewhere to get a few hours sleep. Is that ok with you guys?"

"Fine by me," replied the first helper. "OK with me, too," said the other one. He added, "What's in the backpacks?"

The Pakistani turned around and shot them both between the eyes. The shots caused him to swerve, and he almost collided with an oncoming car. The other driver blasted his horn and drove on by.

He drove along looking for a remote area to pull off the road onto a side road. After about a mile, when he was sure there was no one else around, he pulled off the road, turned off his lights, and dragged the two bodies into a ravine just off the edge of the road. He took their wallets and guns and anything else that might help the officials identify them, walked back to the car and put all their stuff in the canvas bag with the bolt cutters. He was hot and sweating and tired, but he got back in the car and drove to Mexico City.

* * *

Ann was typing on her computer when one of her team members walked up to her workstation.

"I think we may have another lead," George said. "I just had a call from one of our operatives in Mexico. There is a cargo container from Pakistan in the storage yard in Manzanillo, and the authorities just found two dead bodies in the container."

George was Ann's closest friend on her team. He had been at the CIA as long as Ann, but he was clearly not management material. He was your typical nerd who loved computers and research and developing scenarios. He was very good at what he did. He was five ten, a little over weight, with brown hair, which was always disheveled. He was a great team player, and Ann liked having him on her team.

Ann asked, "Pakistani bodies or locals?"

"One of the dead men was a guard in the storage yard and the other worked in the port admin office. They have been dead for a few days. One of the workers noticed some blood near the container, found the container unlocked, and the two bodies inside. The Mexican's are investigating but don't have much to go on.

"The container was about half full of rice, and was shipped from Karachi to a company in Mexico City. The company doesn't exist, and the address and phone number on the paperwork were bogus. It sounds like something else was shipped to Mexico in the container, and the people who retrieved whatever they were looking for, may have been discovered by the guard. He and the port administrator were shot and put in the container.

Ann asked, "Any chance the container was used to get some people from Pakistan into Mexico?"

"No, the container was pretty air tight and there was no evidence of any people being part of the cargo. Not impossible, but unlikely. I think the administrator probably helped others get into the storage yard. Why else would he be in the container?"

Ann replied, "Interesting. And you think the 'something in the container' may have been the yellow cake?"

"Possible. Obviously it also could have been drugs, but as far as we know, this is not a normal way for the drug cartels to import drugs."

Ann suggested, "I think you should call our guy in Mexico and have him do two things. One, take a Geiger counter and see if he can detect any level of radiation above normal in the container. It's a long shot, but we should try. Second, he needs to investigate the dead administrator's background. Maybe we can find some contact he had recently that might give us a clue as to who broke in and claimed whatever was in the container."

"I'll get right on it."

Ann added, "Let's get our team together and brainstorm how they might try to smuggle the yellow cake into the U.S., if in fact that is what was in the container. Let's also draw up a timeline, and see if it suggests that the yellow cake may already be in the U.S. or is still in Mexico."

Ann thought to herself, this is a data point showing that the U.S. may be the target for the dirty bombs. It is still only circumstantial, but I have a bad feeling about what lies ahead. We really need to find the men who are coming with the yellow cake. I wonder if they will risk trying to get the bombs across the Mexican border or will they try to do it some other way. I wonder how hard it would be to smuggle someone into the U.S. by boat, coming into California or Texas by sea? What should we do to try to catch them?

Chapter 3

The U.S. economy was growing stronger after the great recession of the twenty first century. Tax revenues were continuing to grow, and the annual deficit was now under a trillion dollars. The entitlements in the budget continued to grow out of control, which put pressure on the discretionary items in the budget. Allowing for no growth in discretionary items, the estimate for the deficit for the next fiscal year was seven hundred billion dollars. If the economy continued to strengthen, additional revenues could reduce the deficit further, or allow additional spending on discretionary items.

Speaker Wolf met with Bill Sharp, Chairman of the House Finance Committee, and their staffs.

Robert began with his southern drawl, "Bill, thanks for coming today. You probably heard I was invited to my first meeting at the White House with our new President. Minority leader Caldwell was there as were Senators Marino and Banfield. It was a friendly meeting where President Holliday made her case for bipartisanship and the end of Washington gridlock. I will have to say she was impressive and sounded sincere, but I am skeptical. The proof will be in her actions, not her words, but I am feeling cautiously optimistic. If she follows through on what she said in the meeting, I think she will have more problems getting the Democrats in Congress to work with her than she will with us.

"We agreed to a list of broad priorities and the Budget and Debt Limit are numbers one and two on the list. You need to press your committee to have a budget for the House to vote on within sixty days. And you need to think about how we should approach the next debt limit battle that will happen in a few months."

Bill Sharp responded, "Robert, you know Carolyn Holliday is as liberal, if not more so, than the former president? She campaigned on most of the same liberal ideas as her predecessor.

Do you really think she is going to compromise those principles to work with us?"

"Bill, believe me, I know how liberal she is. But I also know she did a pretty darn good job of finding solutions with the opposition when she was Governor of California. She may be trying to set us up, but I think she has realized if she doesn't work with us she will become the "do nothing" President."

Bill smiled and said, "OK, boss. We'll push ahead with the budget process, and hopefully have her budget proposal to work with soon."

Robert thought to himself, the budget is the first test. We need to play hardball with her to see how serious she is. We will appear to be cooperative, but we need to get our fiscal house in order. We need to push for budget cuts just large enough to avoid forcing her into a veto.

Across town President Holliday, dressed in her dark blue business suit, with an off white silk blouse, was having a similar meeting with her new Director of Office of Management and Budget, Tom Flynn.

The President thanked Tom for coming to her urgently called meeting, and said, "Tom, I want your top priority to be completing our budget proposal for presentation to Congress. The Republicans in the House and Senate are waiting to see if I will work with them on a budget for the next fiscal year. I want them to see my eagerness to establish that working relationship. They know I won't sign a budget bill if they just force it through Congress with only Republican votes. And I know they won't give me all I want on the spending side of the bill. So we have to ask for a little and be willing to meet them somewhere in the middle. Here are some guidelines for you to incorporate in our budget proposal.

1. 2% increase overall for discretionary spending.
2. A deficit projection in the $800 Billion range.
3. Use the most optimistic scenario for revenues.
4. Keep the entitlement expense estimates on the low end of the projected ranges.

Do you have any questions?"

"Madam President," Tom responded, "I think I understand everything you have said. Our work on the budget is well underway, as you know, and I'll be sure the final draft meets your guidelines. We should be able to have the budget proposal printed and delivered to Congress on time."

In another part of town Senator Banfield and Congressman Caldwell were having a private lunch in one of Washington's finer restaurants with their old friend, Vice President Jim Townsend.

Senator Banfield had chosen the restaurant, knowing it was Jim's favorite. It was expensive, and frequented by many of Washington's most powerful people. It had high ceilings with lots of light. All the tables had crisp white linen table clothes, with the finest crystal, china, and silverware.

Jim had started his Washington career as a Congressman and after two terms ran for the Senate and won. He had been in Washington for a long time, which was certainly one of the reasons the President had chosen him as her running mate. Additionally, he was from New York, which had been an important state in the election, and Jim had delivered it to her.

Charlie Banfield took a sip of his vodka martini, and with his best Texas drawl said, "Jim, we are going to have problems with Carolyn. Marino and Wolf left the White House meeting almost giddy. They see the President as weak, and they plan to take advantage of her."

Steve followed, "I agree. She will go around Charlie and me and cut deals with the Republicans that will set us back a decade. I can't believe she is willing to gut the Affordable Care Act and cut the other entitlements. Our base will crucify us and throw us all out of office. She doesn't have a clue how Washington works. We need your help."

The Vice President smiled, took a sip of his white wine, and said, "Gentlemen, relax. The President is a very smart lady. True, she doesn't have experience in the ways of Washington, but I will help her with that, and both of you can also help. I wish she had talked to me before her meeting with the leaders of Congress, and I wish she had chosen to meet with you guys first, but she didn't, and we will have to live with that. I think she wanted to take the initiative right away to reach out to the Republicans before they created a confrontation to test her."

Charlie said, "Jim, we need some leverage to control that lady, or she will be the death of us. What was the deal with her husband's death? I heard rumors that he had some sexually transmitted disease that caused his death. Any truth to that?"

Steve looked shocked at Charlie's accusation. He had not heard anything like what his friend Charlie was saying. He looked at the Vice President and waited to hear his reaction.

The Vice President remained calm but firm. "Charlie you are way out of line. Carolyn and John had a great marriage, and she was devastated by his death. I would be very careful about starting rumors regarding her personal life. Trust me, she will be a great President and our liberal principles will prevail."

They switched to lighter conversation for the rest of their lunch and parted with all seeming to be in a jovial mood. Charlie showed them his happy face.

Charlie was not happy, but he was a master at concealing what he really felt. He didn't like the way the Vice President had shut him down about John Holliday's death. He decided he would take matters in his own hands, and contact one of his friends at the FBI to see if he could quietly learn more about it.

* * *

Charlie Banfield was on the phone with his friend, Agent Mike Sewell, at the FBI. "Mike, can I buy you a drink after work tonight?"

Mike agreed but asked, "Is there anything I can do prior to seeing you?"

"No, I don't want to discuss it over the phone. I am seeking advice on how to handle a personal situation, nothing serious."

Charlie and Mike were at a bar just off DuPont Circle. It was a small bar, focusing on upper end clientele. It was fairly dark and had several booths with black leather seats that provided its clients the opportunity for quiet, private conversations. They hadn't seen each other for a while so they spent a few minutes in idle chatter.

Mike had been with the FBI for over twenty years. After college he had joined the Marines, but after serving in Iraq he left the Marines and joined the FBI. He had worked in the Los Angeles Office for several years, but had been working out of the D.C. Headquarters for the last decade. He still looked like he could be a Marine, with his hair cut short, but now he dressed in a suit and tie. He had been married once, but the rigors of his job had taken a toll on his marriage, and they had divorced almost ten years ago. Luckily, they had never had any children. He was now married to his job.

"Mike, I have a very sensitive issue to discuss with you, and I have to ask you to keep it in the strictest confidence."

Mike replied, "Charlie, you know if you have knowledge of a crime I can't be part of a cover up."

"No Mike, it is nothing like that. I haven't committed a crime and no crime has been committed to my knowledge. I just want to have someone look into a person's death for me, unofficially."

"Ok Charlie. Tell me what you need, and I'll see if I can help."

Charlie continued, "You probably know President Holliday's husband died several years ago, while she was Governor of California. He contracted some rare disease or infection while on a trip to Thailand, and in less than a year he was dead. There was never much information about the details of his death or about the disease. I would like someone, very discreetly, to look into his disease and his death. I am not asking for an official FBI investigation. And I can't stress enough how any investigation can't be linked back to me. Have any advice?"

"Drop it. From what I remember, there was nothing suspicious at the time. What makes you think this needs to be investigated now?"

"Just a hunch. But I would not be asking if I didn't think it was important."

"Ok, I know you well enough that you aren't going to take my initial advice, so tell you what. I have a friend in San Francisco who is a retired law enforcement officer. He is probably bored and wouldn't mind discreetly checking this out for me. Can't promise anything, but I'll ask him to have a look."

Mike didn't like where the conversation had gone. He could see a lot of downside and very little prospect of any upside, but Charlie was a friend, so he had agreed to help him. Hopefully his friend in San Francisco could put a quick end it.

A couple days later, during their breakfast together, Judy mentioned to the President that she had heard Senator Banfield was looking into her husband's death. She said, "You and I both know they won't find anything, but I wanted you to know Banfield is an ongoing problem. We need to keep an eye on him."

"Thanks, Judy, for always looking out for me." The President then switched the conversation to the budget negotiations.

* * *

Looking at the big picture, the House Republican budget proposal cut discretionary spending one percent, used a conservative assumption for revenues, and used a realistic assumption for entitlements, and resulted in a deficit of six hundred billion dollars.

The President's budget differed from the House budget by approximately one hundred billion dollars on discretionary spending, and because of the slightly different assumptions on revenue, her budget projected a seven hundred ninety five billion dollar deficit.

The President began, "Gentlemen, thank you all for coming on short notice. I want to re-state my sincere desire to solve problems instead of getting bogged down in a public fight over the budget. Speaker Wolf, I would like to hear your ideas for how we might resolve our differences."

She had called her second meeting with the leaders of Congress. The differences in budget proposals were fairly large, but in her estimation, not insurmountable. She knew this was a critical meeting and she had to be flexible but not weak. She decided to use a little diversion.

"Thank you Madam President. Let me begin with the over riding principle. For too long, both parties have been willing to allow the government to be fiscally irresponsible. We now have a national debt in excess of twenty trillion dollars and the interest alone is sucking more than two hundred billion dollars out of our economy. As interest rates go up, even without increases in the total debt we are looking at approximately four hundred billion dollars each year just to service the debt. Everything we do must move us toward a balanced budget. We can argue about how to do it and how long it will take to get there, but that must be the objective. We must slow down the growth of the debt and get to the point where we can actually begin reducing that giant albatross hanging around our children's necks."

The President smiled and said, "Speaker Wolf, this may surprise you, but I completely agree with you. I am for a balanced budget. The primary solution is a strong, growing economy. And like you said, we may disagree on how to get there and how long it will take, but believe me, I know we can do it.

"I have an idea that might sound a little radical, but let me describe it to all of you. First, assuming we can agree to a compromise on the budget, I think we should change the way we deal with the debt limit increases. Previously this has been a terrible political fight that occurs too frequently. Lot's of posturing, trying to make the other side look bad, and finally the debt limit gets increased. My suggestion is that we deal with the debt limit one time and agree on a number we can all live with for four years, the length of my first term." She smiled, "and maybe my last.

"Just for the sake of discussion, let's say we eventually get to a budget agreement that has a seven hundred and fifty billion dollar deficit. With that deficit for the first year, let's add a five hundred billion dollar deficit for the second year, a two hundred and fifty billion dollar deficit for the third year, and a zero deficit for the fourth year. Wouldn't it be nice to do away with the debt limit fights for four years? We can agree to raise the debt limit one time, by one point five trillion dollars and agree that we will not raise it again during those four years unless an extraordinary event requires it."

Paul Marino said, "Wow Madam President, a few years ago we couldn't even pass a budget through both houses of Congress. Now we are not only talking about an annual budget, but a long-term debt limit increase. I must admit it is a novel idea. I wonder what the odds are that Washington can agree to something for four years and not need to change it sometime before the four years are over? Your idea intrigues me, but I think we should take a little time to discuss it with a larger group of Senators and Congressmen. I suggest we focus on trying to find an agreeable compromise position between your budget proposal and the House budget proposal."

Charlie Banfield jumped in, "Usually I don't agree with my colleague, Senator Marino, but in this case I do. Let's focus on resolving the budget, for now."

Carolyn realized that she had gone too far, too quickly. She had not gotten to know Charlie very well in her short time in Washington, but it was obvious to her that he didn't like surprises, especially from her. She made a mental note to spend some time with Charlie and get to know him on a personal level in the weeks ahead, and try to stroke his ego a little. Inwardly she smiled as she concluded at least I diverted their thinking briefly. Now, maybe they will be willing to compromise more.

She said, "Senators, I understand the debt limit discussion is a little off subject, but I wanted to plant the seed for future discussions. How do we resolve our differences on the budget proposals?" With a straight face, she added, "Do I sense the Republicans want to accept the White House proposal?"

Robert Wolf ignored her comment and grabbed the opportunity again, "Madam President, the part of your budget proposal that is the most objectionable is the two percent increase in discretionary spending. I know it isn't much money, in the scope of the total budget, but that increase is not consistent with our basic principle of moving in the direction of a balanced budget. We are not against some selective increases but the total discretionary budget needs to show a slight reduction. The other differences are just the assumptions used for revenue and entitlements. Reducing the total discretionary spending by one percent, and tweaks to revenue and entitlement assumptions, we can probably agree to a deficit number in the six hundred fifty billion dollar range."

"Speaker Wolf, I appreciate your comments. Seven hundred billion dollars for the deficit number and we have a deal."

"Six seventy five and I think we can get that through the House, assuming some of Congressman Caldwell's associates will vote in favor."

Senator Marino echoed a similar comment. "I think we can pass it through the Senate, again, with help from Senator Banfield."

"OK gentlemen. Get it done so I can sign it.

The President could tell Senator Banfield was very unhappy. He obviously felt she had been too weak, but she would find a way to give him some extra attention.

After the meeting Carolyn told Judy, "That is one small step for the budget, and one giant step for the United States of America."

One month later the House passed the budget, followed by the Senate, and the President signed it a few days later. It held discretionary spending flat and showed a six hundred seventy five billion dollar deficit.

* * *

Mike Sewell called Senator Banfield and asked if they could get together for another drink. That night they met again in the same bar.

After the normal pleasantries and small talk, Mike said, "Charlie, this is a little strange. My friend in San Francisco did some checking and here is what he learned. John Holliday died of an unknown infectious disease. No autopsy was done, at the request of his wife, who was then Governor. He was cremated and his ashes were spread over the Pacific Ocean. But here is the really strange thing. Obviously medical records are confidential, but in his case, no medical records exist. My friend knows a lot of people in the San Francisco area. He asked a medical friend to look into Holliday's medical records at the hospital where he died, and was told that none exist. There is absolutely no record that he was ever a patient. I told my friend not to do anything more for now because I didn't want to risk setting off some alarm bells by asking too many questions. But something is not right with Mr. Holliday's death."

In his slow Texas drawl, Charlie replied, "Isn't that interesting? Thank you, Mike. Now I really have a dilemma. I don't want you or me getting in any trouble, and I really don't want the FBI to open an official investigation, but how do I find out what really happened? Obviously, this is the dead husband of the President. She has some very powerful friends both here in Washington and in San Francisco. I can't have this blowing up in my face. How reliable and discreet is your friend in San Francisco?"

"He is very reliable and he can be very discreet. If you decide to do more, he is the one who can do it for you. I'll give you his name and phone number if you want to talk to him directly. It might be better to keep the FBI out of this for now. If I learned that a law might have been broken, I would be obligated to report it to the appropriate person."

"Ok Mike, I understand. Thanks for your help, and I appreciate your advice."

"Hi Harry, this is Charlie Banfield calling from Washington D.C. Mike Sewell gave me your name and number, and I wanted to have a follow-up conversation with you. Mike speaks very highly of your investigative abilities and your discretion."

Harry Rice was the retired SFPD officer Mike had used to look into John Holliday's death. Harry followed a similar career path to Mike. He had been in the Army Special Forces and after the Army he had joined the San Francisco Police Department. He and Mike had worked together on a couple cases when Mike was working out of the FBI's Los Angeles Office, and they had become personal friends. He, like Mike, had let his career get in the way of his marriage. Actually he had tried marriage twice, but finally gave up on the idea. Just over a year ago, after a thirty-year distinguished career as a police officer, he had retired.

Charlie continued and asked, "Do you have the time and interest in doing some additional work for me on this case? If you do, the first step will be to travel to Thailand to see what can be learned from that end."

Harry replied, "Senator, I am retired with time on my hands. I think I have a few more good years in me, and I am very interested in pursuing this case. I think some kind of cover up occurred, but I will not speculate at this time on who, what, or why. If you want me to go to Thailand, I can make those arrangements. I understand the sensitivity of this case and will be very discreet. No one will know who I am working for, and I will do my best to make it look like a routine follow up to an unfortunate death."

They discussed a financial arrangement and exchanged contact numbers. Charlie gave him his personal cell phone number so no one in his office would be aware of any calls from Harry. Charlie liked Harry right away.

The next morning, Judy mentioned to the President that Senator Banfield had not given up. "He is sending a former San Francisco police officer to Thailand to look into John's medical records. This is going to be a problem. We didn't scrub the records in Thailand like we did in San Francisco."

"Judy, I would like to ask how you got this information, but I think I would rather not know." Changing the subject, she added, "Looks like we have another busy day at the office."

Chapter 4

The next step for Akbar Khan was to send operatives to the United States. He knew they had put together a good plan, but he also was smart enough to know that the probability of success was low. He had to get six of his men into the U.S. without detection, secure some explosives, and find ways to penetrate the targets. The people in the U.S. who were providing the money for the operation and places for his men to stay were critical to the mission. He worried that the U.S. government may have already discovered the locals who were helping with their plan. He knew he had to be careful not to show any doubts to his men. He satisfied himself by looking at the upside. If successful, this could be the greatest terrorist attack since 9-11.

He sent two men, Ahmed and Fahad to Mexico City, on to Colombia, and then over land to Venezuela. In Caracas they took on new identities and secured forged Venezuelan passports with tourist visas for the U.S. They were now Jose and Carlos. The men then traveled to the Dominican Republic. A charter fishing boat carried the two from Santo Domingo into U.S. waters and dropped them off at a Fort Lauderdale marina. The U.S. immigration and customs officials never saw the two men. Jose and Carlos found their way to a safe house that had been prearranged for them. In the kitchen they found a package containing an envelope of American money, two disposable cell phones, a laptop computer, and an envelope with their instructions. They were to wait approximately one week, and then take a train to Washington D.C. Once there, they would take a taxi to the apartment address shown in the letter. Two keys for the apartment were in the envelope. Once they were settled in the apartment, they were to find jobs as bus boys or dishwashers in restaurants near their apartment. They would receive further instructions after they arrived in Washington.

Jose and Carlos had grown up poor in a suburb of Islamabad. They both dropped out of school as teenagers, and did odd jobs for a few years. Eventually, frustrated with life, they found their way into the underground society and soon found themselves in an Al Qaeda group. Fahad/Jose was only twenty-one years old and Ahmed/Carlos was twenty-five. They found friendships and camaraderie in Akbar Khan's group. The life was hard, but they finally felt a sense of purpose.

They had one contact number in the U.S. Their instructions were to call when they arrived in Fort Lauderdale and to not call the number again unless it was an emergency. They didn't know the person who would answer their call, and they had no other contacts in the U.S. They were both fluent in English and had been told before they left Pakistan to be careful, follow their instructions, and keep a low profile. The two had no way to contact the rest of their cell who were also traveling to the U.S. Jose made the call as they were instructed and when a male voice said, "Hello?" Jose said, "We have arrived in country." There was no response, just the click of the phone going dead.

Fahad and Ahmed looked like they could be brothers. They were both medium height, and slender. They wore their hair short and had no facial hair. Akbar had lectured all six of the fighters, who were part of the dirty bomb plan, about their personal appearance. He explained how critical it was for all of them to be invisible. They were to buy clothes after they reached the U.S. and only wear clothes they had purchased in the U.S. They were not to let their facial hair grow, and they were to keep their hair cut fairly short. Baseball caps were recommended, and sunglasses, when appropriate. They were also told not to do or say anything that would draw attention. Always be polite and never argue with anyone.

Two other cell members, Faisal and Jamal, traveled directly from Pakistan to the U.S. carrying student visas to study at American University in Washington D.C. They traveled to Islamabad and then flew to Karachi where they boarded a plane for Hong Kong. They spent a night in Hong Kong and left the next day on a plane for Los Angeles, with a connection to Dulles. Once they arrived at Dulles, they took a taxi to an apartment in D.C. near the American University campus.

When they arrived in the apartment they found two cell phones, a laptop, an envelope with money, and a message to call a number and report that they had arrived. They made the call.

Faisal was one of Akbar's most trusted fighters. They had been together for many years, and had developed a real friendship. Faisal was now twenty-eight. He was excited to be in the U.S. and looked forward to carrying out the plan. In Pakistan, he had grown a full black beard and his hair was full, bushy, and black. He remembered being coached that the success of the plan was dependent on all of them fitting into the American environment. Before flying to the U.S. he shaved his beard off and cut his hair short.

Jamal was several years younger than Faisal. He was quite bright and had no problem learning English. He was a few inches shorter and more slender than Faisal, and much more outgoing. He had gotten into a fight when he was a teenager, and the result was a broken nose that had healed crooked.

* * *

Ann decided to spend time doing what she really enjoyed, tracing the money. Her theory was that an operation in the U.S. by Pakistanis would most likely have someone already in the U.S. to help with logistics and money.

She knew that Pakistan's ISI usually placed people in their embassies around the world just like the U.S. put CIA officials in embassies. She talked to one of her analyst friends who specialized on Pakistan. He gave her the names of the senior ISI person in the embassy and his two assistants, who were likely ISI also.

She made a call to her counterpart at NSA and asked him to put an urgent bug on the three men's incoming and outgoing phone calls, texts, and email messages from all their known phones and email accounts.

She then started looking into their banking practices. After a lot of searches she discovered that the senior ISI person, Mohammad al Babar, had personal bank accounts in his name and in his wife's name, both with sizeable amounts of money in them.

She started to trace the accounts back for several months and found one repetitive item that caught her attention. The wife's account made monthly payments to an Oriental rug company, SPARS Inc. With some digging she discovered that SPARS had showrooms all over the U.S.

She looked at the business account and the personal account of the owner of the Washington D.C. SPARS operation. He made monthly wire transfers to several other SPARS locations in other cities, including New York, Miami, Palm Beach, Chicago, Houston, Los Angeles, Newport Beach, and Phoenix. She also noticed that he made regular payment to various apartment rental agencies around Washington. She thought, maybe he paid the rent for his employees, but just maybe there was more to it than the obvious. Ann made a note to herself to look into this anomaly in more detail.

At the next team briefing, she mentioned what she had learned about the ISI official in Pakistan's Washington embassy and his wife's link to SPARS Inc., an Oriental rug company. She also mentioned the apartment rentals handled by SPARS.

George mentioned that their agent in Mexico had visited the Port Authority in Manzanillo and checked the Pakistan container but found no radiation level above normal. However, when he searched the papers of the dead port authority administrator, he discovered a Pakistani name and phone number. He had the cell phone traced and learned it was now in Mexico City. The CIA agent was having the Pakistani discreetly monitored, but did not plan to interrogate him unless Washington gave the green light.

George said, "Let's summarize. Iran sold yellow cake to someone for one point eight million dollars. An ISI senior official in Islamabad withdrew two million dollars a few days before the Iranian yellow cake sale. We found two dead Mexicans in a Pakistan cargo container that arrived in Mexico from Karachi half loaded with rice. One of the dead Mexicans had the phone number and name of a Pakistani living in Mexico City, who we are now watching. Pakistan's ISI official working in their Washington embassy has large sums of money in two personal bank accounts, and they buy a lot of rugs from SPARS Inc., an Oriental rug company, or they give them money for something else. The owner of the rug company rents several apartments around D.C. We have NSA monitoring all of the ISI official's communications, incoming and outgoing. In summary, we think there is a plot to make some dirty bombs using the yellow cake, but we don't know when, where, or who will carry out this plot. Have I left anything out?"

Ann replied, "That pretty much sums it up. Looks clear to me. Because of the work I am doing on records of people living in the U.S. I think I should bring the FBI and Homeland Security into the loop. Any problems from anybody on that?"

Everyone agreed. The plan was to have their operative in Pakistan continue to try to identify an Al Qaeda group who had links to ISI. Ann would contact the FBI and Homeland Security and bring them up to speed on the potential plot, and she would continue to use her computer to learn more about SPARS.

* * *

Khalid and Masood, the final two of six Al Qaeda operatives, left Pakistan for the U.S. Each carried one small backpack. They carried fake Saudi Arabian passports with tourist visas to the U.S. and to Mexico. Masood was the older of the two, at twenty-six, and Khalid was twenty-four. Masood was usually quiet and very serious looking. Khalid, on the other hand, was the light-hearted, chatty one. Masood was almost six feet and a little stocky, while Khalid was much shorter at five six and slender. Khalid was very respectful of Masood, not only because of his age but also because he was the bomb maker.

Before his departure from Pakistan Masood shaved and cut his black hair short. Khalid had never worn a beard and he had always kept his hair long. He wasn't happy about the advice Akbar had given them, but he had his hair cut a little. It wasn't short but it was not as long as it had been. He wondered if Masood would tell him to cut his hair shorter, but Masood didn't mention it.

They flew from Karachi to Kuala Lumpur, Malaysia and connected with a flight to Mexico City. The Pakistani living in Mexico City gave the slip to the CIA person who had been watching him, and met Khalid and Masood after they cleared immigration and customs. He drove them to a house not far from the airport, and told them to rest for a couple days before they began their trip to the U.S. He gave them a cell phone and told them he would call them later about their departure schedule. The house was on a dirt street in a rundown neighborhood. It was small and dirty, with an old torn sofa in the living room and two mattresses on the floor in the bedroom. Luckily, it had been stocked with some food and drinks. They were told not to go out, and to just rest. This was difficult because of all the sounds outside. Car horns were constantly blaring and planes could be heard constantly as they took off and landed at the nearby airport.

Two days later, the same Pakistani man pulled into the driveway and told them to put their things in the trunk of the car. He said the other three backpacks with "the merchandise" were already in the trunk. The merchandise he referred to was the uranium yellow cake.

They would travel by car to Mazatlan, and from there catch a ferry to Cabo San Lucas. In Cabo their host would leave them, after getting them to the fishing boat that would take them up the coast to California. They would be dropped off to make their way to a safe house for further instructions. Their host gave each of them a small slip of paper that had the address of their safe house in Huntington Beach, California. He said, "Don't lose that address."

The trip to Mazatlan was long, dusty, tiring and boring, but luckily it was uneventful. They were dropped at the Mazatlan Ferry Dock, where the local Pakistani bought three tickets and helped them get all the backpacks aboard the ferry. The local Pakistani spoke Spanish and would travel with them to Cabo to insure they found their ride to the US. The ferry ride was enjoyable and gave them some idea of the boat ride ahead. As they departed Mazatlan, they watched the seagulls following the ferry, hoping some of the passengers would throw them treats. Eventually the birds lost interest and headed back to shore. It was a warm, breezy day with calm seas, and the men enjoyed sitting and relaxing in the sunshine.

Khalid and Masood arrived in Cabo in the late afternoon. They easily found the fishing boat, 'Dos Amigos,' that would take them to the U.S. They boarded the fishing boat, stowed the five backpacks safely below, and thanked their Pakistani friend. They never knew his name and never saw him again.

The Captain of 'Dos Amigos' asked the men, in broken English, if they spoke English. Khalid replied, "Yes, we can speak English but we don't understand Mexican."

The Captain said, "No problem, my friends. My name is Pedro. My son, who will help with the trip, is Pancho." Pedro shouted at his son, "Pancho, say hello to our passengers."

Pancho was up on the bow, turned toward them and said, "Hola, senors."

Pedro was in his forties and had owned the Dos Amigos for ten years. His complexion was normally dark, but working constantly in the sun made him even darker. He was five feet ten and a little stocky. He wore a sombrero, tied below his chin, to keep it from blowing into the sea. His son, Pancho was twenty and hoped to one day own his own charter fishing boat. He looked like a younger version of his father, just not quite as heavy.

Pedro had been paid handsomely to transport the two men from Cabo San Lucas to Catalina Island, off the coast of southern California. The trip was about 900 miles, which would take four or five days depending on the weather and the stops to refuel. They would travel day and night and only stop for fuel, unless the weather forced them to stop more. They were paid triple what they would have normally earned if they had worked ten days in a row on the charter boat.

Luckily, the weather was cooperating and the seas were relatively calm. Their first stop was Bahia Santa Maria. The 'Dos Amigos' had a five hundred gallon diesel tank that gave them plenty of range for the trip. With gentle seas they could travel at ten knots per hour.

Khalid and Masood were happy when Pedro told them they were stopping shortly for fuel. He told them they could walk around the marina if they wanted, but not to go too far and to be back at the boat in an hour or less.

"Are immigration officials at the marina?" asked Masood.

Pedro replied, "No senor, not at this one, but at our next stop you will have to stay on board, below deck."

Khalid and Masood were nervous, but they had never spent this much time on a boat, and they really wanted to get off and stretch their legs.

When Pedro pulled up to the gas dock he said to them, "Remember, back in an hour, no more."

"No problem, Captain."

They casually walked around the docks looking at the other fishing boats. They ventured a short distance from the docks, but when they noticed a couple police walking on the street, they casually walked in the opposite direction and headed back to the boat. They didn't want to get stopped by the police in Mexico before they had a chance to get to the U.S.

After two more stops for fuel, and a total of four days at sea, the captain informed them they had just crossed the border into American waters. They were just south of San Diego.

The captain kept 'Dos Amigos' well out to sea to avoid any possibility the US Coast Guard might intercept them. It was common for Mexican fishing boats to fish in the waters off southern California, and for American boats to fish off the waters south of the border. So it was unlikely they would have any trouble, but the captain didn't want to take any chances.

The next step was to transfer 'the cargo' to a U.S. fishing boat near Catalina, staying far enough away not to be observed. Pedro got on his radio and called the 'Lucky Strike', the boat they were to meet. After a few minutes, the 'Lucky Strike' replied. They talked back and forth about the fishing conditions and then said they would talk later. This was their signal to meet at the pre-arranged coordinates.

On board the 'Lucky Strike' were Captain Joe and his mate, Tommy. Captain Joe was a blond haired, typical southern California surfer dude. He was only thirty years old, six feet tall and quite handsome in a rugged, scruffy way. He had messed up his knee in a surfing accident five years ago, and changed into a charter fishing boat captain for his livelihood. He was well known among the charter captain community as the one to go to when you wanted to do something illegal. Running drugs was a common illegal activity with an occasional gun running trip. Human cargo was less frequent, but Captain Joe was willing to do just about anything to have a good payday.

They had been moored in the harbor at Catalina for two days waiting for the radio call from 'Dos Amigos'. They immediately started the engine, untied from their mooring, and began their voyage to meet Captain Pedro. It was late afternoon when they found each other. About thirty miles offshore, with no other boats in sight, they transferred the two men and all their backpacks. Captain Joe was curious when he saw the five backpacks, but he was smart enough not to ask any questions.

Captain Pedro asked, "How's the fishing?"

Captain Joe said, "We didn't do any. We were just sitting at Catalina waiting for your call. This business is a lot better than fishing any day. Have a safe trip back to Mexico, Pedro."

Khalid thanked Captain Pedro and said goodbye to him and his son. He and Masood stowed the backpacks below. When they returned topside, Captain Joe said, "I don't want to get back to our dock until well after dark, so we are just going to put a couple lines in the water and troll for awhile. Just sit back and enjoy the sunset. Maybe we'll catch some fish. After Tommy gets the lines in the water, he'll get you some sandwiches and drinks."

After a couple hours trolling, Tommy brought in the lines and they headed for home.

They arrived at the Newport Harbor a few hours after sunset. As they entered the breakwater, Captain Joe saw the harbor patrol coming toward them. He said to his passengers, "Just relax and look like you are returning from a fishing trip. As the patrol goes by you may want to just wave to them. Please don't do anything to appear nervous. If they stop us, and I don't think they will, just be polite and only speak if they ask you a question. You are tourists who are staying with friends in Newport Beach, and have been out fishing for the day. We only caught a few and we didn't keep them. Any questions?"

They both replied, "No."

Inside the break wall all boats traveled at five mph or less because it was a no wake zone. The harbor patrol approached, pointed their search light at the 'Lucky Strike', everyone looked at each other, and the boats passed and continued in opposite directions. The Pakistanis let out a sigh of relief.

The 'Lucky Strike' tied up at its slip and Captain Joe helped the men with their backpacks. Khalid and Masood carried the three backpacks with yellow cake and the Captain carried the other two. He walked them up to a place where they could wait for a taxi. Captain Joe said goodbye and Khalid thanked him for his hospitality. A couple minutes later a taxi pulled up, they put the backpacks in the trunk and got in the back seat. Khalid gave the driver, who was from India, the address and he drove up the Pacific Coast Highway a few miles, turned off the PCH and drove to the address they had given him. It was a small house in a quiet area of Huntington Beach, well away from the beach. They paid the driver the fare plus a small tip, retrieved their backpacks, walked up the driveway, past a car sitting in the driveway, unlocked the front door, turned on the light just inside the door, brought the backpacks into the house, and closed the door. They had successfully smuggled three backpacks full of yellow cake into the United States.

"Wow," said Khalid. "I can't believe we made it to the U.S. I wonder if the others have been as successful. I wish we had some way to know if everything was ok."

"The only way we have a chance of success against the Americans is if we follow the plan. The Americans are tricky with all their technology. They have their drones and they monitor phone calls and Internet messages. If we make any mistake they will find us. We have to be really careful, all the time," replied Masood.

Like the others who had gotten into the U.S., there were things neatly arranged for them on the kitchen table. There was a packet of money, keys to the car in the driveway, two cell phones, a laptop, maps for driving from Huntington Beach, California to Richmond, Virginia, and the address of their next safe house in Richmond, with two sets of house keys. There were instructions to call a number and report they had successfully arrived in California, with additional instructions to call the number again when they arrived in Richmond.

Masood made the call and said, "We have arrived in country."

The party on the other end of the phone hung up.

The next day Khalid drove Masood to a shopping mall where they bought pants, belts, tee shirts, sweat shirts, underwear and socks, wind breakers, Nike running shoes, sunglasses and baseball caps. Hopefully, they would now be invisible, looking like everyone else.

* * *

Ann's NSA contact was on the phone. "Ann, we heard something that may be of interest to you. It is not much, but it is something. Last night, your ISI official at the Pakistani embassy received a call on his cell phone that was very brief. The person on the phone said, 'We have arrived in country.' The person making the call immediately hung up and turned his cell phone off. We can tell you it came from southern California, but unfortunately we can't be more specific than that. Your ISI official didn't acknowledge the call or say anything. He just hung up."

"Thanks Cliff," replied Ann. "That is one more piece in the puzzle. Let us know if you get any other communications that might be helpful."

"Will do, Ann. Good luck."

Chapter 5

Fresh on the heels of a successful budget compromise, the debt limit crisis was looming. Traditionally, Congress wanted to tie a debt ceiling increase to some other issue, and the President wanted what was called a "clean" debt ceiling increase. There were three issues in play this time. How large an increase to approve. How long the increase would last before the next debt ceiling increase was needed. And what, if anything, would be tied to the debt ceiling increase?

The President wanted a one point five trillion dollar increase tied to an agreement that she would not ask for another increase during her first term except for an extraordinary unanticipated event.

The Congress was thinking of a one year, seven hundred billion dollar increase tied to the re-instatement of a tax break for corporate research that had recently expired. The leaders of Congress were worried that the President had some momentum coming off the budget deal, and her idea of approving a multi-year debt limit was polling well with the American people.

The House proposed a one point two trillion dollar increase to the debt limit and a proposal to re-instate the tax break for corporate research. Their debt limit increase would take the issue off the table through the mid-term elections.

The President sent the Vice President to visit with the Speaker and the Senate Majority Leader to persuade them that the President really wanted the increase to be enough for four years. She was in favor of the re-instatement of the corporate research tax break, but she wanted to delay that bill, and include it as a provision in the Corporate Tax Reform to be negotiated later.

Senator Marino said to the Vice President, "Jim, my concern is Corporate Tax Reform is going to be a lengthy process, and it is behind the immigration reform on the priority list. By the time we get to corporate tax reform we will be into next year, and that single change for corporate research is important enough to pass this year. Remember, it is only re-instating what was already in the tax code."

The Vice President replied, "Paul, you know the President doesn't want anything tied to the debt limit increase."

"It won't be tied to the debt limit officially Jim, we will pass it as a separate bill, but we will pass it at the same time as the debt limit increase. We just need her assurance that she will sign it when it comes to her desk, this year."

Jim said, "I don't know if I can get her to go along with it. How about you guys agree with her four-year debt limit increase? It will only add three hundred billion dollars to the debt limit for the extra two years."

Robert Wolf chimed in, "Jim, it sounds like we agree to disagree. What if we send her the two bills we are talking about? Is she prepared to veto a two-year, one point two trillion dollar debt limit increase, and cause another crisis? That will look like she is playing political hardball with the full faith and credit of our country. I thought she was trying to work with us. Maybe we should just pass a debt limit increase of seven hundred billion dollars which will cover us for a year."

"Robert, you know she sent me over here to find a solution. I guess we all need to take some more time to think about it and have another discussion in a few days. You guys both know that the next item on our list is health care reform. This is a really difficult issue for all the Democrats, and it is going to be tough to find common ground. The President is sticking her neck way out on this one, but she knows it is important for the country. She wants to get the debt limit increase behind us quickly so we can switch our attention to health care."

Paul responded, "Ok Jim, give us a few days and you kick it around again with the President. We will talk again."

With that they thanked each other and the Vice President left.

After the Vice President was gone, Robert stayed behind in Paul's office to continue their discussion. They both agreed that accepting the four year debt limit increase would not get enough support from the Republicans in the House or the Senate, even with the corporate tax change they were proposing. They also agreed that unless they could get the corporate tax change and the one point two trillion dollar debt limit increase, they would settle for a one year seven hundred billion dollar debt limit increase.

Across town, in the White House, Jim met with the President and briefed her on his discussion with the leaders of Congress. The President said, "Sounds like the honeymoon is over. It didn't last very long, did it?"

"No, Madam President, the Republicans have decided it is time to test us. The budget deal was pretty easy, but I think they have decided it is time to see how easy you are going to be in reaching compromises. You have to decide how important your four-year proposal is to you. I understand their positions on both the two-year compromise and the corporate tax change. But if you let them win they are going to become even more aggressive on future issues. Do we dig in now or do we save the fight for another issue? Obviously Madam President, it is your call."

"What would you do, Jim?"

"I would agree to the two-year one point two trillion dollar deal and the corporate tax change they are suggesting, with the clear understanding that the two issues are separate. I talked to the minority leaders, and they can live with those two conclusions."

"Ok Jim, let them win this one. Wait about a week and then get back to Paul and Robert and tell them we will go along with their proposals. Also, tell the minority leaders at the same time."

A month later, and a few days before the debt limit deadline, the House and Senate passed the bills and the President signed them.

The next priority was health care reform.

* * *

The Affordable Care Act was now the law of the land. Its roll out had been troubled; a disaster if you listened to the Republicans, and it was continuing to be unpopular with a majority of the American people. It was the primary reason the Republicans now controlled both the Senate and the House. The costs of the Act were higher than the initial projections and the health care industry was unhappy with the regulatory burdens and the government's involvement in the practice of medicine.

The President had the four leaders of Congress in another meeting at the White House. This time the subject was health care.

"Gentlemen, welcome to the White House once again. Washington is a strange place. We just signed into law a two-year, one point two trillion dollar debt limit increase and a bill reinstating the corporate tax break on R&D expenses. It is curious to me that on two issues where we basically agreed we still had difficulty reaching an agreement. Washington seems to be more concerned with the game and the process than the actual result. How do we get the members of Congress to think outside the box? How do we get big problems solved that will make our country stronger? Those are not rhetorical questions. They are questions that I would like each of you to spend some time really thinking about, and sharing them with your fellow legislators."

She continued, "Now, health care is our next priority. If I listen to my political base and do things 'the Washington way' my position would be, the Affordable Care Act is the law of the land, and in time, it will be accepted by the health care industry and the majority of the people of the United States. And, Medicare and Medicaid are not perfect, but we shouldn't tinker with entitlements.

"Gentlemen, I think we can do better if we can find the courage to work together on solutions that are good for the American people.

"I want to make my positions perfectly clear to all of you. I will veto any bill to repeal the Affordable Care Act that does not include a comprehensive plan for the country's health care services going forward. So we have a choice; modify the Affordable Care Act or repeal and replace it with something better in a smooth, seamless transition.

"Additionally, I am open to changes in the Medicare and Medicaid programs if the changes are fiscally responsible and cause minimum hardship to the American people participating in these programs.

"We have a lot of work to do. We can spend all our time fighting the old wars on these subjects or we can all agree that this is a new day, and we are going to work together to find solutions that are good for the American people."

Senator Marino spoke next, "Thank you Madam President. I like what I hear. However, your party and my party have many differences. In my opinion the greatest divide is the role of the federal government, especially in health care. Without coming to an understanding on the role of the federal government in our health care system, we will fight endlessly on how to fix it. Your party wants more bureaucracy and more management of the health care system by government. My party wants less government involvement in supervising and managing health care. We want the free market to work for health care just like it works for so many other industries. That doesn't mean we shouldn't have a regulatory role, but let's get out of the way of the doctor patient relationship. Let's do some tort reform that can have more financial benefit to the whole health care industry than any other single item. And finally let's address Medicare and Medicaid head on, and get them going in a direction where they don't bankrupt this great country."

"Senator Marino," responded the President, "thanks for your comments. I understand your concern about our fundamental difference regarding the role of government. However, I also believe we have an opportunity to work together with open minds to find solutions. This opportunity may only come once, but we can have the biggest impact on our country if we can address our total health care system and find changes that are good for the people and fiscally responsible."

Everyone added their comments to the discussion, but Senator Banfield was obviously not on the same page as the others. He was polite, but it was apparent to the President that he was going to be a problem, again.

They all agreed that they would have monthly meetings with the President and Vice President to talk about progress and the major issues to be resolved.

Chapter 6

When Harry returned from Thailand, he placed a call to Senator Banfield's personal cell phone. There was no answer so he left the brief message, "please call me when you have time."

Charlie saw the message when he got home, and immediately called Harry.

"I just got back from Thailand earlier today and wanted to report my findings right away. I hired a local person who came highly recommended and knows his way around the health care facilities in Bangkok. It was not hard for him to find where John Holliday had been treated. Mr. Holliday was a patient in the leading hospital in Bangkok, the Bangkok International Hospital, and was treated by an excellent physician and staff. I have the names of the key players who attended to him during his stay in the hospital. They will be listed in my report. The person working for me was able to make a copy of John's complete hospital medical file without anyone at the hospital being aware.

"It turns out John Holliday contracted two diseases while in Bangkok. The first was syphilis and the second was a virus that is transmitted through oral sex. The virus can lead to cancer and almost always leads to a horrible death. I wanted to get this information to you before I do anything further in San Francisco.

"If there was a cover up after he returned to the U.S., I worry that any attempts to gain information about his case will set off alarm bells with the people involved. We need to be very thoughtful before we stick our nose in the hornet's nest, so to speak."

Charlie replied, "Harry please send your report and a copy of the medical file to my home address. After I have a look at it I'll give you a call and let you know if I want you to do anything further. I agree there is no telling how dangerous this investigation could be. There are some very powerful people who could be involved in the cover up, and there is no way to know how far they will go to protect the President."

* * *

Charlie's office got a call from the President's secretary inviting him to a private dinner meeting at the White House. The secretary explained it would be a working dinner regarding health care reform and therefore did not include his wife.

Charlie felt a little suspicious about a one on one meeting on health care reform, but he was still learning the ways of the President. She had obviously picked up on his concerns, and maybe she was trying to win him over or build a stronger rapport with him.

He arrived at the appointed time and was escorted to the private residence of the President. She was on the phone when he arrived, but shortly ended her conversation and joined him in her private dining room. She asked him if he wanted a drink before dinner, and they both chose scotch on the rocks. She asked about his wife and children, and he gave the obligatory responses that everyone was doing well. His two children were grown, married with a couple children each, and had careers in law in his home state of Texas.

They took their seats at the dinner table and a member of the kitchen staff brought the food to the table for a family style dinner. He also placed a bottle of red wine on the table and a bottle of white wine in a cooler beside the table.

The President said, "I asked the staff to put everything on the table so we can serve ourselves and not be interrupted while we are discussing things. I hope you don't mind?"

"Certainly not, Madam President."

Charlie was sensing something didn't feel right. He didn't know the President well, but he could tell she was a little tense. Maybe she was just tired, he thought, but he was worried that things were not what they appeared.

They served themselves and chose red wine. As Charlie began to eat, the President said, "Charlie, I must admit I called you here under false pretenses. I don't like doing that but under the circumstances, I think you will agree it was the best thing to do."

Charlie looked up from his plate and showed that he was startled by the President's last comment. "What in the world is going on Madam President?"

"Charlie, I hope you don't mind me calling you Charlie. All this formal stuff gets so tedious after a while." She paused for effect and then continued, "It has come to my attention that you have been looking into my husband's death. I thought it best we put the issue on the table and deal with it here and now. As you have learned, my husband was not completely faithful to me, and during a business trip to Thailand, had some indiscretions that lead to him contracting not one, but two sexually transmitted diseases.

"Obviously this was embarrassing to me, but this was not the first time he had been unfaithful. However, it was the first time he had gotten a disease from screwing around. Pardon my use of words. The tragedy this time was one of the diseases proved untreatable, and within a year he was dead.

"Because of my political ambitions and my personal embarrassment, I chose to try to conceal the details of his death. As you learned, the hospital in San Francisco agreed to remove his medical records. But unfortunately, we did not do the same thing at the hospital in Thailand.

"In a way I'm glad you found the information. Deep down I knew I could not conceal the truth about his diseases. But now we are faced with decisions on how to handle the situation going forward. Let me assure you, there is nothing else that has been covered up regarding his death."

Charlie was shocked. He thought he had been so careful. How had she found out about his investigation? He thought Harry was trustworthy, and he was the only person he could think of who knew the details. But right now he had to decide how he was going to respond to the President without destroying his career.

Charlie started, "Madam President, first please let me apologize for not coming to you with my questions. Several of our senators informally approached me about your willingness to compromise with the Republicans instead of fighting for our liberal beliefs. They were uncertain and concerned about your motivation. One senator even theorized that maybe the

Republicans were blackmailing you. I agreed to discreetly see if there was anything in your background that might make you vulnerable. The lack of information about the death of your husband looked like it could be something the Republicans were using against you. I agreed to look into it, quietly, but obviously not quietly enough, to see if there was something the Republicans had found. I am sincerely sorry I did this, but you need to understand many senators are concerned that you are too eager to make concessions to the Republicans."

"Charlie, I am as liberal as you, probably more so. But look at my situation. The Republicans control both houses of Congress. We can agree to disagree on everything, and just drift along for four years, or we can fight to make our country stronger and better. The Republicans had the "do nothing" label for a time when they used their majority in the House to block the previous President and Senate. I will not be labeled the "do nothing" President. I will work to find common ground with the Republicans wherever I can to get things done for the good of the country. If you and your fellow concerned Democrat senators can't live with that, then you need to think about retirement. I can use your support and help. And I hope we can find ways to work together. But going behind my back and using investigators to look into my past is unacceptable. I don't know if you broke any laws. I will assume for your sake that you did not. But you have a decision to make. You can either work with me or fight me. I encourage you to express your views on all the issues, even if your views may be different from my perceived position. I need people around me who I can trust and depend on to speak truthfully, even if your opinion is different from mine. Persuade me, but don't go behind my back. Is that clear?"

"Yes, Madam President."

"Charlie, let's call it a night. Tomorrow will be another busy day."

The President stood and walked out of the room. A moment later a Secret Service agent walked through another door and escorted Senator Banfield to the exit.

When Charlie got home he went into his study and poured himself a stiff drink. He sat at his desk and tried to process what had happened and how the President had found out about his investigation so quickly. It was getting late but San Francisco was three hours behind Washington, so Charlie called Harry.

Harry's phone rang but no one answered. It went into voice mail and Charlie left a message, "Harry, it's Charlie. Call me."

The next day Charlie kept thinking about his meeting with the President, and waiting for a call from Harry. That evening when he got home he called Harry again. Charlie left a second message. "Harry, Charlie. Call me, urgent."

The next day, after lunch, Charlie's secretary came into his office and said, "You had a call from a police detective in San Francisco who said he needs to talk to you urgently." She gave him a note with the detective's name and phone number on it. "Is everything alright, sir?"

Charlie responded, "As far as I know, everything is fine. I'll give this guy a call and see what he needs. Don't worry, Doris."

Charlie was worried, but he was good at concealing his emotions. After Doris left his office and closed the door, Charlie called Detective Sanchez of the San Francisco Police Department.

When Detective Sanchez answered his phone, Charlie said in his best Texas drawl, "Detective Sanchez, this is Senator Charlie Banfield calling from Washington D.C. My secretary said you had called and asked to have me give you a call. What can I do for you?"

Sanchez said, "Thank you for returning my call, Senator. We have an investigation underway and I hope you might be able to help. Do you know Harry Rice?"

Charlie thought, I don't like the sound of that question, but he answered, "Yes I do."

"Sir, can you tell me what your relationship was with Harry?"

"Harry was helping me with a personal matter. He was investigating a private situation for me." Charlie reminded himself, keep your answers short and only answer the question, but be careful not to lie.

"I am sorry to have to ask you, Senator, but can you tell me what and who he was investigating?"

"Detective Sanchez, I am sorry, but it is a private matter and I am not at liberty to discuss it with you. Why are you asking me all these questions? Is Harry under some investigation?"

"No Senator, Harry is not under investigation. He is dead. We found your name and phone number on his phone, and two messages from you on his voice mail showing you have been trying to contact him recently. We are investigating his death."

Charlie was stunned. He didn't know what to say. Finally he asked, "Detective, can you tell me how he died?"

"All I can tell you right now is he died of a gun shot wound to the head. It is an apparent suicide. Harry was one of us, sir, and before we close the case as a suicide, we are going to investigate the case thoroughly to be sure it was a suicide. I can tell you the officers who knew Harry don't believe he would commit suicide. Is there anything else you can tell me about the work he was doing for you?"

"I'm sorry, Detective, I really can't reveal any of the specifics. I didn't really know him personally, only professionally, but during our phone conversations he never gave me any indication that he was depressed or troubled or suicidal. Detective, I am in shock about this. Sorry I can't help you further."

Detective Sanchez ended the conversation, "Thank you, Senator. If I have any further questions, I will give you a call again. Goodbye."

Charlie sat in his office, stunned. His mind was racing. Did Harry commit suicide? Did he keep a copy of the report on John Holliday? Did the police now have the copy of that report? Or, did someone kill Harry and make it look like a suicide? And was that someone working for the President? Should I tell the President that a copy of the Thailand report could be in the hands of the San Francisco police? Too many things to think about, and now he was late for his next meeting.

After a couple more days and no package from San Francisco, Charlie realized that Harry had not mailed the package to him. He had been killed or committed suicide before he was able to mail the package. He still didn't know if the San Francisco police had found a copy of the medical file from Thailand.

Charlie called his friend at the FBI, Mike Sewell, but after a few rings his phone went into voice mail. Charlie left him a message to return his call when he had time.

* * *

Speaker Wolf was meeting with the key congressmen who were leading the work on health care reform. They had been working on an alternative to the Affordable Care Act for years and they had finally reached an agreement on a set of principles for their proposal. They were:

1. Repeal the Affordable Care Act.

2. Replace it with affordable health insurance available for all using free market principles, no mandates, and freedom of choice.

3. Encourage States to offer insurance exchanges for individuals.

4. Portability of insurance plans among states.

5. Tax deduction for individual cost of insurance.

6. Major tort reform, including defined limits on malpractice claims.

7. Tax credit to businesses, large and small, for cost of health care provided to employees, either through insurance plans provided by the employer or as lump sum of cash provided annually to employees for them to purchase individual health insurance. Annual payment of cash to employees considered as income, but actual expense of insurance to individuals considered a tax-deductible expense.

8. Catastrophic health care insurance guaranteed to all citizens, including people with pre-existing conditions. No citizen will pay greater that x% of their income on non-elective health care expenses. Expenses above x% of income are deductible from reportable income for tax purposes.

9. Reform Medicare eligibility from 65 to 70 years of age in increments of 1 year over five years. Example: now-eligibility 65, next year-eligibility 66, following year-eligibility 67, continuing until 70 years of age is reached.

10. Reform Medicare "Doctor fix" permanently with change in the formula that is fair and reasonable.

11. Review Medicaid eligibility requirements and tighten them to eliminate fraud.

Speaker Wolf discussed the set of principles with his colleague Paul Marino. After Wolf and Marino met, they agreed to have a joint meeting with Congressman Caldwell and Senator Banfield to present the set of principles.

The four leaders of Congress met to discuss health care reform. It was obvious from the start that the President had convinced both Democrats that modifying the existing Affordable Care Act was not a realistic alternative. Caldwell and Banfield had done little to develop their own set of principles. They were waiting for the Republicans to go first.

Marino began the conversation, "Gentlemen, Speaker Wolf and his associates in the House have done the major work on a set of principles for health care reform. He will present the working principles that have been developed. I want you to know I support these principles, and I know they are a major departure from where we are today. Philosophically, I know they will be objectionable to you, but in the spirit of the President's wishes, we hope we can work together to develop the legislation needed to implement this set of principles. Robert, why don't you walk our colleagues through the work you have done?"

Speaker Wolf spent several minutes describing each of the eleven principles of health care reform. He ended his comments with a polite but firm statement to the two Democrats, "Senator Banfield and Congressman Caldwell, you know we have the votes to push health care reform through both houses of Congress. We don't want to do it that way. We sincerely want your input to make these reforms represent the thinking of both parties. We want some Democrats to vote for the legislation in both the Senate and the House. Do you have any questions or comments?"

Banfield leaned forward and slowly asked, "Have you discussed your principles with the President yet? Do you have her support?"

Paul stepped in and looking directly at the Senator, quickly responded, "Charlie, we brought this work to you two first. We will let you take it to Madam President if you want, or we can all go together, your choice."

Charlie told Paul he would take it to the President, and after discussing it with her he would call to see how they could move forward.

A week later the four men met again and agreed to form a joint committee with six representatives from both the Senate and House to begin discussions on the principles for health care reform.

Three months later the House passed several pieces of legislation on health care reform and sent them to the Senate. Three weeks later the Senate passed all the health care reform legislation without any changes, and one week later President Holliday signed the legislation into law.

Chapter 7

The first thing Ahmed and Fahad (Jose and Carlos) did, after making the call advising of their arrival, was visit a shopping mall to purchase the clothes they needed. Jeans and tee shirts were the basics, but they had fun buying running shoes and sunglasses and all the other things they needed. They also stopped at the food court and enjoyed their first American pizza.

After a week laying around the house in Fort Lauderdale, Ahmed and Fahad went to the train station and bought two tickets to Washington D.C., for departure the next day.

They cleaned the house, emptied the refrigerator, and took the bags of trash to the small strip mall a couple blocks away and dropped them in one of the dumpsters. They left nothing behind that would show they had ever been there. They boarded the train for Washington D.C. and twenty-seven hours later the trained pulled into Union Station. Ahmed and Fahad were exhausted, but caught a taxi to their new apartment.

The taxi driver was a large man from Ethiopia. He asked, "Do you live here or are you just visiting?"

The driver made Ahmed nervous. He thought to himself, I wonder if he is going to rob us? After a moment's hesitation Ahmed replied, "We are just visiting."

The driver continued, "And where are you from?"

Ahmed again replied, "We live in Florida."

The taxi driver was trying to get some more business. "I would be happy to give you a tour of Washington. I could show you the Capital and the White House and all the sights. I'll give you a special deal for a half-day tour. What do you say?"

Ahmed politely declined.

"Ok. I'll give you one of my cards, and if you want a tour after you have rested, you can give me a call."

"Thanks," replied Ahmed. He hoped that would end the conversation with this pushy big black man.

The driver pulled up in front of an apartment building and said, "This is the address you gave me. Is this the right place?"

Ahmed and Fahad had never seen the building before, but Ahmed said, "Yes, this is it. Thanks." Ahmed paid the fare. They got their bags from the trunk, walked up the steps to the front door, and entered the lobby.

It was a small lobby with mailboxes on the wall to the left and an elevator straight ahead. They walked to the elevator, pushed the button and took it to the third floor. They walked to apartment 309 and entered a one-bedroom apartment with two single beds. The living room was furnished with two end tables and lamps on either end of a dark blue sofa, two beige, stuffed chairs, and a TV, sitting on top of a wooden cabinet, opposite the sofa. All the furniture looked old and worn, and one of the stuffed chairs had a large stain on the seat cushion. There was a small kitchen with the basic necessities and far nicer than their last accommodations in Pakistan.

They had arrived.

* * *

After taking a few days to rest from their long journey from Pakistan to Huntington Beach, Khalid and Masood decided it was time to begin their drive across the United States. The one risk they faced was their lack of driver's licenses. They wanted to be invisible and knew a driver's license would show up in a government database. They had talked about this before they left Pakistan and had decided it was too risky to get a driver's license. All they had to do was drive safely and not exceed any speed limits and the likelihood of getting stopped was miniscule. They would take that risk.

They cleaned the house to remove any evidence of them having been there. They put the three backpacks containing the yellow cake in the trunk of the car, placed a blanket over the backpacks, and added a couple small, light boxes on top of the blanket. They put their other two backpacks and a suitcase filled with their clothes, in the back seat along with two bags of trash they needed to drop somewhere.

It was a warm, sunny day when they headed for their first destination, Flagstaff, Arizona. It was only about 480 miles, but they decided that would be enough for their first day. Khalid had the most experience driving and he volunteered to be the driver. Masood would navigate.

They found a gas station within their first mile and dropped the trash bags in a dumpster on the edge of the parking lot. They were surprised to learn the gas station was actually a small store with gas pumps in front of it. Khalid tried to fill the gas tank but couldn't get the pump to work. He wondered what he had done wrong when he heard a woman's voice over a loud speaker saying, "You have to pay for the gas before you can pump it. Please come inside to pay." He was embarrassed when he walked inside to pay. He told the woman behind the counter that he wanted to fill up the tank. She told him to give her sixty dollars and she would give him any change after he finished pumping the gas. Khalid was shocked when he put fifty-nine dollars of gas in the car. He had no idea it cost that much to buy gasoline in the U.S. After he got his dollar back, he and Masood walked around the store looking at all the bags of potato chips and Doritos, and aisles full of candy, crackers and cookies. Then they noticed rows of refrigerated cabinets with soft drinks and beer and bottled water. They had never been in a store like this. Khalid bought two bottles of water for the trip.

Their car was a beige Chevrolet Malibu with California license plates. It looked in pretty good condition, but in reality it was twenty years old.

Khalid watched the speed limit signs and drove about five miles under it. All the other cars were passing him and he realized almost everyone on the road was driving faster than the speed limit. After the first hour he decided to increase his speed and drive the speed limit. Cars were still passing him, but he couldn't take the chance of being stopped for speeding. He wondered if the U.S. had a law about driving too slow? He didn't think they had a law for that, but he knew that Americans did some weird things, and were strange people.

They arrived in Flagstaff without incident to end their first day on the road. They found a small motel and checked in for the night. There was a cute girl behind the check in counter who was very nice, and actually seemed to be flirting. Khalid was puzzled but didn't say anything to Masood about it.

* * *

Ann briefed her liaison contacts at the FBI and Homeland Security. They thanked her for bringing them into the loop, but after her discussions it was obvious to her they planned to do nothing on this potential threat.

She went back to her computer and spent time looking at SPARS business records. They imported oriental rugs from Pakistan and several other countries in the Middle East. It appeared they had a very successful business selling rugs in the Washington D.C. area. They also advertised a rug cleaning service, but she learned they used another company to do the cleaning work. That company was located in Arlington, Virginia, just outside Washington. Upon closer examination, she learned the owner of the cleaning company was the son of the owner of SPARS.

Ann discovered the SPARS owner and his wife lived at a very exclusive address in Georgetown, and the company actually owned their home. In addition, the company rented five apartments in the D.C. area. One was in the exclusive Watergate building, and the other four were spread around the District.

SPARS had six full time employees plus the owner, and a few additional part time employees. Three of the full time employees lived at the address of one of the apartments rented by SPARS, and the other full time employees lived at other addresses around the city, apparently paying their own rent. The part time employees were not occupying any of the other apartments rented by SPARS.

Ann had one of her team members visit all the apartments to see what could be learned.

During the next team meeting Ann reported, "We have a little more info on the SPARS apartments in D.C. They pay for a total of five apartments. One is upscale, fully furnished at the Watergate. It is occasionally used by the owner, possibly for some hanky panky, and is occasionally used by guests visiting Washington from Pakistan. It is empty most of the time. Three employees of SPARS share one of the other apartments, and have lived there for more than two years. Two apartments are empty and one other apartment has two men living in it. The apartment manager does not have their names and said they have only been living there a few weeks. He said he assumed they work for SPARS because when they arrived they already had keys. He thinks they are middle eastern, but said he had only seen them a couple times.

The team debated whether they should ask the FBI to watch the apartment, but they agreed that for now they would do it themselves. They wanted to get photos of the two men to see if their facial recognition software could be used to identify them.

George and one of his colleagues on the team staked out the apartment and took photos of people coming and going. On the second day, two Pakistani men exited the building, and George captured good images of them using the telephoto lens on his digital camera. He couldn't be sure these were the men living in the apartment, but watching the other people coming and going, he was pretty sure he had the right guys. He could show the photos to the building manager, but he decided not to risk it.

He had the photos checked with immigration records but no matches were found. He also had the photos run through databases of known terrorists, the FBI, Interpol, and a couple other databases, but nothing matched.

George stopped by Ann's desk and told her, "We have two men, most likely Pakistanis, living in the SPARS apartment for only a few weeks, but they don't show up on any databases I searched, and I have searched a bunch. They are unknowns."

Ann asked, "Are you sure you got the right guys?"

George replied, "Pretty sure, not a hundred percent, but I think these are the guys. I can show the pictures to the apartment building manager, but I don't want to risk him saying something to one of them and spooking them."

Ann called the FBI and told them she had two suspects that she wanted observed for a few days to see what could be learned about their activities. Her FBI contact asked how credible the information was about the men, and Ann replied, "It's very credible. We need to know more about them, but we don't want them to know they are being watched." She gave him their apartment address and said she would email photos of the two men to him. "Please keep me informed of everything you learn."

Her contact said, "I have to run this up the ladder. I know I am going to get some resistance to committing manpower but I will see what I can do."

Ann said, "If you can't spare the manpower, we will do it ourselves, but I just didn't want the FBI to get all bent out of shape by us working on your turf. If these guys are as bad as we think, you will be glad to get some of the credit when we stop a major terrorist plot."

"I'll do my best. Thanks for the heads up, Ann."

Ann's phone rang. "This is Ann."

"Hi Ann, this is Roger Meyers with the FBI. We have a detail watching a couple guys for you, and we want to give you a report on the status. Can you come over to the FBI this afternoon?"

"Sure, Roger. What time?"

"How about two?"

"I'll be there. If you don't mind, I'll bring another team member, George, with me?"

"Fine. See you at two."

A few minutes before two, George and Ann walked into the FBI headquarters and asked to see Agent Roger Meyers. When the man behind the desk asked to see their IDs they complied. He made a phone call, turned to Ann and politely informed her that someone would be right out to escort them to the meeting room.

A minute later a very attractive young lady walked up to Ann and asked, "Are you Ann Hunt?"

"Yes ma'am."

"Hi, I'm Betty, please follow me." Betty led Ann and George down a hallway to an elevator and up a floor to a conference room. Three men were waiting.

Roger began, "Ann, I'm Roger Meyers. These are my associates Bill and Tom. They are involved in the surveillance you requested so I asked them to sit in."

Ann shook hands with Roger, and introduced George.

They all sat, and Roger began. "Ann, we think you may have found some people up to no good. We put a surveillance team on them, as requested. One of them works as a dishwasher at a restaurant a few blocks from the apartment, and the other works in another restaurant a few blocks in the opposite direction. It appears they only work part time based on watching them for a few days. Other than working and going to the store occasionally for food, they seem to spend all their time in the apartment watching TV.

"We decided to check out their apartment when they were both at work. Other than a few clothes, they don't have much. What we found of interest was a wad of money and two passports. Both passports are Venezuelan with U.S. tourist visas in them. We have their names and the photos used in the passports. The passports are fakes. They are pretty good fakes, but they are fakes. The photos look like the guys we are watching. The names in the passports are Jose and Carlos. They don't look like a Jose or a Carlos to us. We would guess they are from Pakistan or Afghanistan. We have tried to identify them through facile recognition, to no avail. They have over $9,000 in small bills in an envelope in one of the dressers in the bedroom. We didn't find any guns, and frankly there wasn't anything else in the apartment, except a laptop. We downloaded the laptop and are still looking but there are no files on it. It doesn't look like it has been used. They haven't sent any emails, or done anything with it. They haven't even used it to look at porn.

"They might have other things on them when they are at work that could help us learn more about them, but they are being very cautious. I would guess at least one has a cell phone on him, that they can use to contact someone or that someone can use to contact them. But we won't know that unless we pick them up. We have followed your instructions to follow and observe, but not get caught."

Ann responded, "Thanks, guys. We appreciate your work. We might want to bug their room to hear what they talk about and to listen to any phone calls they make or receive."

Roger said, "Oh, I forgot to mention that. We put a bug in their living room and one in the bedroom. If we hear anything, we'll let you know."

Ann smiled, "Memory lapse, huh? Anything else you forgot?"

"No Ann, nothing else."

Ann said, "We could have you pick them up and question them and then deport them, but I think we are better off watching them and listening to them to see if they eventually are contacted by someone. Can you keep them under surveillance for a while longer?"

One of the other guys with Roger said, "It is the most boring surveillance you can ever imagine. But I'm convinced they are up to something. As long as it is ok with Roger, we will sit on them for as long as it takes."

Roger added, "We will watch them for a while longer. If we get pressure from above, I'll let you know."

Ann thanked them for their information. She and George drove back to CIA Headquarters, got their team together and gave them the information they had learned from the FBI.

Chapter 8

At their private dinner in the White House, Judy said, "Madam President, I just had a call from Senator Banfield's aide informing us that the Senator was found dead earlier today at his residence. The aide said the EMS attendant told him it was an apparent heart attack, but they would not be certain until after the autopsy. The Senator's wife is in Texas visiting one of their children. The aide said the Washington Post would have it in the paper tomorrow morning, and the evening news will probably get the story in time to run it tonight on the late news."

"Oh my," uttered Carolyn. "What a shame. I know I was causing him a lot of stress, but what sad news. Please get me his wife's phone number after dinner. I would like to call her and offer her my condolences."

"Will do. I hope this doesn't sound cold, but your life will be easier with Charlie gone."

The President decided not to respond to Judy's comment. They ate without talking for a while, and Judy realizing Carolyn had not appreciated her cold remark.

The following day The Washington Post had a huge article about Senator Charlie Banfield, the Senate Minority Leader, announcing his sudden death from a heart attack. It chronicled his career as a Senator and his many achievements.

* * *

FBI Agent Mike Sewell walked into his boss's office and asked if he could have a minute. His boss, George McDowell said, "Sure, what's up Mike?"

"I need to bring you up to speed on a couple possible coincidences. Several weeks ago I had a call from Senator Banfield, whom I have known for quite a while. He asked me for some confidential advice. I warned him if it involved a crime or a potential crime I was obligated to report it to the proper authorities. He assured me he was unaware of any crime, but needed some guidance. He wanted to learn more about the death of President Holliday's husband, and wanted to know if I knew anyone in San Francisco that might help him look into the situation. I told him my advice was to forget it, but if he was determined to look into it, I volunteered to talk to an old friend who was retired from the San Francisco police force. I talked to my friend, Harry Rice, and he spent some time looking into the death. You may remember it. John Holliday started a tech company and made millions, and the President worked for him right after graduating from law school. They met at Berkeley and married several years later. While she was Governor of California, he went to Thailand on business and contracted some rare, untreatable, infectious disease, flew back to the U.S. and was dead within a year. When Harry inquired into his medical records he got the brush off by the hospital, but upon further snooping found out the medical records were gone. There was no evidence of Mr. Holliday ever being in the hospital in San Francisco. Holliday was cremated and his ashes spread over the Pacific.

"I told Senator Banfield what Harry had found, and suggested that if he needed to talk directly to Harry I would give him Harry's full name and phone number. Again, I suggested he should let it go, that it was probably just the Governor trying to protect her privacy.

"Well, the Senator didn't let it go, he talked to Harry and asked Harry to fly to Thailand to see what else he could learn. A few days ago I heard from another friend with the SFPD that Harry Rice apparently ate his gun and committed suicide. His friends on the force don't think Harry would do that and are investigating. They said it was strange that Harry had apparently deleted everything from his computer and there was nothing in his apartment that indicated what he had been working on. They did find his cell phone and heard two urgent voice mails from Senator Banfield asking him to return the call immediately. They talked to

Banfield and he said he knew Harry and that Harry was working on something for him that was personal and he could not divulge what it was.

"Now I read in the paper that Senator Banfield had a heart attack and is dead. Coincidence? I don't know, but it is strange. Do you think I might take some time to look into this a little?"

George said, "What are you suggesting? That a suicide is not a suicide? And a heart attack didn't kill the Senator?"

"Don't know, but I knew both these guys. I liked the Senator and I liked Harry. They were basically good people. I just don't want us to miss something, but I don't have any evidence to support my gut feeling."

"Ok. Let's not open an official case. You can spend a little time being sure the locals in San Francisco and here in Washington do a thorough job of looking into the alternatives, but do it in a way that doesn't ruffle any feathers. I don't want a call from upstairs because somebody is complaining that the FBI is meddling in a local matter. Understood?"

"Yes sir, and thanks."

* * *

The President ordered all government flags flown at half-mast.

Charlie's wife chose to have the funeral in Washington and then fly with the casket to Texas where she would bury her husband. The Washington funeral was held at the National Cathedral. The President spoke fondly of Charlie and praised him for the service he had given to his country.

Standing in the wings, listening to the service were two interested individuals. Judy Webber listened to her boss speak and partially listened and watched the others who spoke. Mike Sewell, out of respect, listened to everyone who spoke, and continually watched the crowd. He was asking himself if some foul play was involved in Charlie's death, and if the guilty party were in the audience.

After the service, Mike made a courtesy call on the medical examiner. They had met a few times over the years, and Mike greeted him casually as he entered his office. "Hi, Dr. Jim, how's your day been?"

"Just another day," said Jim. "What brings you to this uninviting place?"

"Doc, I'm here on unofficial business. Please look at this as a courtesy call for now, and I hope it doesn't develop into anything more. I understand you did the autopsy on Senator Banfield. Can you tell me, off the record, if there was anything unusual about the autopsy?"

"Mike, when an FBI agent comes into my office and asks a question like that, off the record, I immediately think, he knows something I don't. I would be interested to know what that is, off the record of course. But, to answer your question, there is a 100% probability that Senator Banfield died of a heart attack. The real question is what caused the heart attack. I would answer that one, if you had asked, that there is a 95% probability that the heart attack was from natural causes. However, there are several things that can be given to someone in his medical condition that could trigger a heart attack. Most but not all of those triggers can be detected by an autopsy. I looked for that possibility, being a thorough medical examiner, but I did not find any of the known triggers. Would I stand up in court and swear that he died of natural causes? No, I would always leave a small out, just in case some very smart person used something that is undetectable. Why are you here, Mike?"

"Because the Senator was a friend, and because my gut doesn't feel right. I have no evidence that it wasn't natural, Jim."

"Mike, if you were to bring me something that you thought was used to trigger a heart attack I could test it specifically to see if any of that substance remained in his organs. But without a sample of something, I have done everything I know to be sure this was not foul play."

"Thanks, Jim, I appreciate your candor. Trust me, I am not questioning your skills or competence. Others may take short cuts, but I believe you when you say you did everything you could to rule out foul play.

"Jim, just one more thing. How difficult would it be to stage a murder to look like someone shot himself in the mouth with his own gun?"

"Why do I think this question is somehow related to your earlier question? Well, to answer your question, the medical examiner will again need to be very thorough. Look for evidence that the person was restrained, either physically or possibly chemically. Was he incapacitated in any way like alcohol or a sedative, or had he been given a shot of something? Toxicology screens would need to be extensive, and the examiner should look for bruising or puncture marks from a needle. Care to share what's going on?"

"Jim, I introduced the Senator to an individual recently. The Senator just died of a heart attack and the other individual just allegedly committed suicide by gun in the mouth. I hate to think I may be responsible for their deaths. I have no evidence of any kind in either case that foul play was involved, but I owe it to them to be sure their deaths are not somehow related. Thanks, Jim. You've been helpful."

Mike drove back to his office and had his secretary book him on the next flight to San Francisco. He also asked her, just in case, to get him a visa for Thailand.
When he arrived in San Francisco it was a beautiful sunny day, a little cool and windy.

Mike called a friend who worked for the SFPD and said, "Jerry, I just happen to be in San Francisco and was wondering if I could come by and see you?"

Jerry wondered what had brought Mike to San Francisco, but they hadn't talked for a while and he looked forward to seeing his old friend. "What time can you be here?"

"It's almost lunch time. Do you have any plans? I can pick you up and buy you a burger if you are interested."

"I never turn down a free burger. Just give me a call when you arrive at our building and I'll be right out."

Mike drove to a small, dinghy restaurant they had frequented before, where they knew the burgers were excellent, and they could enjoy a private conversation. The two old friends enjoyed their burgers and fries and caught up on each other's activities since they had last been together. Both were in the business of catching bad guys and it never seemed to stop.

After a while, Mike asked, "I was really sorry to hear about Harry Rice. Had you seen him lately?"

"Not for some time, but we talked regularly. Last time I talked to him was only a few weeks ago, and he sounded great. He was doing some private work for somebody, and sounded like he was keeping busy. He didn't give me any indication that anything was wrong."

"Is the case still open or have they closed it as a suicide?"

"A guy named Sanchez is the lead on the case. He's like a terrier. He won't let them close the case. He is convinced Harry didn't kill himself, but all the evidence says he did. His boss is leaning on him to close it and move on."

"Jerry, I talked to Harry several weeks ago and actually asked him to look into something for a friend of mine. I don't want to step on any toes in the SFPD, but I would really like to talk to Sanchez to see what he has to say. Think I should talk to his boss so he doesn't get pissed at the FBI?"

"Yea, Mike, that would be a really good idea."

They drove back to the precinct and Mike walked in with Jerry. They walked to the Captain's office and Jerry introduced Mike to his boss, Captain Joe Simons. Jerry excused himself and left Mike and Joe to get acquainted.

"Captain, I am not here on official Bureau business, and I can assure you I don't want to step on anybody's toes at the SFPD. I knew Harry Rice for a long time and considered him a friend. I was shocked to hear about his death. Do you know anything about what he had been working on lately?"

Joe said, "If I were a betting man, and I am not, I would bet you already know the answer to that question. What's going on?"

Mike responded, "I talked to Harry several weeks ago and asked him to do some private work for a friend of mine in Washington. He did the work, and I passed the results to my friend in D.C. I gave Harry's name and phone number to my friend, and said I would get out of the middle. They could communicate directly if any more was needed. I am pretty sure my friend asked Harry to do more work for him. Then, I heard Harry committed suicide and I was shocked. He sounded great when I spoke to him last, and I personally want to be sure it was a suicide."

Joe said, "Let's get Sanchez, the lead investigator on the case, in here.

He walked to his door and hollered for Sanchez to come to his office. Sanchez was of Mexican heritage, but his parents had brought him to the U.S. and they were now U.S. citizens. He was five foot ten and solid as a rock. He grew up across the bay in Oakland. After high school he joined the Army and after two years and an honorable discharge he returned to the bay area and graduated from college. He had been with the SFPD for almost fifteen years, was married with four kids. Sanchez walked in and Joe introduced him to Agent Sewell. The Captain said, "This is an unofficial inquiry by an FBI agent. The FBI is not getting involved in your case, understand?"

Sanchez said, "Sure, what do you want to know?"

Mike looked at Sanchez and said, "I'd like your take on the case. What are the things keeping you from closing it as a suicide? And, with all due respect, I would like the opportunity to look at the case file, visit the scene, and talk to the medical examiner who did the autopsy."

Joe said, "Sanchez, I think Agent Sewell knows more about this case than he has shared so far. But I don't care about jurisdiction. I just want to know if Harry did it to himself or if someone helped him. I want the case closed unless there is some evidence that it was a murder. If the FBI can help us get to the bottom of this, fine. Have at it. Sanchez, give him everything he wants, understand?"

"Yes, sir." Sanchez turned to Mike and said, "Let's go to my desk and I'll show you everything I have."

They spent part of the afternoon going over the case file, and then Sanchez took Mike to Harry's apartment, where he had been found. He walked him around the scene, describing where things were located. Things like Harry's computer which had been on the kitchen table, had been taken by the police as possible evidence.

Sanchez described the scene to Mike and explained there was no physical evidence of foul play. The bigger problem was the lack of evidence. In particular, Harry or someone had wiped the computer clean. There were no files on the computer. It still worked but it was like Harry deleted all his history of computer activity. One would have thought that he would just leave the computer with all his personal files and work files on it, but he took the time before killing himself to wipe it clean. There were also no paper files of any work Harry had done since he retired. Why would someone suicidal go to all the trouble of getting rid of all paper files and computer files before he shot himself? And how had he destroyed the paper files? There was no evidence he burned them, and they were not in the trash. Had he taken them to the dump in plastic bags? Sanchez said he even talked to the regular trash pickup guy to see if he remembered picking up an unusual number of bags at Harry's address, but the guy said he didn't think so, but he really couldn't remember.

Then Sanchez told Mike about his phone conversation with Senator Banfield. He said, "The Senator confirmed that Harry had been doing some work for him, but he said it was personal and he wouldn't reveal any of the specifics of what Harry was doing for him. But at least that confirmed Harry was working on something. I was about to call the Senator again and try to lean on him to give us some details about what Harry was doing, and suddenly I read in the paper that the poor guy dropped dead of a heart attack."

Mike asked Sanchez if he could arrange a meeting with the medical examiner in the morning. Mike suggested that he not mention to the medical examiner that Mike was with the FBI. "I don't want him to get all nervous. Just tell him you have another guy helping to put a fresh set of eyes on things."

Sanchez arranged the meeting for nine am. He asked Mike, "Where are you staying? I can pick you up at your hotel in the morning if you like."

"I'm staying at the Fairmont. I will be at the front door tomorrow morning at eight forty five, ok?"

"Fine. See you then."

The medical examiner was relaxed and after introductions asked, "What brings you by this time Detective Sanchez?"

"I am still investigating Harry Rice's death, and Mike wanted to hear first hand your conclusions from the autopsy."

"How many times do I have to tell you, it was a clean autopsy? Unfortunately, everything points to suicide. We did all the toxicology screens to see if we could find anything in his system that shouldn't have been there, but we came up empty. It was his gun, he held it in his right hand, and he was right handed. We checked all that. No suicide note, nothing on his computer, no files around the house, no indications from his friends of any problems. Those are all curious, but medically the case is straightforward.

Mike asked, "Sir, I don't mean to question your professionalism, but did you inspect the body for physical bruising, and did you look for needle puncture marks all over his body?"

"Yes, I did."

Mike took a different tack, "If you were a professional and wanted to make a retired police officer look like he had committed suicide with a gunshot in his mouth, how would you do it?"

"Knowing what I know about forensics, I would find a way to drug the guy with a spiked drink to make him near comatose and then stage the event. But the killer would have to use something that would not remain in his system. The digestive system stops when the heart stops pumping, so most chemicals would still be in the body during autopsy. We didn't find anything unusual.

Mike pressed, "Your operative word was "most" chemicals. What chemical could be used to control someone that would not remain in the body?"

"Let me think about that one. I'll get back to you after I do some research."

Chapter 9

Masood and Khalid's second day started earlier than the first because their destination, Amarillo, Texas was over 600 miles away. They enjoyed the free breakfast offered in the lobby of the motel and then headed east. It was another beautiful sunny day, with not a cloud in the sky. Their route took them through Arizona, New Mexico, and into the Texas panhandle. Again, the scenery was spectacular. Khalid wondered what Masood thought about the country they were passing through, but he was afraid to say anything to him for fear of sounding weak.

Finally, Masood said, "I had no idea that America was so beautiful. If you want to stop along the way and enjoy looking at some of the things we are passing, I wouldn't mind. I always thought America was crowded, with people everywhere, and just a bunch of big, dirty cities. Except for the few cars and trucks on the road, there aren't any people around this part of the country. Strange, don't you think?"

Khalid was shocked at the words coming from Masood. Masood had always been quiet. This was the most Khalid had ever heard Masood say at one time. He took advantage of the opportunity, and agreed with him. "This is a really beautiful part of America, and I had no idea it would be like this. I don't know how much we should stop because we have over 600 miles to travel today, but why don't we see as we go."

Masood replied, "Yea, we probably should keep going. Maybe after we get to Amarillo tonight and find a place to stay, we can look around the city a little. It is not like Akbar is watching us. We can do whatever we want."

"Good idea. It could be fun to look around Amarillo tonight."

They stopped when they needed gas, and they stopped for lunch. Somewhere around Amarillo, after about a twelve-hour drive, they found a motel and pulled into the parking lot. Khalid was tired because of all the driving, but he hoped Masood still wanted to look around. They took showers and then walked next door to a little restaurant. The waitress, Penny, was friendly, just like the girl behind the counter in Flagstaff. Neither Khalid nor Masood knew how to act around her.

She asked them where they were from and Masood responded, "We started in California and we are driving across the country."

"No silly, I meant where are you from, where were you born?"

Masood was embarrassed by not answering her question correctly, and he didn't like being called 'silly'. Khalid could tell he was upset so he told the waitress they were from Saudi Arabia, like their passports said. "We are visiting your country for the first time."

"Are your daddies rich oil barons?"

Neither Khalid nor Masood knew what a baron was. But after a pause Khalid said, "Sorry, but we are just learning your language. Maybe we should order our food."

She smiled and asked, "I'm Penny. What can I getcha?"

Khalid, feeling worse said, "I don't understand"

She wrinkled her brow, "What would you like to eat, silly?"

Khalid and Masood noticed she had said "silly" again. Khalid almost asked her why she called them silly, but he didn't want to embarrass himself and Masood.

 Khalid said. "I would like a cheeseburger and some french fries please."

Masood added, "I will have the same."

Penny asked, "Anything to drink?"

"Just water, please," said Khalid. "Me too," added Masood.

A little while later, Penny brought their food, and said, "I hope you like it. Say, I get off work around 9 o'clock tonight. Would you guys like to go to the Lonestar Bar just down the road with me? I can teach you how to dance like a cowboy."

Khalid looked at Masood to get his reaction, and Masood looked terrified. Khalid tried to think what to say and finally responded, "Penny, we have to get up early tomorrow morning, but maybe we will see you there for a short visit."

Penny added, "OkeDoke."

They finished their burgers and fries, paid the bill, and walked back to the motel.

Masood said, "What do you want to do? I would like to go see the place, but she called me 'silly'. I didn't like that."

Khalid responded, "I don't think she meant to offend you. 'Silly' must mean something else to her. I would like to go, just to watch.

'Ok, we'll go at nine, but we will just watch and only stay a short time."

They lay on the bed watching television until it was almost nine.

Khalid said, "It is time to go. Do you still want to?"

"Sure, let's go see what a Texas bar is like and watch the cowboys dance."

The bar was about a mile down the road, away from the highway, and they found it easily. It had a big neon sign outside and there were quite a few cars in the parking lot. They walked in and the first thing they noticed was how loud the music was. There was a long bar with barstools along the wall opposite the front door and a dance floor in the middle of the room. Around the dance floor on three sides were tables and chairs. Most of the tables were occupied, but there were a few empties. Masood walked to one and sat down, facing the dance floor. A waitress in a red and white checkered blouse, short skirt, and cowboy boots came over and said, "What can I get you gents?"

Masood said, "We will both have cokes, please."

"Coming right up."

Just after the waitress came back with their drinks, Penny walked over and sat down at their table. "Hi, guys. Glad you could come. Which one of you wants to learn how to dance first?"

Khalid responded, "We want to watch the others dance for awhile. Neither of us knows how to dance."

"Well, I sure would like to teach you. You could tell all your friends back home that Penny from Amarillo taught you how to dance like a cowboy."

"Thanks, Penny, but not right now."

"Maybe at least you could buy a girl a beer. Have you ever had a beer? Is it against your religion?"

"Our religion says we should not consume alcohol, but not all of us always obey all the rules. Tonight we are just having cokes, but I would be happy to buy you a beer," Khalid said.

Penny waved to the waitress and she brought over a beer for Penny.

As Khalid was paying the waitress, Penny said, "Thank you. Are you sure you don't want to try just one while you are in Texas?" As she took her first sip she added, "You know guys, I don't even know your names. You know mine but I don't know yours. That ain't fair."

"My name is Khalid and this is Masood."

"Hi Khalid and Masood, nice to meet you. Welcome to Texas."

Penny kept chatting away and Khalid listened and smiled. Masood focused on the dance floor. He was fascinated with the people dancing. There were a lot of big men, and they all wore big cowboy hats. The girls were all wearing short skirts. Clearly, this kind of place would be unacceptable in Pakistan. Masood wasn't offended with what he saw; rather it made him curious to learn more.

Penny tried again to get Khalid to dance with her, but he was too shy. Finally, Masood said to Khalid, "I think it is time to go."

They said good night to Penny, walked to their car, and drove back to the motel. On the way to the motel Masood said, "We shouldn't tell anyone about going to that bar."

"I agree."

The next day when they walked out of the motel it was raining. They drove to Little Rock, Arkansas, and it rained all the way. Two days later they were in Richmond. They had a map of the city, and the address of the safe house, but even with the map it was not easy to find their way. After driving around the city streets for almost a half hour, finally Masood recognized the street sign they needed. About halfway down the block was the address they wanted. It was a small, single story house similar to the other ones on the street. It had a two-car garage attached to the house. They pulled in the driveway and walked to the front door. The key worked and they walked into their new home.

After looking around they decided to pull the car into the garage. There was a door in the kitchen that opened into the garage. Khalid walked into the garage, opened the garage door and drove the car in. They took their backpacks and suitcase into the house, but left the three backpacks in the trunk. They would hide them later.

Back inside the house, they noticed it was very similar to the house in Huntington Beach. One bedroom, two single beds, a nice living room with television, and a nice kitchen.

They had arrived.

* * *

Ann was at her computer in her cubicle when she got a message indicating that she was being hacked. She had the latest software to block attacks and she had developed her own advanced software that also identified where the attack was coming from. She confirmed that the attack had not penetrated any of her systems, and then opened a file that showed where the hacker was located.

She was shocked to see that someone in the Pakistan Embassy in Washington was doing the hacking. After a few seconds, when the hacker realized he had hit a wall and was not able to penetrate her system, he broke communication.

Ann walked to George's workstation and told him what had happened. She said, "This really bothers me that they would be trying to hack my computer. I was sure when I was looking at the ISI official's computer, I was not leaving any trace of being there. But it can't be just a coincidence that someone from the Pakistan Embassy is now trying to hack my computer. I'll send a message to our IT group alerting them about the attempted hack, and suggest they send a memo to all personnel to be on the lookout for hackers."

She asked George to round up their team for a brainstorming meeting.

The next day Ann's Al Qaeda Team met in their conference room. Ann brought everybody up to speed on all the pieces of info they had.

1. Yellow cake sale by Iran's Republican Guard to unknown parties.

2. Possible link, regarding the money used for yellow cake purchase, to Pakistan's ISI in Islamabad.

3. Two dead Mexicans found in Pakistan cargo container in Manzanillo, Mexico. One dead man had name of Pakistani living in Mexico City.

4. Senior ISI official in Washington Embassy has large financial dealings with SPARS Inc., a company owned by a U.S citizen, originally from Pakistan.

5. Company has business locations in several major cities in the US.

6. SPARS owner has five rental apartments throughout DC. One is in the Watergate and is used for special guests and possibly private entertaining, three employees are using one apartment, and one other has two Pakistani (?) men living in it. They have Venezuelan passports, but look Pakistani. Facial recognition has been unsuccessful. FBI is watching them. Other apartments are currently empty.

7. NSA picked up a phone conversation between ISI official in Washington and someone in southern California. The message was, "We have arrived in country."

8. Two suspected Pakistanis are living in one of the SPARS apartments. They have fake Venezuelan passports using the names Jose and Carlos. The FBI is watching them and bugged the apartment. The men work part time in restaurants and are being very cautious.

Ann said, "This list all seems to be related, but it is all pretty thin. We don't know who bought the yellow cake. We don't know if the container in Mexico had yellow cake in it or drugs or something else. And, we don't know if the ISI official is involved in a terrorist plot, or if the owner of SPARS is involved in a terrorist plot. We don't know how many dirty bombs are planned, where they will be set off, when, or who the players are.

I think we need to keep pursuing the leads we have, but I think we need to start thinking much broader. Are they planning to hit other cities? What are the likely targets for dirty bombs in D.C.? When are some likely dates for this attack, like the next anniversary of 9/11? Osama bin Laden's birthday or date of his death? Who are the players in the plan, and what tools do we use to identify them? Which other countries might be leading this terror plot if we are wrong about Pakistan? Who are the first responders to a dirty bomb attack, and when do we alert them to the potential threat? And finally, currently the FBI and NSA are involved in limited roles. What other resources should we reach out to for help?"

George was the first to respond. "Ann that is a good list of the things we know and the things we don't know. I think it is time to brief the boss, and recommend that he brief the President on the current status of the information. I know there are a lot of holes, but there is a reasonable possibility that the yellow cake is now in the U.S. and possibly two or more terrorists may already be in the country. It doesn't take long to convert yellow cake into a bomb that can be easily detonated. It could happen at any time. The President needs to know."

The group was in agreement with getting the information to the Director of the CIA with the recommendation that he bring the President up to speed. Ann was selected as the one to brief the Director of the CIA, Warren Simpson.

Ann scheduled a meeting with the Director for late afternoon, and when she walked in his office he said, "Hi Ann, how's your father doing?

Ann replied, "I think he is doing fine. He is in the middle of Russia with the Peace Corps teaching business courses at a university. But somehow I think you probably already know that."

"Tell him I said hi the next time you talk to him. He did a great service for his country while he was with us. What brings you up to the top floor to see me?"

Ann gave him the briefing with all the important details but keeping it as brief as she could make it.

When she finished, the Director said, "Ann, it is time for you to meet our new President. I want you to go with me when I brief her. I'll let you know when it's scheduled."

The next day Warren and Ann rode in the back of his chauffer driven black Lincoln to the White House.

In the Oval Office were the Vice President, the President's National Security Advisor, and the President's Chief of Staff. When they walked in the room Warren greeted each one and introduced Ann Hunt to them all. They were standing, finishing their greetings, when the President walked in.

She started, "Everybody have a seat. Thanks for coming, Warren. Who is this young lady you brought with you?"

"Madam President, I would like you to meet Ann Hunt, our lead analyst on the Al Qaeda and Affiliates Team."

"Hi Ann, welcome to the Oval Office. Have you been here before? As you know, I'm a little new here."

"First time, Madam President. It is a pleasure to meet you."

"Well Warren, I hear you have some information you want to share with us about a possible terrorist attack. The floor is yours."

Warren went through the briefing covering all the separate pieces of information that had been collected and the broader things the team would continue to work on. He also mentioned the roles of the FBI and NSA.

As Warren finished, the President said, "Warren and Ann, I am glad you are not taking this evidence to a court of law. You would be laughed out of the courtroom. I will assume that the Iranians sold yellow cake to someone, and possibly it could have been the Pakistanis. Two dead Mexicans in a storage container in a place where the drug cartels are killing each other on a regular basis is hardly strong evidence that the yellow cake was smuggled into Mexico. And two poor Pakistani men living in an apartment in D.C., rented by a friend of a person working in the Pakistan Embassy? Well that isn't the strongest evidence either. I know when 9/11 happened there was criticism that our agencies were not communicating with each other and because of that we missed connecting the dots. My concern is that you are connecting dots now that maybe should not be connected. I think you have a lot of work to do before we can conclude we have a credible treat of a terrorist attack."

The President asked if anyone else had any comments or questions for Director Simpson, and when no one volunteered, the President said, "Warren, thanks for coming. Don't let my comments influence your pursuit of more leads. Yellow cake in a dirty bomb is not something I want happening in our country while I am President. Use all your resources to find that yellow cake before someone uses it to make a dirty bomb."

Warren and Ann walked to their car and climbed in the back seat. Warren said, "Well Ann, how did you like your first meeting with the President?"

"I am not totally surprised by her reaction, but I thought she was pretty cruel in the way she delivered her message. There is too much circumstantial evidence for us to be wrong. There is a real threat out there, and we need to find more clues before they decide to act."

"I agree with you Ann, but to the inexperienced eyes of the President, things often look different to the way we see them. You and your team have my support. Keep working on it, and work as fast as you can."

When Ann got back she quickly briefed her team, and then headed for home. She lived in the northwest part of the city and had her own condo, which her Dad had helped her buy. She enjoyed the drive back and forth to work using it as time to relax and think about other things for a while. She especially liked driving the Rock Creek Parkway because it was a beautiful drive and a winding road where she could enjoy the handling of her little BMW.

As she took a curve to the right, out of the corner of her eye she saw another car next to her getting very close, like it was going to hit her car. Suddenly the other car collided with hers and she felt her car jump the curb and begin to roll to the left. A few seconds later she woke up and realized her car was upside down and had crashed down a grassy slop and stopped when it hit a tree. She was dazed but didn't think she was seriously hurt. She tried to unbuckle her seatbelt but it was jammed. The windshield was severely cracked, but it was still in place. She tried to open her door and realized she was hanging upside down. Suddenly a police officer was at the passenger side door and yanked it open. He asked her if she was ok and she said, "I'm ok, I think, but I can't get the seat belt to release." He crawled in, released the seat belt, and she collapsed in a heap. The officer dragged her out of the car and helped her walk away from the car for safety.

A few minutes later an EMS vehicle arrived and two paramedics came down the slight hill to where she was sitting. They wrapped her in a blanket and talked to her about her condition. After they determined she was ok to move, they walked her up the hill to the EMS unit, had her lay on the gurney, and drove off to the hospital with the siren blaring.

Ann had a couple lacerations on her forehead, but she had no idea how they had happened. She also told the attendants that she felt like she had been punched all over. They gave her a complete exam, and declared that she was a lucky lady. Other than the two lacerations and bruises she was in good condition.

When the medical people were finished, the police questioned her about the accident. All she could remember was driving in the left lane going around a curve and seeing out of the corner of her eye a car on her right that seemed to be coming closer to her, like it was trying to force her off the road. She told them she thought she was going about forty-five miles per hour at the time.

The police told her the other car did not stop. The car immediately behind her stopped, but the driver said it all happened so fast he had no idea what kind of car hit her or what color it was.

When the police finished questioning her, the nurse said the hospital was releasing her and she was free to go home. The policeman who helped her out of her car gave her a ride home to be sure she was ok. He gave her his card and told her to call if she needed anything.

She walked to her bathroom and looked at her face in the mirror. She was puffy and red, but the cuts had not required any stitches. She just had a couple Band-Aids on them. She was exhausted, but before she climbed into bed she called her Mom to let her know she had an accident but she was fine. Then she called her boy friend to say hi and tell him what had happened. He offered to come over, but she said she needed to sleep. They didn't see each other as often as she would have liked, primarily because of her work, but he was also busy with his teaching career. They had been seeing each other for almost two years, but they had both avoided conversations about the future. She liked him a lot, but for now she preferred their current relationship to a more permanent commitment. She sensed he felt the same way.

The next morning when her alarm went off she couldn't believe how badly she felt. She had a terrible headache and she hurt all over. She called her friend and co-worker George and told him what had happened. She said she was really sore all over and was going to take the day off to rest and take care of getting her car towed somewhere. She promised to call him later in the day to check in.

As she lay in bed her phone rang. The caller ID didn't show anything, but she answered it with a "Hello?"

"Hi sweetheart, how are you doing?" It was her Dad's voice on the other end of the line.

"Dad, where are you? You sound like you are next door. What are you doing calling me? It must be the middle of the night for you."

He responded, "First, I am still in Russia. I got a call earlier this evening saying that you had been in an accident. How are you?"

She told him what happened, at least what she remembered. "I only have a couple scratches on my forehead, but I feel like I have been run over by a herd of water buffalo. I ache all over."

"A friend of mine will probably pay you a visit in the next couple days. Remember the name I gave you, when we lived in Hong Kong, to contact if you ever had a problem and I wasn't around? That is the guy who will stop by to see you. He might be able to help identify who ran you off the road. How is everything at work?"

"You know Dad, we are just trying to connect some dots. Right now we need some more dots."

"Remember Ann, always look at the extended families. Amazing what you can learn sometimes. Sorry I can't talk any longer, but I wanted you to know you are in my thoughts, even if I am on the other side of the world. The next time you talk to your Mom tell her I am doing fine, but miss her. Love you and bye for now."

"Bye Dad. Love you."

Later in the morning Ann called her BMW dealer, told them about her accident, and asked them to retrieve the car, inspect it to see if it was fixable or if she needed a new one. She asked if they could deliver a loaner to her apartment for her to use temporarily. They told her they would take care of everything, and she would have a loaner at her condo later that afternoon. She thanked them and went back to bed.

She awoke a couple hours later and realized she had been dreaming about work. The dream was about the Iranians who were behind the whole terrorist plot. They had tricked the Pakistanis into buying yellow sand packaged in lead to prevent radiation leaks. They were planning to make some dirty bombs themselves and have it all blamed on the Pakistanis. Could this be real or was she just hallucinating after the accident?

* * *

The next day Ann drove her temporary loaner to work and told George to assemble the team. She told them about her dream, and asked them if it was possible that they were following the wrong dots?

George said, "Personally I think we have the right dots, but it is certainly possible that the Iranians sold the Pakistanis junk. We should talk to our contacts in Iran to see what chatter they are hearing.

Ann also planned to work on her Dad's advice. Look deeper at the extended families. She would search deeper into the family tree of the ISI official in the embassy and she would go deeper into the owner of SPARS.

When Ann arrived at work the next day she had a message on her desk from the man who her Dad had told her about when they were in Hong Kong. He left a phone number and asked her to call him when she had time.

She dialed the number. "Hello Ann, this is Ben Stokes. I'm in the building. Can I come down and see you for a short visit?"

Ann said, "Sure, I assume you know where I am, so I'll see you when you get here."

A few minutes later a tall man about her Dad's age, or maybe a little older, walked up to her and said, "Hi Ann, I'm Ben. I've known your father for a long time, and have watched you grow up, from afar. I was delighted when you joined the Agency, and I am sure you will make some great contributions.

"I heard about your accident and have been doing some work, behind the scenes. It turns out we sometimes have some surveillance in the sky over Washington and can see things when we need to. We got lucky and were able to see your accident. The car that pushed you off the road was registered to Mohammed Masori, an American citizen, of Pakistani origin. He was actually born here, and now lives in Richmond, Virginia. His father immigrated to the U.S. many years ago, and is the owner of an Oriental rug business named SPARS. I think you have heard of it, yes?"

"Ben, you are amazing. His father is a person of interest in an investigation my team is working on. Do we know for sure that Mohammed was driving the car or only that it was his car?"

"Only that it was his car, unfortunately."

"Do the police have this information?"

"No, the police don't have it, and we can't give it to them. No one can know we have this capability, sorry."

Ben stood to go and said, "Ann, it is great to finally meet you. Use what you have learned to help you with your investigation. Good luck."

"Thank you, Ben. I hope we can meet again sometime."

* * *

Ann assembled her team for another review. They were all concerned about her accident and asked it she knew any more about what happened.

She told them, "I had a visit from someone in the Agency who has access to some video from over head surveillance. We know Mohammed Masori owns the car, and he is the son of Waheed al Masori, the owner of SPARS. We don't know if Mohammed was driving the car. Unfortunately, this information is classified and we can't share it with the police.

"The other thing of interest is someone tried to hack my computer. They didn't get in, but the hacker was working from the Pakistan Embassy. My guess is that somehow Mohammad al Babar discovered I was hacking his computer. He must have some new technology that set off an alarm. I will have to be more careful because I didn't think they had that capability. I must have really pissed him off. He is probably behind my accident.

"Have we heard anything from any of the field operatives in the other countries that could be involved with the yellow cake?"

George responded that most of the operatives had responded and there was no chatter about yellow cake coming from Yemen, Iraq, Syria, Afghanistan, or Libya.

Ann mentioned her dream about Iran and said she was going to contact the operative in Iran to do some more digging to see if he can learn anything more about Iran's Republican Guard and any activity that might be suspicious. She also told them she would be spending more computer time looking into Mohammad al Babar's family and Waheed al Masori's family. She also planned to talk to their contact in Islamabad to see what he can learn about the two men.

* * *

After talking to the station chief in Islamabad and spending time searching computer sources, she had a more detailed understanding of the two individuals. Mohammad al Babar grew up in Karachi and after going to college had joined the ISI in Islamabad. After college he married his wife who was also from Karachi, and they had two sons, both living and working in Islamabad. His wife was with him in Washington.

Waheed al Masori and his wife were also from Karachi. They had immigrated to the U.S. almost thirty years ago, and had three sons, all born in the U.S. When he came to the U.S. he started SPARS Inc. and built it into a very successful Oriental rug business importing rugs from all over the Middle East. Their three sons were Kareem, Omar, and Mohammed. They all used Masori as their last name which is not the traditional naming system used by most Muslims in the Middle East. The tradition was to adopt the father's first name as their surname, which would have been al Waheed, but they apparently chose the western approach to last names.

Kareem was off the grid. He had gotten a Virginia drivers license when he was eighteen, but the DMV records showed that the license had expired. He had a couple arrests for assault when he was a teenager, got probation, but did not serve any time. There was no trace of him currently. Omar had gone to a small college in the Washington area but did not graduate. He was now the owner and general manager of the rug cleaning business used by SPARS. Mohammed, the youngest, was a student at the University of Richmond studying physics.

The surprise Ann discovered was that Mohammad al Babar's wife and Waheed's wife were sisters.

* * *

Faisal and Jamal spent a few days walking around American University and walking around Washington visiting the sites, playing tourists. They visited the Lincoln Memorial, walked all the way to the top of the Washington Monument, walked around the Capital and the White House, and visited the Smithsonian Institute. They were amazed at all the government buildings and the beauty of Washington. It was late summer, which is hot and humid in Washington. They blended in well with all the other tourists.

They felt comfortable walking around the city and enjoyed the opportunity to just relax. Faisal said, "I think it's time for us to register for classes and try to find part time jobs, like we were instructed."

Jamal responded, "I guess you are right. It is time for us to get back to work. I wonder how long it will be before we are contacted?"

"There is no way to know. We don't know if the others have arrived, and we will just have to be patient and ready when we get the call. I hope we can get the kind of work they want us to find."

It was another hot and humid day when they walked to the administration offices of American University and asked where to go to register for fall classes. A cute co-ed at the information desk asked if they were new students. When they responded yes, she said she would be happy to sit down with them and explain everything they needed to do. She said, "My name is Sue, what are your names?"

Faisal said, "I am Faisal and this is my friend, Jamal. We are both from Pakistan, and we are really excited about being here."

Sue smiled and said, "Welcome to America." Then she told them the first thing they needed to do was get their university ID cards. She gave them a map of the campus and showed them where to go to get the IDs. She explained that once they had their ID cards they could register for classes online. She showed them how to get to the university website and explained how to use the IDs to register for classes. "If you have any problems just come back to the information desk and I can help you. If I am not here, another student will help you.

Faisal said, "We also need to find part time jobs. Can you tell us the best way to go about finding a job?"

"Sure," responded Sue. "We have a placement office available to help students find temporary jobs. There is some information about jobs on the school website, but I think it is easier to just go to the placement office and talk to someone there." She showed them on the map where the placement office was located and then added, "But they can't help you unless you have your ID cards, so do that right away, today, if you can. If you have any trouble, come back and find me."

Faisal and Jamal thanked her for all her help and walked off in the direction of the office where they would get their IDs.

They each filled out the form necessary for their ID and gave it to the girl behind the counter. She entered Faisal's information in the computer and then asked him to stand in front of the camera to have his picture taken. Two minutes later she handed him his laminated photo ID card. Then she repeated the process for Jamal and both men walked out as official American University students.

They looked at the map again and saw a place nearby where they could get something to eat. They both wanted a snack before going to the placement office. There were many students in the snack bar when they entered. It was cafeteria style, so they walked through the line and each bought a hamburger, fries and a coke. Faisal paid for both meals and they walked to an empty table and enjoyed eating their meals, among the other students.

Their next challenge was to find jobs. They found the placement office and saw a sign on the door that said, "CLOSED, back at two pm." They walked around for a while, then found a bench near the placement office and sat to wait for the office to re-open.

Shortly after two, they walked in and were greeted by another co-ed. She politely asked, "How can I help?"

Again Faisal took the lead, "Hi, we have just gotten our university IDs and will be registering for classes this fall. We need to find some part time work to make a little extra money. Can you tell us how to go about it?"

"Sure. My name is Sandra, but my friends call me Sandy. Do you have any ideas what kind of work you want?"

Faisal continued, "Well, we both worked for a food delivery company in Pakistan, and we were hoping maybe there was something similar to that."

"That sounds interesting. I've heard some students work for the company that delivers the food to our campus, so maybe you can find something like that. Let me see if I can find the company name and address and phone number. A lot of companies like to hire students who are taking classes here, so hopefully we can find something you will like."

She started looking at her computer and after searching for a minute she said, "We're in luck." She wrote the company name, address, and phone number on a piece of paper and handed it to Faisal. She pointed to her right and said, "There are some desks over there with phones. You are welcome to call the company using one of our phones if you want. Or if you prefer, you can call them later from your residence."

Faisal said to Jamal, "Let's call them now." He turned back to Sandy and said, "Thank you very much, Sandy. If they don't have any opportunities we will be back to look for something else."

"Good luck."

They walked to one of the desks and Faisal said to Jamal, "Why don't you make the call for us?"

Jamal talked to a nice lady, who told him they should come by to fill out applications. She said the office was open until five pm. Jamal thanked her and said they would be there before five.

A few days later, the company called their apartment and invited them both to come in for short interviews.

Two days later they had jobs working on food trucks that delivered food all over Washington.

Chapter 10

Mike Sewell decided he needed to go to Thailand. He called his secretary in Washington and asked her to make a reservation for him from San Francisco to Bangkok with a return flight about a week later back to San Francisco. She said she would take care of it and send him an email with the flight details.

He called Detective Sanchez, "Detective, how are you today?"

"I'm fine, but still frustrated about the Harry Rice case. What can I do for you?"

"I've decided a trip to Thailand is in order and I'm flying out tomorrow. Do you still have Harry's cell phone?"

"Yes, it's being held in evidence."

"Can you take a look at the phone and see if there is a number in his contacts for anybody in Thailand?"

"Sure, I'll have a look and call you back. How can I reach you?"

Mike gave him his cell phone number and asked him to call as soon as possible if he found anything. Sanchez said he would call him in a little while.

About two hours later Mike's cell phone rang and it was Detective Sanchez. "Mike, there was no one with a Thai named in his list of contacts, but there was a contact listed just as 'Thailand' with a number that looks like it is not in the U.S." He gave the number to Mike and said he hoped it was someone who Harry talked to when he was in Thailand.

The next day Mike boarded a flight to Hong Kong, with a connecting flight the following day to Bangkok. When he arrived in Hong Kong he took the train from the Hong Kong airport into the city. The airport and train were air conditioned, but when he walked out of the train station in Central, a blast of hot humid air hit him in the face. He had forgotten how hot it could be in Hong Kong. He checked into the Mandarin Hotel, which was a short walk from the train station, but he was dripping wet by the time he got to the lobby. After one of the staff escorted him to his room, he took the elevator to the restaurant on the top and enjoyed a delicious meal. He was exhausted after the flight, but slept off and on during the night, suffering from jetlag. The following morning he took the train back to the airport and boarded his flight to Bangkok.

When he walked out of the airport it was as hot as Hong Kong, but it was also pouring rain. He checked into the Mandarin Oriental Hotel in Bangkok and made a phone call. When a man answered the phone Mike said, "This is Mike Sewell from the United States. May I ask you if you know Harry Rice?"

The man said, "Yes, I know Harry Rice."

Mike continued, "I'm sorry, but I don't know your name. I would like to meet with you if that is possible?"

"I too am sorry, but I don't know you. Why do you want to meet me?"

"I know Harry visited Thailand recently investigating a case. I am interested in learning who he talked to and what he found."

"My work was of a confidential nature, and I am not at liberty to share that information with anyone without Harry's approval."

"Sir, are you aware that Harry is dead?"

"What? No, I can't believe Harry died. How did it happen?"

"I will explain everything to you if you will just meet with me. Harry was a friend of mine, and it is possible he was murdered. I have reason to believe his death may be related to the case he was working on when he was in Thailand. Sir, I am an FBI agent and I can give you a contact at the U.S. Embassy who you can call to confirm I am who I say I am."

Mike gave the man the contact at the embassy and his phone number.

The man said, "I'll call you back."

Mike said, "Thank you. I am at the Mandarin Oriental Hotel. I will be waiting for your call."

About an hour later Mike's room phone rang and it was the man he had called earlier.

"Mr. Sewell this is Chumpong. I am in the lobby of the Mandarin Oriental and will be happy to talk to you."

Mike said, "Thank you, Chumpong. I am in room 407. Please come up."

Chumpong was a small and slender man with a bronze complexion. His features were fine and his demeanor, like most Thais, was calm and humble. He wore brown slacks and a traditional Thai white shirt.

He explained that Harry had called him to seek his help investigating John Holliday's medical problems when he was visiting Bangkok. He told Mike he was able to find the hospital where John was admitted, and with his contacts, he learned about the medical problems. He went on to explain he had been able to make a copy of the complete medical file at the hospital, without the hospital being aware he had made the copy. He said Harry had taken the copy of the medical file with him when he flew back to the U.S.

Mike said, "I need to visit the hospital to see if I can get access to the file. Do you think they will cooperate? Would it help if you accompanied me to the hospital?"

Chumpong replied, "I am not sure if they will give you access to the medical records. They will be suspicious and probably tell you that the records are protected by confidentiality. They only talked to me because I know people. It might help if I accompany you, but they will probably still not cooperate. They will be suspicious that they might have done something wrong, and they will try to protect themselves. We can try, but I doubt if we will be successful."

Mike took a different approach. "What if you go back on your own and make another copy the way you were able to the first time?"

"That might be a better approach. Let me see what I can do. Tell me more about Harry's death. You think he may have been murdered? Couldn't you tell?"

"Harry's death looked like a suicide. There is no hard evidence that it was murder, but his computer had been wiped clean and there were no files around his apartment indicating that he had travelled to Thailand and no files about him working on the John Holliday case. That is obviously suspicious, but it is possible he destroyed the files himself for some reason."

"Harry seemed like a nice guy. I can't believe he would commit suicide, and I can't imagine why he would have destroyed the files he worked so hard to get. Give me a couple days and I'll see what I can do."

Mike said, "Great. But please be careful. There are some powerful people who may be trying to conceal the details of John's death and the disease he had. They apparently were willing to kill Harry and do it in a way that concealed what they had done. They will try to stop us if they find out we are still investigating John Holliday's death."

"I understand and I will be careful. That is why it is more important I try to do this quietly instead of you walking in the hospital yourself. Give me a couple days and I will give you a call."

Chumpong called Mike's hotel room and asked for another meeting. Mike invited him to his room again.

Chumpong started their meeting by saying, "This is getting serious. I tried to get the file to make a copy again, but the files are all gone. They are not in the hospital. I talked to a very close friend who works at the hospital. She said someone from the U.S. Embassy came to the hospital and met with a senior official of the hospital. The person from the embassy demanded the hospital give him all the files related to John Holliday's stay at the hospital. He told the hospital official that this was an issue of national security to the U.S. He went on to say that there was evidence that a foreign government was trying to blackmail the President of the United States. The hospital gave him the files, and instructed the doctor on the case not to talk to anyone about the case and to advise the embassy if anyone visited the hospital asking questions about the case. Unfortunately my friend does not know the name of the man from the embassy."

Mike said, "This is amazing. Whoever is involved is one step ahead of me. Did you give your name to my contact at the embassy when you called him?"

"No, I refused. He asked, but he didn't push when I refused. He simply told me he knew you and you were legit."

Mike continued, "Without a name of the man who visited the hospital I can't be sure he was really an embassy official. He may have just said he was from the embassy and maybe he had fake credentials. I will have to risk asking my friend at the embassy if he knows anything about this national security thing, but I have a feeling the man who visited the hospital was bogus. But I guess it is possible that he was telling the truth."

"Mike, I didn't tell you the first time we met because I was still a little suspicious, but I think I need to come clean. This is too big for me, and I need to go underground for a while. I made two copies of the medical file I got from the hospital. Harry took one copy with him when he returned to San Francisco. I want to give you the copy I kept for myself."

Mike smiled. "That is the sign of a cautious and excellent investigator."

Chumpong opened his briefcase and handed a file to Mike. "Don't try to contact me again. My family and I are taking a trip to points unknown. I hope for your sake that you are very careful, and I hope you get to the bottom of this case."

"Thank you, Chumpong, if that is your real name. I wish you well, and I hope you will be safe."

Chumpong smiled and said, "Goodbye, Agent Mike Sewell, and good luck. Be safe."

After Chumpong left, Mike sat in his room and read the medical file on John Holliday. Then he wrote a report about the case. He emailed a copy of the report to his boss, George, and a copy to the Director of the FBI. He included in the report that he believed his life may be in danger, and if something happened to him, he had no doubt it was related to this case. In the report he said he planned to talk to his intelligence contact at the U. S. Embassy in Bangkok to see if he knew anything about the John Holliday medical file being part of a national security issue.

* * *

Mike called his contact at the U.S. Embassy and arranged a lunch meeting at a restaurant near the Mandarin Oriental Hotel. He had known John Adams when he worked for the State Department in Washington. John had graduated from George Washington University in D.C. and had gone into the intelligence business working for the Department of Defense. He had spent his whole career in various parts of the intelligence services of the U.S. government.

When Mike left the hotel, it was raining again. Mike carried a hotel umbrella and took a short taxi ride to the restaurant. He arrived first and sat at a table in a private section of the restaurant. John arrived right on schedule and with a smile said, "Hi Mike, it's been a long time. I hope my endorsement of you to your friend worked out. What brings you to Bangkok?"

Mike smiled and said, "John, it is good to see you again. How is life in Bangkok?"

"It's a good posting. My wife enjoys living here and has fun shopping and entertaining friends who come to visit. She also likes to travel with the other wives to see other parts of Thailand and the countries near by. It's a good life."

Mike continued, "Let's order our lunch and then I'll explain the purpose of my trip."

He signaled to the waitress who arrived with a warm smile and took their orders.

As she left, Mike said, "Let me ask you a question first, and then I'll give you the background. Were you involved in a national security issue recently that involved someone visiting a hospital in Bangkok to obtain some medical records?"

"No, Mike, that would be news to me. And as you know, national security is my business. Nothing close to that has happened that I am aware of."

"Mike pushed a little more, "Is it possible that the Ambassador might have gotten a message directly from Washington, and had someone visit the hospital without your knowledge?"

"Anything is possible, but that is extremely unlikely. I have a very good working relationship with the Ambassador, and he would come to me with anything involving national security. I can always talk to the Ambassador to see if he bypassed me for some reason."

"Ok, let me give you some background. Someone visited the Bangkok International Hospital and allegedly showed them his embassy credentials and said he was involved with a national security threat to the U.S. government. He demanded the hospital turn over the medical records of a U.S. citizen who had been treated at the hospital. He also demanded that if anyone contacted the hospital regarding the medical records they were to contact him. It sounds to me like the man was using fake credentials.

"I came to Bangkok to look into a possible murder that happened to a friend in San Francisco. He had visited Bangkok as part of an investigation into the death of a U.S. citizen who had been hospitalized in Bangkok a few years ago. The medical records taken from the hospital recently were those of the same man my friend was investigating."

John had listened carefully to Mike's explanation and replied, "It sounds like you would prefer not to tell me who the U.S. citizen is who was treated in the hospital."

"John, this whole case has me a little spooked. If I am right, some very powerful people in Washington may be involved. I would like to think there is some logical explanation for what has been going on, but it looks like these people will do anything necessary to cover up what they have done. You might be better off not knowing for now."

"Mike, I am thinking out loud, but I think we need to visit the Ambassador and see if we can confirm that the person who took the records was not an authorized embassy employee, and indeed someone using fake embassy credentials. If that proves to be the case, you and I should visit the hospital and see what we can find out about this impersonator. Maybe they caught him on one of their security cameras."

Mike asked, "What can you tell me about the Ambassador? Is he a career diplomat, and can he be trusted not to say anything about this investigation to his bosses in Washington?"

"He is a career diplomat, and I think he can be trusted not to say anything to Washington, unless he thinks this is going to cause a problem for the U.S. with the Thai government. If he is worried that it will become an international incident then for sure he will send up a red flag to Washington.

"But what is your alternative? Without knowing who this guy is, you are at a road block, aren't you?"

"Not completely, but it would really help if we could find out who he is. You have pretty much assured me the guy was not an embassy person, but to be absolutely sure I guess we need to confirm it with the Ambassador."

John asked, "Can I call the Ambassador's secretary and see if I can get on his calendar sometime this afternoon?"

At three o'clock Mike walked out of his hotel. It had stopped raining, but now it was just hot and muggy. The aroma of Bangkok was more evident now that it had stopped raining. It was hard to describe the smells because they were a combination of many things. Pollution, in the air, from all the cars, trucks, and three wheeled taxis called 'Tuk Tuks' was one of the smells. Others were raw sewage in the ditches along the side of the roads, and rotten fruits that had been discarded along the roads. All those smells in the hot, humid environment combined to offer a harsh, pungent odor. The opposite extreme was the beautiful fragrances one smelled in the hotel lobbies and hotel rooms where many beautiful orchids and other flowers were used for decorations and for their beautiful fragrances.

At the U.S. Embassy, Mike asked to see John Adams. They walked together to the Ambassador's office.

John introduced Mike to the Ambassador, who asked, "Mike, what brings the FBI to Bangkok?"

"Mr. Ambassador, I came here with the knowledge of my boss, but on unofficial business. A personal friend and retired police officer in San Francisco either committed suicide or was murdered. It is an ongoing investigation by the SFPD, but the man had recently visited Bangkok working as a private investigator. I came here, unofficially, to follow up on the case he was investigating. What I would like to ask is if you recently asked someone to visit the Bangkok International Hospital to retrieve the medical records of a U.S. citizen, based on a threat to our national security?"

The Ambassador looked somewhat confused for a moment but then replied, "Mike, if there were a national security issue, I assure you John would know about it. That is his area of expertise.

I can't imagine being asked to do something like that without involving John, and I can assure you I have no knowledge of any such activity."

Mike said, "Thank you very much sir. I appreciate your candor."

The Ambassador went on, "It troubles me that someone represented himself as an employee of our embassy. John, do you have any idea how this could happen?"

"No sir, I don't. It probably isn't too hard to create a fake ID that looks like an embassy ID. People at the hospital have probably never seen an official embassy ID so it could have been made by almost anyone. Mike and I are considering a visit to the hospital to question them about the man. I will show them my ID and see how it compares to the one he used. With a little luck we might at least get a description of the individual."

"Mike, is there any chance this thing is going to create an international incident between our government and the government of Thailand?"

Mike responded, "No sir. We will be careful when we talk to the hospital administrator and be sure he understands there was no way he could have known the person was an imposter. The important thing is for us to try to learn as much about him as we can.

"One final comment sir. It is important that we keep this investigation as low profile as possible. I hope you don't feel the need to alert anyone in Washington about what we have discussed."

The Ambassador said, "Mike, I can accommodate that request. Good luck on your investigation. How long will you be staying in Thailand?"

"My plan is to return to the U.S. after John and I talk to the hospital personnel. Thank you, Mr. Ambassador."

John and Mike walked in the lobby of the Bangkok International Hospital, regarded as the finest medical facility in Thailand. They both looked around to see if they could spot any security cameras, but they saw none.

They walked to the reception desk where John introduced himself, showed the receptionist his ID, and asked if they could talk to the head of security for the hospital. She made a phone call, spoke softly briefly, then turned to John and Mike and said, "Please have a seat, Mr. Chanchai will be with you shortly."

After a few minutes, a short, well-dressed Thai man approached them. He looked at John and Mike and said, "Hello, I am Chanchai. Are one of you Mr. Adams?"

John and Mike stood and John said, "Yes, I am John Adams and this is my friend, Mike Sewell. Thank you for seeing us. Is there somewhere we can talk privately?"

Chanchai said, "Of course. Please follow me to my office."

When they arrived at Chanchai's office, he asked them to have a seat and asked if they would like a cup of coffee or tea? Both John and Mike declined. Chanchai started the conversation, "What can I do for you gentlemen?"

John responded, "Chanchai, I am with the U.S. Embassy in charge of our security. We have learned that someone recently visited your hospital and represented that he worked for the Embassy. He apparently had an ID but we assume it was a fake. We are trying to identify this individual. Can you review for us your security system for the hospital? I didn't notice any surveillance cameras when I was in the lobby, but they may be concealed."

Chanchai showed a small smile and replied, "Mr. Adams, we will help you and the U.S. Embassy any way we can. We only use a limited number of surveillance cameras around the hospital entrances, but there is one that watches the front entrance where you came in. We try to make them as difficult to see as possible. The Thai people don't like the idea of being watched by cameras, but as you know, it is becoming more necessary in this world."

John continued, "If this man came to the hospital to talk to someone about obtaining medical records on a patient, who would he have talked to?"

"I suppose he would have visited our Managing Director of Administration, Khun Niran."

John asked, "Would it be possible to see if he is available to meet with us? After we talk to him, we may want to impose on your time again and watch some of your surveillance tape, once we can pin down when this man visited the hospital.

"Let me call his secretary and see if he is available." Chanchai made a call and spoke for a moment, and then turned to John and Mike, "He is available to see you in a half hour."

John replied, "That would be fine."

Chanchai thanked the secretary and told her he would bring the two gentlemen to Niran's office in a half hour.

Chanchai offered them tea or coffee a second time. John accepted this time and asked for black coffee.

Mike, who had not said a word, said, "Black coffee also, please."

Chanchai walked outside his office and asked his secretary to please bring three black coffees for them.

As he walked back into his office, he asked John how long he had been living in Bangkok, and how he and his family liked it?

John replied, "My wife and I have been here just over two years. I enjoy the assignment and my wife loves living here. She spends much of her time shopping and learning about the Thai culture. Many of the embassy employee's wives go on trips together to see the country outside of Bangkok. You have a beautiful country."

The three men enjoyed their coffee, and continued their light conversation. When it was time for their meeting, Chanchai walked them to Khun Niran's office, and his secretary told them they could go in. Chanchai introduced John and Mike to Niran and said he would leave them to have their conversation. He told John to have the secretary bring him back to his office when they were done.

As Chanchai left he closed the door.

Niran welcomed John and Mike to his office and asked, "What can I do for you?"

John started, "Khun Niran, I am with the U.S. Embassy, in charge of security, and Mike is visiting us from America. I want to begin by assuring you that you have done nothing wrong so please do not worry. I believe you were visited recently by a man who claimed to be from the U.S. Embassy and he demanded you give him the medical files on a U.S. citizen who was a patient in this great hospital a few years ago. This man was not a representative from the U.S. Embassy. We believe he had a false ID and gained the files under false pretenses. We are trying to identify this individual and track him down."

"Mr. Adams, I am shocked," replied Niran. "A man named Robert Jones visited me several days ago, and like you described, he said he was from the U.S. Embassy and showed me his ID. He said it was a matter of national security for the U.S. and he needed to take all the medical files on this individual. He also said I was never to speak of his visit to anyone, and if anyone visited regarding the files I was to say nothing and call him as soon as possible. He gave me his card with his phone number."

Niran pulled out a handful of business cards, and found the one Robert Jones had given him. He handed it to John. John looked at it and showed it to Mike.

John said, "It looks official enough, but I can assure you it is a fake. It does have the phone number of the U.S. Embassy on it, but there is no one working at the embassy named Robert Jones. Can you tell us specifically what day he visited, and can you try to describe him for us?"

Niran was clearly looking uncomfortable. "I am so embarrassed. Our medical records are private and confidential and we never give outsiders access to this sensitive information, but he was so believable. I was afraid if I didn't do what he wanted he would call someone in our government and get me fired."

"Please don't worry, Niran. You could not have known, and you are not in any trouble. We just need to find this man and any information you can give us will be greatly appreciated."

"Thank you, Mr. Adams." Niran looked at his calendar and continued, "He was here a week ago, Monday, in the morning at eleven o'clock. He was tall, around six feet, clean-shaven, probably about fifty, with short, brown hair, slightly thinning. He wore a shirt and tie, just like you gentlemen. No coat, because it is so hot here. I would describe him as a fairly big guy, not fat, but just solid, kind of like a rugby player. He was also very stern and serious. He didn't smile, and actually now that I think about it, he was not very polite."

"Niran, thank you very much. You have been very helpful, and again, please don't worry." John continued, "I want to leave my card with you. If you think of anything else after we leave please feel free to call me. I promise, I do work at the Embassy and if you call I will be there to talk to you." John stood and shook hands with him and gave him a warm smile.

For the first time Mike finally spoke, "Khun Niran, I want to thank you for your help. It has been a pleasure to meet you. We are going back downstairs to Chanchai's office to spend some time looking at his security tapes to see if we can get a glimpse of our mystery man. Again, thank you."

Niran's secretary walked them back downstairs to Chanchai's office.

John told Chanchai the date and approximate time of the mystery man's meeting with Niran, and Chanchai called one of his security people to give him the information. Chanchai said, "Let's walk to another office and look at the security footage."

They watched the security tape starting with the footage at ten am. At ten forty a man fitting the description walked through the front door of the hospital. The only difference from Niran's description was he wore sunglasses. Unfortunately, the quality of the image was fair to poor. It was not good enough to positively identify someone, but it was better than nothing. Chanchai had two still photos made of the individual and gave one to John and one to Mike.

The two men thanked Chanchai for his help. As they left the hospital they decided it was time for lunch. Mike said, "You choose the place and I'll buy."

John took Mike to a nice Thai restaurant on the bank of the Chao Phraya River that flows through Bangkok. They were seated at a table with a great view of the river.

Mike suggested they treat themselves to Thai beer. John ordered two Singha beers, and when the waitress brought them, they ordered their food. As they enjoyed the cold beer, Mike said, "John, I can't thank you enough. You were great with the administrator, Niran. I thought he was going to pee his pants at one moment. I think he was obviously worried he might lose his job."

John replied, "Yea, I felt sorry for the guy. He got duped. It happens. Do you think the photo is of any use?"

"I'm not sure. I kind of doubt it, but I will have our tech geeks enhance it and see what they can do. They are pretty amazing, sometimes. When an American visits Thailand he needs a visa and needs to include a photo with his application, right? My secretary always takes care of that stuff now so I am a little out of date."

John said, "That is the requirement. What are you thinking?"

"I wonder how many Americans arrived in Bangkok the week prior to our man's visit to the hospital? And I wonder if I have enough clout to get the Thai immigration officials to make a list for me of all the Americans who arrived in Bangkok during that time who fit his description?"

John said, "This thing is about to take on a higher level of visibility if you try to do something like that. You had better talk to your boss about that one, if you want my opinion."

"No way to keep it low profile?" asked Mike.

"Let me think. Who do I know who has contacts with Thai immigration? And what will it cost us for a little favor?"

Mike said, "I am going to call my boss tonight and bring him up to date on what we learned. I will also send a copy of the photo to the computer guys to see what they can do with enhancement."

John added, "I'll keep my copy of the photo. If you leave for the U.S., I'll see what I can come up with, and maybe find a way to ask some people at the immigration office for a favor."

"I'll give you a call tomorrow morning. Great restaurant, I enjoyed the lunch."

"I look forward to hearing from you tomorrow morning, Mike. Thanks for lunch."

* * *

Because of the time difference between Bangkok and Washington, Mike had to wait until later in the evening to call his boss. When he called, he told George what he had learned during his stay in Bangkok. He told him about his discussion with the administrator at the hospital, and the description he gave of the mystery man, and the image that they were able to get from the hospital security system. He mentioned wanting to ask the immigration people in Bangkok to help identify the individual, but had to admit that it was probably a long shot.

George encouraged him to leave the immigration contact in the hands of his friend at the embassy. He told Mike that it was time to come home.

Mike agreed and told George he would fly back to San Francisco to update the SFPD on what he learned in Bangkok, and then fly back to Washington. He said, "I will see you in about three days."

Chapter 11

The President and her Chief of Staff were having their normal breakfast. Judy said, "Carolyn, I think it is time to kick off immigration reform. Now that Senator Banfield is no longer with us, maybe the new Senate Minority Leader, Senator Lehman will be more enthusiastic in finding bi-partisan solutions. What can I do to help with getting this agenda item moving forward?"

"Judy, you won't be surprised that I was just thinking the exact thing, except for your comment on poor Charlie Banfield. I know he was not pleased with my actions on health care and the debt limit and the budget, but I didn't want to see him have a heart attack and die."

The President added, "I think it is time to get the leaders of Congress together again and have a kick off discussion about immigration reform. This is going to be even harder than the health care reform we just completed. I need to come up with something to convince the Republicans to think outside the box. Their insistence on building a damn fence from the Pacific Ocean to the Gulf of Mexico is crazy. We have to find a way to get them off that idea. Reagan got the Berlin wall torn down, why do we have to be the only country in the world that wants to build a fence to keep people out? There must be a better way."

The President added, "Judy, you know what upsets me most about the Republican approach to fixing our immigration system? It is the fence. They use the phrase 'secure the border first', but their definition of securing the border is build a fence."

Judy responded, "I agree totally. However, if we dig in our heels on the fence issue, and say we won't support building a fence, or if we even try to slow it down, we will not get to a bipartisan solution. We need to find a Republican, with some influence, and is technology savvy and more modern thinking.

Then we need to convince him to guide the Republicans to a non-fence way to secure the border. Let's call it a virtual fence."

"Great idea, Judy. Why don't you talk to the new Senate Minority Leader and the House Minority Leader and see what they think of the idea and see who, of the Republicans, are the best targets for our virtual fence idea. We should hold off on a leadership meeting until we have found one or two Republicans who will champion the virtual fence idea. The best solution would be one in the House and one in the Senate."

The President said, "Looks like it's time to go to work. I enjoy these breakfasts, Judy. This one was particularly productive. Thanks."

Judy added, "One more thing on a completely different subject, Natalie Jefferson asked me to get a small time slot for her to see you today, if possible. I squeezed her on your schedule as your first appointment.

Natalie Jefferson was the President's Chief Legal Counsel. She was a medium height, slender, very attractive black woman. She sometimes wore wire-rimmed glasses, but apparently she only needed them for reading, because most of the time she didn't wear them.

* * *

As the President walked to the oval office she saw Natalie sitting waiting to see her. Carolyn walked up to her and said, "Natalie, good to see you. Come on in."

"Thank you, Madam President."

"What do we have cooking today, Natalie?"

"Some sad news, Madam President. I received a hand delivered letter from Justice Clyde Henderson yesterday asking me to inform you that he has decided he must retire from the Supreme Court. As you know, he has been fighting cancer for about two years. Recently it has taken a turn for the worse. He is at home, and unable to travel. He is very weak, and unfortunately the prognosis is not good. He told me, for our ears only, that the doctors have given him only a few more months to live. He wanted to inform you personally, but under the circumstances he chose to ask me to do it for him."

"Oh my," uttered the President. "Such a dear man and what a brilliant legal mind. Do you think he is well enough to take a call, if I call him?"

Natalie responded, "I believe he is, and I know he would appreciate receiving your call."

"Natalie, in addition to everything else on your plate, would you head a small group to recommend candidates for consideration to replace Clyde?"

"Yes, Madam President, I would be honored."

"Please work with Judy to decide who else should be on the search group."

After Natalie left, the President buzzed her secretary and asked her to get Justice Henderson on the phone. "And tell Judy to hold my next meeting until after I have finished talking to the Justice."

One minute later the President's intercom buzzed and her secretary said Justice Henderson was on her line. Clyde sounded very weak.

He said, "Thank you very much for calling, Madam President. I assume Natalie has informed you of my situation?"

The President replied, "Clyde, I am so sorry to hear the news. I want you to know how much I have admired your work on the Supreme Court. You have been a tremendous voice for the Court, and your legal perspective has served this country well. You should be so proud of your contributions. Is there anything I can do for you and Mary? As the President, you would think I should be able to do something, but I feel so helpless."

Clyde spoke softly, "Madam President, thank you for your call and thank you for your kind words. The doctors are doing everything they can, which now is pretty much limited to keeping me comfortable. Mary and I have things in order and she will be able to spend more time with our three daughters and their six kids. Everything will be fine, Madam President. I am happy you were the first woman to be elected President. You are doing a great job, and I know you will continue to do what is best for our country."

"Thank you Clyde for your kind words. I would like to come by and see you sometime in the next few days, if that is ok?"

"I would be happy to see you, but please don't feel it is necessary. I know you are very busy."

"See you soon, Clyde. Bye for now."

* * *

Judy met with Senator Joe Lehman, the new Senate Minority Leader, and Congressman Caldwell. They had agreed to meet in Senator Lehman's new office.

Senator Lehman was from Illinois and was very different from Charlie Banfield. Physically, he was medium height and weight with brown hair that was thinning and beginning to turn grey. His personality was much different than Charlie's. He was much more of a leader and consensus builder and someone who was not afraid to reach across the isle to find solutions with the Republicans.

Judy began, "Senator Lehman, congratulations on your new position as Minority Leader, and Congressman Caldwell, it is good to see you again. The President asked me to meet with you to plan our strategy for the upcoming immigration reform legislation. Have the Republican leaders had any discussions with either of you on the subject recently?"

Congressman Caldwell went first, "Judy, I have not heard a word from the Speaker. I would guess he is waiting for the President to make the first move."

Senator Lehman said, "As you know I am new at this, but Senator Marino hasn't reached out to me. I haven't heard a word on the subject, other than from some of my fellow Democrats. They are a little worried that the President will yield too much to the Republicans on this important issue."

Judy said, "Well let me tell you the idea the President came up with recently.

The concept of a fence stretching from the Pacific Ocean to the Gulf of Mexico is offensive to her. As you know the Republican position forever has been secure the border first and then we can discuss immigration reform. Regrettably, the Republicans have always believed to secure the border means building a fence.

Well, the President agrees with them that we need to secure the border, but where she strongly disagrees is how to secure the border. We are living in the twenty first century not the nineteenth or twentieth century. A physical fence is out of date. We need the Republicans to come up with the idea of a "virtual fence" instead of a physical fence. The President worries that if this proposal comes from her or the Democrats in Congress, the Republicans will immediately reject it. But if we can get the idea to come from an influential Republican or two, we might just succeed at getting the Republicans to abandon their idea of a physical fence."

Senator Lehman asked, "Exactly what does the President mean by a virtual fence?"

"More border patrol officers, electronic surveillance, use of drones, and the use of satellite surveillance. The technology advances that have been made in these areas couldn't have been imagined thirty years ago. But today we don't need a physical fence, we can use technology and border patrol officers to prevent illegals crossing the border. The President believes the virtual fence will be more effective and probably cost less. But the question is, how do we find a Republican Senator and Congressman who will champion this idea within the Republican Party?"

Caldwell said, "I like it. The challenge will be to find the right guy, or gal, to champion the idea. And we need to keep this whole idea quiet so it doesn't leak that this is the President's idea. Let Senator Lehman and me spend some time talking about the right people to approach in the Republican caucuses."

Judy reported back to the President about her meeting with Senator Lehman and Congressman Caldwell. She told the President both men liked the idea and were thinking about who might be receptive to the idea.

The President told Judy about Justice Henderson's planned retirement.

Judy commented, "He is a great Justice, and because of his liberal leaning it should be relatively easy to replace him with another strong liberal."

I have asked Natalie to lead the search committee, and I want you on her team.

"Thank you, Madam President. I am honored by the opportunity."

Two days later the White House made a press release announcing the retirement of Justice Henderson, due to medical reasons. The announcement also mentioned the formation of a search committee and said the White House hoped to have a nominee for his replacement in a few weeks.

* * *

Senator Lehman called the President's Chief of Staff to discuss immigration reform. He told her he and Congressman Caldwell had come up with two individuals they believed would be receptive to the idea they had discussed regarding the virtual fence. He suggested Senator George Shuster the Chairman of the Senate Intelligence Committee and Congressman Sam Goodman the Chairman of the House Budget Committee. He asked Judy if she supported them talking to the two Republicans. His plan was to have one meeting with both Republicans in attendance.

Judy gave them the green light to have the conversation. She thanked him for their ideas and wished him good luck.

Senator Lehman called Judy again a few days later and told her they had a good meeting with the two Republicans. He said they were optimistic that the Republicans were receptive to the idea if the President assured them that she supported the idea and would support the costs associated with the virtual fence. Judy said she was sure the President would guarantee her support for the costs involved assuming the other issues with immigration reform were within the scope of what she could support.

Judy said, "The President would like to have another leadership meeting with the leaders of Congress in the White House to try to outline the basics of the complete reform package. Do you think it is time to arrange that meeting?"

Senator Lehman replied, "Please tell the President that the Democrat leadership is ready for such a meeting."

The Speaker and Minority Leader of the House and the Majority and Minority Leaders of the Senate arrived at the White House for the meeting on immigration reform. Clouds were building in the west like a big storm was on the way. How ironic.

"Gentlemen, welcome to the White House once again. This time our attention will be on immigration reform. This issue is long overdue and I am glad we are going to give it a serious try once again. I envision a comprehensive reform that addresses both illegal immigration and reforms to our legal immigration system. With today's technology I believe we can come up with programs that address both of these issues. I know the Republicans have been consistent with the idea that we need to secure our southern border with Mexico before other immigration reform can move forward. I must tell you that building a fence from the Pacific Ocean to the Gulf of Mexico is still a problem for me. If we can find a solution to this old fashioned idea, I think we can then focus on dealing with the issue of the millions of illegal immigrants now living in the country. I know we have different ideas on how to address these illegal immigrants, but I am willing to listen to ideas from both sides to find a bi-partisan solution. Senator Marino, do you have any comments you would like to share with us?"

Senator Marino began, "Thank you, Madam President. You are correct in your understanding of the Republican position of securing the border with Mexico. The current fence in clearly inadequate. We must find a way to secure the border as the first step toward comprehensive immigration reform. Clearly a major increase in the number of border patrol officers is one important part of any security system we deploy. Our members of both houses of Congress have spent time discussing this issue recently, and we are willing to consider a more modern approach to the problem. We believe the use of technology can play a larger role in securing the border. For example, increases in the use of electronic surveillance can be a big help to the border patrol officers. Additionally, we think the use of drones should be added to our security system, and even the addition of surveillance from existing satellites can be an effective addition to the security system. But, most importantly, we need to be able to count on you, Madam President, to make a public commitment to securing the border, and including that commitment in the legislation to be enacted. We simply cannot compromise on securing the border without the commitment from you, both in what you say and what you allow to be included in the legislation. It must be enforceable. We have been down that road before and we got burned."

"Thank you, Senator. Your idea of using technology plus increasing the number of border patrol officers is totally acceptable to me. I am delighted to hear you and the other Republicans believe that an alternative to building a fence along the entire border is an acceptable possibility.

"I also believe that our modern technology should be used as part of the ongoing challenge of insuring legal immigrants do not overstay their legal visas. As you know, part of the problem is a huge number of immigrants come to the U.S. on student visa, tourist visa, and other visas of limited duration, and then stay beyond their legal time in our country and simply disappear. We need to be able to find these people, and with changes to our tracking system using technology, we should be able to manage this problem much better than we do now.

"I also support the concept of verification of the legal status of people before employers can hire them. A verification requirement on the employers should be a part of our immigration reform legislation.

"I am sure we will have differences in the timing of a path to citizenship and the requirements for current illegals to get on that track, but I will leave those details for the Congress to negotiate.

"Any other ideas or concerns by the other leaders around the table?"

The Speaker of the House spent time talking about some of the other critical issues to the Republicans in the House, and the minority leaders also added their thoughts.

The President let them voice their ideas and concerns without challenging any specific details. Finally, she asked, "Does anyone feel there is a deal breaker that has not been mentioned?"

There was silence, and after a pause, Senator Marino said, "I am more optimistic today than I have been for a long time. There is still a lot of work to do on the details, but with strong, clear wording around securing the border component, I am hopeful we can finally come to an agreement on this divisive issue."

"Thank you, Senator Marino. On that we definitely agree."

* * *

Natalie and Judy were sitting in the Oval Office when the President entered.

The President said, "Hi ladies, sorry to keep you waiting. Needed a brief conversation with my National Security Advisor. I hope you have made some progress on the search for our next Supreme Court Justice."

Natalie replied, "Yes, Madam President. We believe we have a great group of potential candidates. An initial screening has been done, but we will only fully vet your first choice. Based on our group discussion, we believe all six would make excellent nominees, and we have included a brief summary for you on each candidate. You are obviously free to choose anyone on the list, or send us back to do additional work, but based on our discussion we are in unanimous agreement on our top recommendation. She is Circuit Judge Diane Kline, currently sitting on the United States Court of Appeals for the Ninth Circuit."

"Ladies, you have done excellent work. I know Diane quite well, and I am familiar with much of her legal work. She is brilliant and believes in interpreting the law to the benefit of the little guy. She is pragmatic, and will make an excellent Supreme Court Justice. I will hold my complete support until I have looked through the other candidates you have given me, but I like your recommendation. I will give you a call tomorrow, Natalie, and we can talk about the process of getting our nominee confirmed."

The President called Natalie, as promised, and told her she agreed with the committee's recommendation. She instructed Natalie to oversee the vetting process and to keep her informed of any unexpected issues.

The vetting process was completed without any red flags. The President knew the only red flag standing in the way of Diane Kline's nomination was her activism as a judge and her strong liberal leaning. She also knew the Republicans would not like her, but there was little they could do to stop her.

The President chose Senator Collins from California to champion Diane Kline through the informal meeting process with the Senators that goes on before the actual confirmation hearings begin. All went well.

The President received a call from Senator Marino regarding the Kline nomination.

He started, "Madam President, I want you to know that the Republicans in the Senate are not overjoyed with Diane Kline as your nominee for the Supreme Court. She is a fine lady, but she is way out there on the left on many of her legal opinions. However, I wanted you to know, in the spirit of cooperation that you have brought to Washington, there may be some tough questioning during the hearings, but she will be confirmed as our next Supreme Court Justice."

The game went on in Washington with Senators using the confirmation hearings to state their position on various issues to gain political points for their next elections. After the confirmation hearings were completed, the committee recommended her nomination to the full Senate where she got all the Democrats to support her and a dozen Republicans.

Diane Kline was sworn in as a Justice of the Supreme Court. One week later, retired Justice Henderson lost his battle with cancer.

Chapter 12

Mike Sewell arrived in San Francisco and after checking into the Fairmont, called Detective Sanchez. He scheduled a meeting with him for later that afternoon.

Mike told Sanchez, "A mystery man visited the hospital in Bangkok, and posing as an official from the U.S. Embassy demanded the hospital give him all the medical records on the individual who Harry Rice had been investigating. We got him on the hospital's security camera, but the quality of the image is pretty poor. We don't have much to go on, but I am even more convinced that Harry's death was not a suicide. Something is going on, and I believe some very powerful people in Washington are involved. I am headed back to Washington, but this investigation is a long way from being over. Have you heard anything more from the medical examiner?"

Detective Sanchez said, "No, he hasn't gotten back to me. It is too late to call him today, but I will check with him again tomorrow, and let you know if he came up with anything."

Mike flew out that night on the redeye to Dulles. When he arrived he caught a taxi home, showered and headed for the office. He was dead tired, but he knew his boss would be interested in hearing first hand about his trip.

He walked in his office and asked his secretary to get him a big cup of black coffee and to call George to see if he was available for a meeting.

His secretary delivered his coffee and said "Mike, you look like you haven't slept. Don't you think you should take the day off, and come back tomorrow after you get some sleep?"

Mike said, "Sleep is greatly over rated. I can sleep when I'm dead. Let me know when I can see the boss."

She walked briskly back to her desk, made the call, and told Mike that George was tied up but wanted to see him in two hours.

Mike walked down to the lab where he had sent the image of the mystery man. Frank, the technician, was sitting in front of his computer working on something. Mike said, "I hope that is the image I sent you."

Frank said, "You need to suggest to the hospital they invest in a higher resolution camera. I did all the enhancement I could and it improved it a little, but it is still far from what you want."

Frank reached in a file and handed Mike a copy of the enhanced image.

"That is a long way from a clear image. Is it worth running this through facial recognition to see if we can get a hit?"

"I seriously doubt there is enough clarity of the features for facial recognition to work, but I have a feeling you are going to say, 'why not give it a try', so I'll try and maybe we'll get lucky. Do you want a global search or just the U.S.?"

"Start with the U.S., Frank. Give me a call when you find out who it is."

Frank just grinned at Mike and said, "Right."

Mike walked to his boss's office and his secretary said, "You can go right in. He is waiting for you."

George greeted Mike, and said, "Don't sit down, the Director wants to be in this meeting so we are going to his office. I wanted to talk to you first, but he insisted we could save time by just meeting all together. You look tired. Did you get any sleep last night?"

"I took the redeye from San Francisco and got to Dulles early this morning. I slept a little on the plane, but I will admit I am a little tired. Maybe I'll go home early today and get caught up tonight. What's the Director's mood?"

"He's worried. He doesn't want a government scandal, but he will support you, when you have the evidence."

They arrived at the Director's office and his secretary said he should be available in a few minutes. She asked if they wanted coffee and Mike asked for a cup, black. George declined.

The Director opened his office door and said, "Gentlemen, please come in. Welcome back from Thailand, Mike." Then sarcastically said, "Did you have a nice vacation?" He paused a moment and then added, "That doesn't require an answer."

Mike responded, "Thank you, sir."

The Director said, "We got your report from Bangkok and it sounded like you were a little worried. Bring us up to date on your 'unofficial' investigation.

Not knowing exactly how much his boss had told the Director, Mike decided to walk them through the case from the time Senator Banfield approached him requesting his advice and help, on John Holliday's death. He explained he had suggested to Senator Banfield that he leave the subject alone, but when the Senator said he was going to look into it somehow, he decided to contact Harry Rice, a retired SFPD officer that he had known for a long time, and ask him to look into the details of John Holliday's death.

Mike continued, "Harry reported back to me that Mr. Holliday had died in a San Francisco hospital after having contracted a rare infectious disease during a trip to Thailand. At the time, his wife was the Governor of California, and she requested no autopsy and they honored her wishes. He was cremated and his ashes spread over the Pacific Ocean. Harry was able to confirm that all his medical records were no longer in the hospital. I reported all of this to Senator Banfield, and at his request, gave him Harry's full name and phone number so he could talk directly to him, and get me out of the middle of this situation. It is clear the Senator talked to Harry and asked him to go to Thailand to continue the investigation. Upon Harry's return, I believe Harry either talked to the Senator or tried to talk to him. What I do know is that the Senator called Harry twice and left messages on his voice mail to return his call, urgently.

"Harry may have already been dead when the Senator left the voice mails. Shortly after the Senator left the second voice mail, he died of a heart attack.

"The medical examiner confirmed the Senator died of a heart attack, but he would not say positively that the heart attack was from natural causes. However he did say there was no evidence from the autopsy of any foul play.

"The medical examiner in San Francisco who did the autopsy on Harry said similar things. Is it possible to stage a suicide of someone shooting himself in the mouth? Yes. Was there any evidence to support that conclusion? No.

"In both deaths, there was no physical evidence of bruising or no observed puncture marks, and there was nothing unusual from the lab tests on the bodies.

"I went to Thailand to see if I could find out what Harry had found during his visit. I found the local investigator he used, and he is the one who discovered for me that someone posing as a U.S. Embassy employee recently took all the medical files related to John Holliday's stay in the hospital in Bangkok. That person told the hospital administrator that the files were part of a national security issue regarding the United States.

"I confirmed through my intelligence contact at the Embassy, John Adams, and we confirmed at a meeting with the Ambassador that no one from the Embassy went to the hospital on any orders from the Ambassador or from John Adams.

"We then obtained from the hospital security camera a blurry image of the mystery man plus a general description of the man from the hospital administrator. Our lab is running an enhanced copy of the photo through facial recognition, but it is doubtful it is clear enough to make a match.

"The good news is the investigator Harry used in Thailand got a copy of the Holliday medical file. We know Harry took a copy with him when he returned to San Francisco, but no file or any records of his work were found at his apartment. The Thai investigator also kept a copy of the medical file. He gave me that copy. I sent you a copy with my report from Thailand, and I brought the copy home with me. The report shows that Mr. Holliday contracted two diseases while visiting Thailand. One was syphilis and one was a virus transmitted during oral sex. The virus is the precursor to cancer of the mouth and tongue, which is usually fatal. However, the normal life expectancy after a person contracts the virus is a few to several years.

"Someone is going to a lot of trouble to conceal this information. Stealing medical records from a hospital is one thing, but killing a retired officer of the SFPD and possibly a Senator is over the top. Do I have the evidence I need? No. Do I believe there is a high probability that one or both deaths were murder? Yes. All I can say is that someone is going to great lengths to protect the President from the embarrassing details of her husband's death. How far they have gone is not clear."

The Director asked, "First Mike, thanks for the review and the timeline of events. I think there may be two possible scenarios in play. One is the one you mentioned that someone is going to great lengths to protect the President. Another possibility is that someone is going to great lengths to gain information that could be used against the President. Do you agree?"

Mike thought for a moment and then replied, "Yes, sir. I agree that both scenarios are possible based on the evidence we have at this time."

The Director followed up, "Mike regardless of which scenario is in play we need to continue to pursue this case. You need to find your 'mystery man'. He is the best lead you have."

Mike and George walked back to their offices. As they were parting, his boss said, "Thanks, Mike. Good review for the Director. In addition to looking for the mystery man, have another go at both medical examiners. Tell them they need to look harder."

Mike checked with his lab tech and confirmed that after running the mystery man's image through countless databases for facial recognition they had come up empty.

Mike was sitting at his desk, enjoying a cup of coffee and leafing through some files on other cases he should be working on, when his phone rang.

When he answered, the voice on the other end said, "You are at work pretty early, aren't you? This is John in Bangkok. How are you?"

"Hi John. Yea, I am in the office pretty early, and just sitting here wondering what to do next. I have several other cases that demand my attention, but I am still frustrated with the Harry Rice case. What's happening in Bangkok?"

"Not too much. It's another beautiful day in paradise. Just thought I would give you a call and catch up on what's happening on identifying the mystery man at your end?"

"Not much, John. I had the image enhanced a little, and ran it through every database known to man, but the image quality just isn't good enough to give us a match."

John replied, "How would you like a couple names to investigate?"

"What do you mean, John?"

"Mike you must not have slept enough last night. You're a little slow on the uptake. Would you like to know the names of two people carrying U.S. passports, who were in Bangkok when the mystery man visited the hospital, and who match the description given to us by the hospital administrator, and sort of match the blurry image from the security camera?"

Mike exclaimed, "John, did you find something? Why didn't you just say so? Out with it!"

John laughed and said, "I had to tease you a little before I gave you the news. It took a little while, and a little bribery, but I finally got a friend in the Thai immigration service to go through their records and look for someone fitting the description of our mystery man. We got two hits. Both men are in their fifties, and fit the description given by our friend at the hospital. They also match the security camera image, but that would never stand up in court.

"One man, Edgar Harmon, lives in San Francisco. The other one, John Webber, lives in New York. They were both here at the right time and generally fit the description. That is all I have for you this fine day. I'll leave it in your hands to carry on. It's nice to know a lowly embassy employee can be of assistance to the FBI."

Mike didn't recognize either name.

Mike said, "This is amazing. I can't believe it, John. I am still in shock. I'll get right on it and start looking into these guys. Interesting, one of them is from San Francisco. Gee, is that a coincidence? Thanks a million. I will be eternally grateful. I owe you one, big time. I'll let you know if anything develops with these leads. Thanks for the call, John. Good night."

"You are welcome. It's nice to be able to help. Have a good day. Bye for now."

Mike was elated. He couldn't contain himself. He walked to his boss's office and stuck his head in the door. "Have a minute?"

His boss said, "Yea, what's up?

"I just got off the phone with John Adams in Bangkok. He persuaded the Thai immigration people to quietly look through their visa records, and they found two men who were in Bangkok at the right time and fit the description of our mystery man. One man lives in San Francisco and one lives in New York.

"I'm going to discreetly check out these two guys. I will let you know what I learn."

"Ok Mike," replied George. "Good job. Don't get too excited yet, but check them out. Keep me in the loop."

It was a little early to call San Francisco, but he decided to try anyway. He called Sanchez's number and on the second ring Sanchez said, "Hello?"

"Detective Sanchez, surprised you are already at work. This is Mike Sewell calling from Washington."

"Hi, Mike. Actually, you called my cell number, so I could be anywhere, but believe it or not, I am in the office. I just walked in. What's happening?"

"I have some work for you. I just got a couple names of men fitting the description of our mystery man in Bangkok, who were there at the right time. One of the men lives in San Francisco. His name is Edgar Harmon. Could you check him out to see what we can learn about him? Don't talk to him directly. I don't want to tip him off, but see if he has a record, what he does for a living, you know, all the basic stuff."

Sanchez said, "Sure Mike. I'll check him out and let you know what I find. Thanks for the call."

Mike thought about calling the New York FBI office to check out John Webber, but he decided he would wait for Sanchez to get back to him. The fact that one of the names was from San Francisco couldn't just be a coincidence. This was the break he was looking for.

Just before Mike was planning to leave for the day, his phone rang. Detective Sanchez was on the line.

Sanchez said, "Mike, I think Edgar Harmon is a dead end."

Mike sighed with disappointment, "What did you learn about him?"

"He is a professor of anthropology at the University of California, Berkeley, specializing on Southeast Asian studies. He goes to Thailand and Malaysia and Indonesia all the time. He has a clean record, no arrests, and looks like your typical academic. Only thing I can see unusual about him is he doesn't have long hair like most of the left over hippies who work at Berkeley. I could talk to him just to get a better handle on the guy and ask him what he was doing in Bangkok on this trip, but on the surface, I don't think he is our guy."

Mike said, "You're probably right, but why don't you talk to him just to be thorough. Let me know if any bells go off. Thanks for the call."

Mike drove home to his apartment in Alexandria, had a couple beers, fixed himself some dinner, watched TV for a while, and went to bed. At 2 o'clock in the morning he sat up in bed and said, "Holy shit! Webber, the President's Chief of Staff is named Webber. That can't be a coincidence."

Mike got up, threw on some clothes, and walked to the kitchen to make a pot of coffee. He brought his laptop to the kitchen table and logged on. He went to a government site and looked up Judy Webber.

Born in New York City, graduated from NYU with a bachelor's degree in Political Science, and got a law degree from Stanford. Worked for Governor Holliday in California. Worked on her campaign for President, and is now Chief of Staff to President Holliday.

He went to another database and searched for John Webber.

Born in New York City, went to CCNY but did not graduate, served in the U.S. Army as a medic. Currently works as a medical technician on an EMS unit in the Bronx.

Mike sat at his kitchen table, drinking coffee, and said to himself, "I wonder how high this goes?" He went back to bed and tried to sleep, but he was too wired to sleep. He got up early, put on his running gear, and went out for a run. He knew he did some of his best thinking when he was running, and this was the time when he needed some clear thinking. This case just became bigger, and he needed to be sure he didn't do anything to mess it up. He also thought, as he was running, if this guy killed Harry Rice and

Senator Banfield, he will stop at nothing. I have to be really careful about my personal safety, or I might end up as another apparent suicide.

Mike got to work a little early, before his secretary, and made himself a cup of coffee. He called his boss and left a voice mail saying he needed to see him as soon as possible. He busied himself reading emails and looking through other papers in his in box.

His secretary looked through his office door and said, "George's secretary just called and said he can see you now."

Mike said, "Thanks. I'll be back in a little while."

Mike walked into George's office and said, "Hi. Had your coffee yet?"

"Why, do I need it? What's up? Your message sounded like it was urgent."

Mike began, "I woke up at two o'clock this morning, startled. One of the two men in Thailand that we are looking into is an Anthropology Professor a Cal Berkeley. Pretty sure he is not our guy. The other man is named John Webber. Didn't mean anything to me at first, but at 2 am I realized he is the brother of Judy Webber, the President's Chief of Staff."

"Good Lord, Mike. Are you sure?"

"Not a hundred percent yet, but it won't take long to confirm they are sister and brother. I will confirm they are siblings right after this meeting, and then I think you or we need to inform the Director. Obviously all we have currently is circumstantial, but it is enough to now have an official investigation. We need to be sure we keep the investigation confidential until we develop more evidence. I would like to propose that we get a warrant to tap John Webber's phones right away."

George looked at him and said, "What you are saying is that you think Judy Webber is behind the cover up of the details of John Holliday's death, and possibly including the murder of Harry Rice?"

"Yes, sir. And it is also possible that Senator Banfield's death was not from natural causes. We have a guy, John Webber, who had access to medicines and needles and the knowledge of how to use them. He could have administered something to Harry to incapacitate him and put the gun in is mouth for him. And he could have given the Senator something that induced the heart attack."

George said, "It is going to be hard to prove, but I guess that is why we pay you so well. I'll get us a meeting with the Director this afternoon. Go check to be absolutely sure Judy and John are sister and brother."

Chapter 13

Ann was perplexed why she and her team could not find Kareem Masori. He had disappeared leaving no footprint. Ann had checked all the databases looking for a trace. She checked legal records to see if had changed his name. She checked IRS records, but found he had not filed a tax return for several years. She searched the criminal files to see if he was incarcerated somewhere, and checked to see if he had any outstanding warrants against him, but everything was a blank.

Finally, she decided Kareem had no digital footprint, but maybe she had become too dependent on her computer. Maybe a field trip was in order.

The Islamic Center of Washington D.C. was on Massachusetts Avenue NW in the area known as 'embassy row'. Ann thought it likely that Waheed al Masori, because of his wealth and success, might be active in the Center. She knew there was some risk involved in her visiting the Center, but if she could find Kareem, it would be worth the risk.

She drove her new, black BMW to the Center and asked at the information counter if she could meet with Dr. Khan, the Executive Director. She had learned his name from their website. The man at the desk asked if he could inquire why she wanted to talk to Dr. Khan, and she replied she was looking for someone and she believed Dr. Khan might be helpful. Ann added, "I will only need a few minutes of his time."

The gentleman called a number and after speaking on the phone hung up and said, "Dr. Khan will be with you shortly. Please have a seat and I will let you know when he arrives."

"Thank you."

After a ten-minute wait, a distinguished man walked to the information counter and Ann was pointed out to him. He walked over to Ann and said, "I am Dr. Khan, how may I help you?"

Ann introduced herself, and explained she worked for the U.S. government. She began, "Dr. Khan, I appreciate you taking the time to see me. In a study, the name Kareem Masori came up, and I have been trying to locate him, without success. Do you recognize his name?"

Dr. Khan replied, "Ms. Hunt, may I ask why you are looking for him?"

Ann put on her best smile and said, "Sir, I knew you would ask me that. Unfortunately, I cannot tell you the specifics of the study. I am very sorry, but it is very important to me to find him."

"You appear to be a very nice lady, Ms. Hunt," Dr. Khan said. "We are always a little suspicious of inquiries from your government, especially when they are not clearly explained. However, because you have been polite and not like some of the other demanding people who visit us from your government, I will answer your question. I can't see what harm it will do.

"Kareem Masori was the oldest son of Waheed al Masori, a very prominent member of our community. Kareem is no longer with us. Several years ago, he was visiting Pakistan and was killed in a drone strike launched by your government. He was an innocent victim, or what your government calls 'collateral damage'. The loss was devastating to Waheed and his wife. They are immigrants to the U.S. and came when they were very young, to get away from the violence and bloodshed that so frequently occurred at that time in Pakistan, only to have their son die in their homeland at the hands of the U.S. government."

Ann responded, "Dr. Khan, I am very sad to hear this. Do you happen to know where this incident happened?"

"No, I don't. But I will always remember the date. It was December 15th, which coincidentally is my first son's birthday."

Ann returned to her office and called her team together for a brief meeting.

She said, "Finally, after searching every data base known to man, I decided to go native and actually talk to a real person about my search for Kareem Masori. I went to The Islamic Center of

Washington D.C., turned on my charm, and voila, I found Kareem. Or rather, I found what happened to Kareem. He was killed in Pakistan by a drone attack, allegedly an innocent killed as collateral damage. I didn't get the location of the drone strike, but I did learn it happened on December 15th. George, will you go through the records and see if we can learn any more about where the drone strike happened, what year, and who the target or targets were?

"This could be the reason Waheed and his sons are involved in this planned terrorist attack, revenge for Kareem's death."

Chapter 14

Washington was rocked by the sudden death of the Chief Justice of the Supreme Court, William Stone, of an apparent heart attack.

The President had learned the news when she was having breakfast with Judy. A Secret Service agent approached them and said, "I apologize Madam President, but I was just informed by the Head of the Secret Service that Chief Justice William Stone was found dead at his home. It is speculation at this time, but it appears he had a heart attack. The FBI has been notified, and they will lead the investigation. Again, I am sorry, Madam President. Is there anything you want me to do for you?"

"No, Bill. Thank you. I'll finish my breakfast and then head to the Oval Office."

The Secret Service officer backed away and disappeared.

The President said to Judy, "This is terrible news. I think he was only seventy. That is so young. What is going on in this city? First Senator Banfield drops dead and now Chief Justice Stone. It is so sad."

Judy responded, "This is really tragic. Please don't think me cold, but it is an opportunity for you to appoint another Justice."

The President was not happy, and said, "Judy, that was uncalled for. You are a better person than that."

"I am sorry, Madam President." Judy realized she had gone too far and felt embarrassed.

The Director of the FBI had just gotten the news about Chief Justice Stone's death. He called George McDowell and told him he wanted Mike to handle the investigation. He said, "You tell Mike that he can tell the Medical Examiner that the Director of the FBI is on this case personally.

And he can tell the ME that we want to know what caused the heart attack, if indeed it was a heart attack."

Mike heard the news as he was driving to work. When he arrived he had a message from his boss to call immediately. He called and learned he was the lead agent on the investigation of the Chief Justice's death and the Director would be breathing down his neck.

Mike drove to the crime scene and found two Secret Service Agents and the crime scene investigators from the FBI already there. Right after Mike arrived the Medical Examiner and two assistants arrived.

Mike walked over to the Secret Service Agents. The agent told Mike he had discovered the body. He introduced Mike to his boss, who was the other Secret Service Agent now present. He had called the Director of the FBI.

Mike asked the agent to walk him through the timeline.

"I arrived at the Chief Justice's house at seven thirty am to escort him to the Court. When he didn't answer the doorbell, I unlocked the door, and entered. His wife is out of town, visiting one of their children in Florida."

Mike interrupted, "Has anyone notified the wife?"

"I called her," replied the Secret Service supervisor.

Mike said, "Ok, please continue."

"I called out to the Chief Justice but got no response. I walked to the kitchen and saw that no one was there and no one had eaten breakfast. The kitchen was clean. I then called out again, and walked upstairs to his bedroom. He was lying in bed like he was asleep. I said, 'Sir, are you awake?' He didn't move so I gently shook him. Then I put two fingers on his neck to see if I could feel a pulse. That is when I knew he was dead. I then called my boss, and he told me to stay with the body until the FBI arrived. And here you are."

"Have you been assigned to the Chief Justice for long?"

"Going on six months, sir."

"What can you tell me about how he was feeling, both physically and emotionally?"

"He was in good health as far as I know, both physically and emotionally. He was basically in good spirits. He always seemed to be happy, and it was no different lately."

"Did you notice any signs of anyone else having been in the house?"

"No, everything was in its place. Even the kitchen was spotless. Sometimes when his wife is out of town, he would leave the kitchen a little messy. Not bad, but he didn't always put everything away. He must not have had dinner at home last night, because if he had, I think there would be some dishes still out. They have a maid who comes in for a few hours every day to straighten up, after he leaves for the Court."

Mike finished by saying, "Thank you, Agent. I'll try to check where he had dinner last evening. Can I have your card and your supervisor's card, in case I have any other questions? You can both go. Again, thanks."

Then Mike added, "Agent, do you know if the Chief Justice used any sleeping pills or anything else to help him sleep?"

"No sir. He didn't like to take any pills. We talked about that once. He didn't even like to take aspirin. I am pretty sure he didn't take any sleep aids. He even told me once he never had any trouble sleeping."

The Secret Service Agents left, and Mike went back to have another look at the Chief Justice. He looked relaxed, as if he was sleeping. Mike stood over him and looked carefully at his face and neck. Then he noticed a small spot on his black pajama top. It looked like he had spilled some water or something on the pajamas.

Mike walked over to the lead crime scene investigator and asked, "Have you found anything that looks suspicious?"

"No sir, not yet. Looks pretty straight forward so far."

Mike asked, "Have you done anything yet in the kitchen?"

No, we haven't been there yet. Anything special we should look for?"

Mike said, "I am going to have a look at the kitchen, and I'll talk to you again before I leave."

He walked down to the kitchen and noticed that it was spotless. It showed no sign that the Chief Justice had used the kitchen the night before. He opened the dishwasher and found it was empty.

He went back upstairs and entered the bathroom off the master bedroom. Everything was in order. He looked in the drawers and the medicine cabinet. There were no prescription drugs in any of the drawers or the medicine cabinet. He surmised if his wife took any prescriptions she probably had them with her. There was no evidence that the Chief Justice was on any medication.

He went back to the lead crime scene investigator and said, "Ok, I have some things for you. First, I think there is a spot on the Chief Justice's pajama top. It might be just a water spot, but be very careful to analyze whatever is on the pajamas. He may have drunk something and spilled a little bit on his pajamas. But there is no glass in the bedroom. Then I want you to check the sink in the bathroom to see if there is any evidence that something may have been poured down the drain. Do the same thing in the kitchen. Also, I want you to take all the glasses from the kitchen and test them for residue of any kind. Take the water glasses and the small juice glasses. Take them all. Don't leave anything to chance. I am looking for evidence that the Chief Justice was forced to drink something and someone cleaned up after himself, really well. It is a long shot, but we don't want to miss anything. One other thing, please check all the doors to see if there is any evidence that someone entered the house without a key."

The Medical Examiner was waiting for them to release the body to him. Mike walked over to him and said, "Dr. Jim, we meet again. Do you see anything suspicious?"

"No Mike, it all looks like he died in his sleep, but we won't know any more until we do the autopsy."

"I won't tell you to be thorough, because I know you will be. But I want you to go over the body in minute detail. If there is a puncture mark anywhere on his body, I want you to find it. And pay particular attention to the possibility that the Chief Justice drank something, willingly or not. He has a small liquid spot on his pajama top, which we will analyze. If he was forced to drink something, we may not be looking at a natural death. When do you expect to have a time of death, and preliminary cause of death?"

"We'll take the body as soon as you give us the green light. I will do the autopsy as soon as I get back to the morgue. It may take a little longer than normal, because we are going to be very, very thorough. I will give you a call as soon as I have the preliminary results. Some of the lab tests may take a little longer, but obviously this one is a top priority. If you can keep your Director off my butt, I will be grateful. Phone calls from him and others will just slow us down."

Mike replied, "I understand, Jim. I can't promise you that I have any influence over the Director, but I will do my best to give you the privacy you need. I am ready to let you have the body, but check with the lead crime scene investigator to be sure he is done with it."

Before he left he talked to the FBI guy who had arrived to sit on the crime scene to be sure it wasn't disturbed by anyone after everyone left. Mike mentioned to him that the Stone's had a maid who came everyday, usually mid-morning. He said to send her home and be sure she doesn't touch anything in the kitchen, master bathroom or master bedroom.

When Mike returned to his office he had a message from the FBI office in New York, marked urgent. He needed to brief his boss and maybe the Director, but he closed his door and placed a call to the New York office.

He talked to Joe Spagnola, his contact in New York. "Hi Joe, it's Mike Sewell in Washington. I had a message to call you, marked urgent. What's up?"

Joe responded, "Thanks for the call Mike. After you got the warrant for us to listen to John Webber's phone calls, we have been listening. We got a hit last night that we thought you might be interested in. I'll send you a digital copy of the message, but maybe you want to listen to it now. The interesting thing is it came from John's cell phone and we tracked it to Washington. He was in your town last night. At four o'clock this morning he made a call to another cell phone. We don't know whom he talked to, but it was a woman, and she was talking on an unidentified cell phone, probably a burner. But, she was somewhere in the White House. Let me play it for you."

Mike waited and then heard a man's voice say, "Hi, wanted you to know the mission was accomplished. Everything went fine." Then a woman's voice, "That is great news, thanks." The man's voice, "I am headed home unless you need anything else." The woman's voice said, "No, I think we are done. I'll call you this weekend. Have a safe trip home."

Joe came back on the line. "I'll send you a copy, and keep the original in a safe place. We'll keep our ears open and let you know if we hear anything further."

"Thanks, Joe. Great job. I am about to brief my boss and probably the Director, and I will include your information. Keep up the good work. Bye for now."

When Mike called his boss, George said, "Come on up." He walked to his boss's office and was met at the door. I called the Director and he said to bring you to his office and we will both listen at the same time.

The Director was a pretty serious guy, but today he seemed extra serious. Mike wondered if he was feeling the stress of the job. The Director had no time for small talk today, and said, "What's the status?"

Mike walked them through the crime scene. He told them the scene looked like the Chief Justice died in his sleep. There was no evidence of any foul play. Then he mentioned the stain on the Chief Justice's pajama top and said the forensic guy promised to give it top priority. He reviewed his conversations with the Secret Service agent who found the Chief Justice in his bed, and his conversations with the crime scene investigators and the medical examiner. Then he added, "Please don't be offended, but the medical examiner pleaded with me to keep everyone at the FBI from calling him so he can focus on his job. He promised to call me as soon as he has his preliminary report."

Then Mike changed subjects to tell them about the phone call from the New York office. He walked them through the recorded message from the notes he had taken. Then he explained, "The man on the recording is John Webber, talking to a woman on a burner phone. The woman was somewhere in the White House, and John was calling her at four am from somewhere in Washington."

The Director said, "My God, do you think Judy Webber used her brother to kill the Chief Justice of the Supreme Court?"

Mike replied, "The message could be about something else, but the timing sure is suspicious. First, we need to confirm that there is evidence the Chief Justice was murdered, but if we find that evidence, then we have another piece to this strange puzzle.

"When we get the recording of the message between John Webber and the woman, maybe we can use voice recognition to confirm it was, in fact, Judy."

The Director said, "Good job, Mike. It sounds like the next steps are to get the forensic evidence and the ME's report. I won't call him, as much as I want to, but let me know as soon as you get his report."

* * *

The voice recognition expert confirmed that the woman on the recorded phone conversation was Judy Webber.

The forensic expert called to give Mike his findings on the Chief Justice's pajama top. It was water with two active ingredients, a heavy sedative and potassium chloride. He explained that potassium chloride in a high enough dose can change the electrolyte balance in the body and lead to death with the same symptoms as a heart attack. He said he would send a copy of the report attached to an email right away. He also added that they were still testing the glasses from the kitchen and the residue taken from the bathroom sink and the kitchen sink, but so far there was no evidence of either the sedative or potassium chloride in anything tested.

Mike thanked him for his hard work, and said he would await the copy of his report.

Shortly after the call from the forensic expert, Mike received a call from the medical examiner. Dr. Jim said, "I don't know how busy you are, but if you have time, why don't you come to my office and I will talk you through my preliminary report."

Mike said, "I can be there in about a half hour, if that is ok?"

"See you when you get here."

Mike excitedly drove to Dr. Jim's office. His office was across the hall from the morgue where the formaldehyde and bleach odors never seemed to go away. When he arrived, Jim said, "Have a seat and I'll walk you through the preliminary findings.

"First, I estimate the time of death between two and three am on the day the Secret Service agent found the body. There are some suspicious aspects to the Chief Justice's death, leading me to a preliminary conclusion that he did not die of natural causes. We found evidence of the sedative Valium in his body, which in itself would not have caused his death. But it is possible someone may have given him the sedative to make him relax, and to more easily control him. More importantly we found an imbalance in his electrolytes, showing his potassium to sodium ratio was way out of balance. That imbalance could lead to death and the symptoms would be very similar to a heart attack. There were minute traces of both the sedative and potassium chloride on the mucus areas in the mouth, suggesting he ingested them, or simply put, he drank them.

"There is no way to determine if he drank that mixture of his own free will or if he was forced to drink it. Certainly, if he were trying to commit suicide, drinking that mixture would do the job. But being forced to drink it would have the same effect. I have no way of determining if he committed suicide or was murdered."

Mike said, "This is consistent with the spot found on the Chief Justice's pajama top. It showed the same chemicals, indicating to me that while he was drinking the death potion, he spilled a little on his pajamas.

Jim added, "One more thing. You were insistent on checking for puncture marks. I have examined the body in detail, and I was unable to find any marks that could be puncture marks. I also found no evidence of bruising caused by restraints or someone forcibly grabbing him.

"Without additional evidence from some of the other tests, that are not yet completed, I will rule the cause of death was a heart attack caused by an excess of potassium in his system."

Mike switched subjects on Jim. "Will you review the autopsy of Senator Banfield to see if there was any evidence he had an electrolyte imbalance similar to the Chief Justice's and whether he too had a sedative in his system?"

Dr. Jim said, "I'll take another look and let you know what I find."

He thanked Jim for his hard work, and said he would brief the FBI Director on his findings.

Back at FBI Headquarters, Mike briefed his boss and the Director. "I just got back from the Medical Examiner's office, and heard his assessment of the death. He found evidence of a strong sedative and potassium chloride having been ingested by the Chief Justice. This is consistent with the spot found on the Chief Justice's pajama top. Potassium chloride can be fatal and the symptoms are generally the same as a heart attack. Unfortunately, the Medical Examiner can find no evidence that will tell him if the Chief Justice drank the potion of his own free will or was coerced. He has additional tests that are not finalized, but he is sure the potion is what killed him. Additionally he puts the time of death between two and three o'clock in the morning. There is no forensic evidence yet indicating someone else was in the house at the time of his death. Would it be possible for someone to drink a glass of sedative and potassium chloride and have time to wash the glass and put it away and then climb into bed and die? The answer is yes."

The Director asked, "Where do we go from here?"

Mike replied, "I asked Dr. Jim to review Senator Banfield's autopsy to see if it showed an excess of potassium in his body and if it showed he had taken a sedative. I am going to ask the Medical Examiner in San Francisco to also look for evidence of a sedative in Harry Rice at the time of his death. I'm going to check the Chief Justice's medical file to see if he was ever prescribed any sedative, and I will check if his wife took sedatives. I checked the master bathroom when I was in his house, and there was not a single prescription drug bottle in the bathroom or the bedroom.

"I am also going to send a photo of John Webber to my friend in the Embassy in Bangkok and ask him to show it to the administrator at the hospital to see if we can confirm that it was John Webber who took the medical files.

"Anything else you want me to do, sir?"

The Director responded, "We have good circumstantial evidence that John Webber killed the Chief Justice, and that his sister, Judy, was aware, based on their phone conversation. I hate to ask this, but do you have any circumstantial information that would suggest the President of the United States is aware or involved?"

Mike said, without hesitation, "No sir. It looks to me like Judy is the mastermind and her brother is the killer."

"Thank you, Mike. For the country's sake, I hope you are right."

Because of the time difference with Bangkok both men were never in the office at the same time. Mike decided to send John Adams an email and attach a photo file of John Webber. In the email he asked John to show the photo to the hospital administrator and see if he can give us a positive ID that Webber is the man who took the medical files.

Next, he called Detective Sanchez in San Francisco. After the pleasantries, Mike asked, "Will you please check with the Medical Examiner again to see if Harry's autopsy showed evidence of any sedative in his body? And also while you are at it, check with Harry's doctors to see what medications Harry was on before his death, and go through the inventory of things in his house to see what medicines were in the house."

Sanchez asked, "Have you found something you are not telling me, Mike"

Mike replied, "I have to be careful, but I have another case that may be related where there was evidence of a sedative in the victim's system. That is really all I can say for now. Please give me a call as soon as you have the answers."

Evidence started pouring in. Dr. Jim called Mike to inform him that Senator Banfield's autopsy showed a small amount of the sedative Valium in his system. It was disregarded initially as something that is almost normal. It certainly would not have caused the heart attack. There was no evidence of an electrolyte imbalance.

Sanchez called Mike and reported, "The Medical Examiner confirmed that Harry had the sedative Valium in his system. He apologized for not mentioning it earlier, but said it is common in suicides for the person planning to kill himself to take a sedative before to help calm his nerves."

"Did you ask the Medical Examiner if the sedative would make it easier for a person to force Harry to shoot himself?"

Sanchez said, "Mike, we think alike. I asked him and he confirmed that the Valium could have made Harry easier to control, and with enough Valium in Harry's system, someone could have forced him to pull the trigger with the gun in his mouth. I also checked with Harry's doctor, and he had never prescribed any sedative to Harry. The only medications we found in Harry's apartment were some arthritis pain medication, blood pressure medication and cholesterol medication. The doctor confirmed prescribing all of those for Harry."

Mike received an email from John Adams that said Niran positively confirmed that the photo of John Webber was the same man who visited, claiming to work for the U.S. Embassy.

Mike decided it was time to have another update with his boss. Mike explained, "We now have a link. Valium was used in three deaths, Harry Rice, Senator Banfield, and Chief Justice Stone. Each of them had Valium in their system at the time of death, but none of them had ever been prescribed the drug. I still can't determine how Senator Banfield's heart attack was induced, but I am confident that it was murder."

Mike asked George, "I sort of would like to arrest John Webber and get a warrant to search his house, car, and place of business for Valium, and also review his work schedule to see if he was absent from work when the crimes were committed. But I know once we arrest him or initiate a search we tip off his sister. I am unsure how we should proceed? Should we talk to the President first, or should we confront Judy first, or should we go after John Webber?"

"Gentlemen," the Director said. "I have a piece of interesting news. I had a call recently from Judy Webber. She claimed she was calling on the President's behalf, and said the President didn't want to appear to be interfering in an FBI case, but she was curious to know if there was anything to report on Chief Justice Stone's apparent heart attack? I explained that it was still an ongoing investigation, and that I really couldn't say anything at this time. She was a little pushy asking if there were any things suspicious. I said we were just dotting the i's and crossing the t's. I told her I would call the President as soon as I can.

"She is a pretty smooth lady, and didn't give any hint that she was nervous or anything like that. I don't know if she was really calling on behalf of the President, but I will give her the benefit of the doubt. I know the two women are really tight. They have breakfast together almost every day and they eat dinner together frequently. Judy actually lives in a suite adjacent to the President's residence."

Mike and his boss briefed the Director on the latest evidence that had been collected. They expressed their joint opinion that additional investigation into John Webber would likely tip their hand.

"Mike," the Director said, "I will ask you again, do you have any evidence, circumstantial or even a hint, that the President is involved?"

"No sir. But she has not been the focus of our investigation. To completely rule her out, we would need to monitor her private conversations with Judy. Sir, I can't see that happening, and I am certainly not suggesting it."

The Director said, "I think it is time we have a private conversation with the President of the United States. I am not sure how to do that without tipping off Judy, but I will come up with some scheme.

A week later the Director of the FBI and Agent Sewell met with the President of the United States. They met outside the White House and only the President's Secret Service detail knew the location.

The Director introduced Mike to the President and told her he was the lead agent on the Chief Justice's death investigation.

The President began, "Gentlemen, this meeting makes me feel a little strange. I hope you have a good reason for not meeting me in the White House. The situation room is about as secure as it gets, and if that worries you, then I am really worried."

The Director replied, "Madam President, we wanted to have a private conversation with you, and this was our best hope for concealing it from people in the White House. Please let me explain. There is considerable circumstantial evidence that the Chief Justice was murdered. I can go through some of the evidence with you later. The primary suspect in the case is John Webber, your Chief of Staff's brother. We are at the point of the investigation that any additional collection of evidence will likely tip off John and, or Judy.

"Madam President, there is evidence that John Webber traveled to Bangkok recently and posed as a U.S. Embassy employee and confiscated the medical records of your late husband, John. There is also evidence that John Webber may have killed a retired police officer that was doing a private investigation into your husband's death at the request of Senator Banfield. Finally, Senator Banfield's heart attack may not have been from natural causes."

The President was in shock. She was white as a ghost, and actually trembling. She asked if she might have a drink of water. Mike fetched a bottle of water, poured it into a glass, and placed it on the table in front of her.

She drank a sip of water, and said, "This is the most shocking thing I have ever heard. I have known Judy since she was a student at Stanford. Other than John being her brother, do you have any evidence that shows Judy is involved?"

"Madam President, we have a recording of a phone conversation between Judy and John, approximately one hour after the Chief Justice was killed, at four am in the morning. Judy was in the White House at the time and John was calling from somewhere in Washington D.C. The content of the phone conversation is very suspicious."

The President paused to think. She was still stunned. She tried to think back to all the times she and Judy had been together and whether she had ever given any indication she was capable of something like this. Other than a few cold remarks from time to time about someone, she couldn't think of any signs she had seen.

Finally, the President spoke. "As a minimum, for national security reasons and safety reasons, I need to suspend Judy from all her duties immediately. Lord, she lives in the suite in the White House next to my residence. She will have to leave the White House immediately, until the investigation clears her or she is charged.

"Gentlemen, I am thinking about the legal issues involved, but what I would really like to do is have a private, one on one meeting with Judy and confront her. We could do it in a place where you could monitor the entire conversation and be close by if she becomes violent, which she would never do. I think I can get her to tell me what she has done and why. My concern is whether

her confession would be admissible in court in the prosecution of her and her brother?"

"Madam President, unless we somehow could Mirandize her first, anything she said would be inadmissible in court."

The President said, "I really need to know why she did what she did. This could destroy my presidency. I need to talk to her."

The Director asked, "Do you think you could get her to sign a Miranda waiver before you talk to her? She obviously has some issues with right and wrong. I think possibly she was doing these things thinking she was helping you."

"I think she would sign a Miranda waiver if I asked her. We have a very close relationship. We have worked together for years. She has always been there to help me, even when my husband died. She never wanted to be in the spotlight, actually preferring to work in the background. I had to twist her arm to get her to take the Chief of Staff position."

The Director said, "We will arrange to have John Webber arrested at the same time you are scheduled to talk to Judy. You will have a Miranda waiver for her to sign, and we will have the room bugged for recording. Agent Sewell will be near by and take her into custody immediately after your meeting with her. Agreed?"

The President said, "I would love to see all the evidence, but my judgment tells me to let you guys do your jobs. This has been the most difficult meeting of my presidency. Dealing with Congress is a lot easier than this. The country is in for a shock and some difficult times ahead. I hope I have the strength to get through it."

The Director said, "You do, Madam President."

The President and Judy met for breakfast the following morning like they had done almost every morning since they moved into the White House. Judy already had her coffee when the President walked in the room. Judy noticed she was carrying a small leather folder with her and she looked tired, like she hadn't slept well.

Judy said, "Carolyn, are you ok? You look like you didn't sleep very well last night."

The President replied, "You are very observant, Judy. I didn't sleep very well. We need to talk, but first I must tell you a couple things. The FBI took your brother, John, into custody this morning. And immediately after our discussion, the FBI will take you into custody. I very much want to have a conversation with you but before I do I want you to sign a Miranda waiver."

The President opened her leather folder and handed Judy the Miranda waiver and a pen.

Judy looked at her and saw in the President's eyes how much she was hurting. Judy took the Miranda document and signed it. She placed it on the table, and said, "Carolyn, I did it for you. Men have always been out to hurt you. It started with that lousy man you married. He couldn't keep it in his pants. When he went to Thailand he got what he deserved. He was going to be in that hospital in San Francisco for years, and the truth was going to come out about what an evil man he was. I couldn't let that happen to you.

"Senator Banfield was going to use it against you and hold it over you to get what he wanted. I couldn't let that happen.

"And then the Chief Justice. He was a pompous ass. He was standing in the way of your ability to change the United States the way we know it should be. With him gone, you could nominate a young, liberal Chief Justice who would lead the court for decades. I know that is what you want."

The President had tears in her eyes. "Judy, where did we go wrong? We had it all, but you missed the most important lesson. Leadership and working with others to form a strong bi-partisan agreement will always be better than ruling like a dictator. Diversity of opinions, listening to other's ideas, and finding ways to work together are the foundation of our success. We have endured troubles, and I could have gotten through the humiliation that would have come when people learned about my husband's infidelities. Hell, most people already suspected it. We could have gotten through it."

Judy said without showing any remorse, "Carolyn, I did what I did to protect you. I love you and will always love you."

The President walked to the door and opened it for Agent Sewell. Judy stood and turned around while he put handcuffs on her. Mike and another FBI agent escorted Judy to a waiting car and drove away.

* * *

The next day, at noon, the Director of the FBI held a press conference. Standing with Director Postles were Supervisor McDowell and Agent Sewell. The Director began, "Ladies and gentlemen, today we have a series of related announcements to make. First, after completing the autopsy of Chief Justice William Stone we determined that the Chief Justice did not die of natural causes, as was initially assumed. An extensive investigation was conducted, lead by Agent Mike Sewell, who is here today, which led to the arrest of two individuals.

"Judy Webber and John Webber have been taken into custody and will be charged for the death of Chief Justice Stone.

"In a related case, we recently lost one of our elder senators, Senator Charlie Banfield. The initial autopsy indicated he died from a heart attack. Upon further investigation it was determined the heart attack was triggered by an external substance given to the Senator. Judy Webber has confessed and implicated her brother in both crimes. In addition, there are other charges that will be brought against both suspects.

"I want to compliment Agent Sewell for his fine work and tenacity in pursuing these cases.

"I will answer a few questions, if there are any?"

The Director spent the next few minutes answering questions from the press, being careful not to reveal any specific details of either case. When asked what other charges will be brought, he danced around that question too.

It was the lead story on the evening news of all the major television stations. The stories all included a profile of the President's Chief of Staff, Judy Webber.

At nine o'clock the President went on television to give a special address to the country.

The President began, "Ladies and gentlemen, I come before you tonight with a heavy heart. Yesterday my trusted Chief of Staff, Judy Webber, confessed to her involvement in the murders of Chief Justice William Stone and Senator Charlie Banfield. She was taken into custody by the FBI, and will be charged for multiple crimes. I cannot describe the shock and sorrow I felt when I learned the news. First, I was greatly saddened with the lose of Senator Banfield and Chief Justice Stone, but to learn that they had been murdered and that my Chief of Staff was involved was almost too much to comprehend.

"Judy Webber has been a friend and loyal advisor to me for many years. Tragically, she lost her moral compass sometime ago. I feel the need to apologize for the tragic loss of life that one of my senior advisors caused. I can't go back and change what she did, but I can promise you that I will continue to devote the rest of my presidency to making this great country financially and morally strong. The people of this great nation deserve a government that works for all the people and creates the environment that allows everyone to pursue their dreams.

"Thank you and good night."

The day after the President spoke to the nation, Mike Sewell placed a call to Detective Sanchez at the SFPD.

Sanchez said, "Hi Mike. Sounds like you have been pretty busy back there in Washington."

Mike replied, "Yes Sanchez, it has been a busy time. I am calling because I want you to know we have a confession that confirms positively that retired officer Harry Rice did not commit suicide. The same people who murdered the Chief Justice and the Senator murdered Harry. I don't know how, when or where all these cases will be tried, but I can assure you the perpetrators will be going away for a long time.

Sanchez said, "Mike, that is great news. His friends on the force will be pleased to hear this. Thanks for all your hard work. Any time you want to help the SFPD with another case, you are always welcome."

"Thanks Sanchez, but I think I already have enough to keep me busy for awhile. Please tell your Captain and the Medical Examiner the news. Thank both of them for their help and support. It was great working with you."

* * *

The President spent time talking to her advisors and staff to get recommendations on candidates for Judy's replacement. There were many candidates suggested, but eventually the President decided she needed someone with fresh ideas and a non-Washington perspective on things. She chose an old friend, Walter Bennett, who she had met through her late husband, John. Walter was from San Francisco and, like John, had made a fortune in the technology business world. He had been an unofficial advisor to her when she was Governor of California, and she was very comfortable with his political philosophy and him personally. He was married to a lovely lady, Sarah, and they had two beautiful, grown daughters.

Carolyn called him one evening when it was ten o'clock, Washington time, and seven o'clock, San Francisco time. She made the call herself from her residence in the White House. Sarah answered the phone and Carolyn said, "Hi Sarah, you probably won't believe this, but this is Carolyn Holliday, how are you?"

Sarah responded, "Is this some kind of joke? Who is this, really?"

Carolyn laughed and said, "Sarah, I get that all the time. But, really, it is the President. I was hoping I could talk to Walter. Is he home?"

"Carolyn, or Madam President, I am sorry. I thought it was someone playing a prank. I'll get Walter for you."

Carolyn could hear through the phone, "Walter it's for you. It's the President. Yes, of the United States."

Walter picked up the phone. "Do I have to call you Madam President?"

Carolyn said, "Only in public. Tonight, you can call me Carolyn. How are you Walter?"

"Fine Carolyn. I am fine, Sarah is fine, and the children are fine. More importantly, how are you. I was sad to hear about Judy. What can I do for you?"

"Well Walter, I decided it is time to disrupt your beautiful life. I need you to come work for me. I want you to become my Chief of Staff. We need a fresh perspective on things, and only someone outside the Washington system will do. We will have to check you out to be sure you are not a terrorist, but if you are agreeable, I can start that process immediately. If you want to fly to Washington to sit down and talk about it, fine. But I really need you."

Walter said, "I always wondered what it would be like if the President called and asked me to do something. You always hear, 'You can't say no to the President.' Now I know that feeling. Madam President, I am honored to be asked and I humbly accept your offer. Have me checked out and see if they can find anything in my past that will disqualify me. It will be an interesting conversation with Sarah and the girls. I predict Sarah will stay here to be close to the girls. But don't worry; we will work out the family details. When do you want me there?"

"I'll put a rush on the vetting process, but hopefully in about a week to ten days you should be cleared. Why don't you tentatively plan on being here in about ten days, ok?"

"Ok, Madam President. I won't mention this to anyone except Sarah and the girls, and I will swear them to secrecy. I'll start putting my business things in order, that won't be a problem. Thank you, Carolyn. I look forward to being your Chief of Staff."

"Thank you Walter. I look forward to having you on board."

The President asked her secretary to arrange a meeting with Natalie as soon as possible. Later that day Natalie was sitting in the Oval Office with the President.

"Natalie, you did such a great job finding the last Supreme Court Justice that I want you to lead the search committee again. Unfortunately, this time it might be a little more work."

Natalie frowned and wondered what the President meant. Natalie was thinking they already had five good names.

The President continued, "This search will be quite different considering the circumstances. First, I want you to start with a clean piece of paper. I know the other five names you had from the last search were all good candidates, but the requirements have changed. I will not put a liberal leaning woman in the Chief Justice position replacing William Stone. I want you to find a moderate candidate. Too liberal is out just like too conservative is out. I want you to find a middle of the roader who will be acceptable to both Republicans and Democrats.

"There are three people I want you to talk to about potential candidate names. First, talk to Chief Justice Stone's law clerk and see if he has any names that the Chief Justice would have liked. Also talk to the other two oldest Justices and ask them for suggestions. Coincidentally the oldest Justice is conservative and the second oldest is liberal, so we will get both viewpoints. Then assemble your team again, and add names from their recommendations. I assume this process will take you longer than before. I need a quality search, and I want the best candidate."

Natalie called the members of the last search committee, excluding Judy, and invited them to participate again and called the first meeting. At that meeting she explained the different criteria the President had described. They all talked about it and went away to start their individual research.

Natalie arranged meetings with the law clerk and the two oldest Justices. The two Justices promised to get back to her after they had given her request the appropriate amount of thought. The law clerk gave Natalie two names the Chief Justice had mentioned who he thought would be excellent Justices for the Supreme Court. One week later Natalie had six names, two from each of the Justices and two from the law clerk.

She got the search committee together for their second meeting and by the end of the meeting they had a list of fifteen candidates, five women and ten men.

Natalie put together profiles on each of the candidates and sent the packet to each search committee member, with a note scheduling the next meeting a week later.

Then Natalie arranged a meeting with the President.

The President said, "Hi Natalie, are you all done with the search, already?"

"No Madam President, but we are making progress. We have fifteen candidates, with six of them coming from the sources at the Supreme Court. We have five women and ten men. I thought this time around you might want to be more involved in the process, earlier."

"Sure Natalie, I will be happy to read the profiles on the fifteen candidates you have assembled. Thank you."

Two weeks later the President had her nominee for the new Chief Justice of the Supreme Court.

* * *

The President called the four leaders of Congress to another meeting in the White House. In addition to those leaders, also in attendance were the Vice President and the President's new Chief of Staff, Walter Bennett. The President introduced Walter to the leaders of Congress.

The President began, "Gentlemen, as you know, this has been a difficult time for me. Judy Webber was one of my closest friends and advisors. It is still hard to believe she concealed such an evil side of her life for so long. But, for the sake of the country, we will move on, and we will move forward together.

"I am honored that Walter Bennett has agreed to put his business career on hold for awhile and become my Chief of Staff. I know he plans to spend time meeting and getting to know all of you plus all the movers and shakers in Washington. That could be a full time job for him, just meeting people in Washington, but in addition, he will find time to keep me focused on the important things going on that need my attention. Welcome Walter.

"Now, to the purpose of this meeting. I want you all to know we have been busily working on finding a nominee for the Chief Justice of the Supreme Court. Some of you might expect me to use this opportunity to nominate the first woman as Chief Justice, and you might also assume she will be somewhat liberal. That is what my base expects, and I can assure you I have had many unofficial advisors suggesting names for my consideration.

"As my Democrat friends in the House and Senate know, I have offended many in my base with the compromises I have been willing to make so far in my Presidency.

"But this time is different."

All in the group noticed that the President had started her comments with almost a whimsical attitude, but now her demeanor had changed to a very serious one.

She continued, "The senseless killing of Chief Justice William Stone was life changing for me. As much as I previously wanted to appoint the first liberal woman to become Chief Justice,

I will not use these terrible circumstances to accomplish my wishes. I will not nominate a liberal and it will not be a woman.

"My search committee was given specific instructions and guidelines quite different for this search compared to the last one.

"I want to use this nomination to begin the healing process of losing a Chief Justice, and to bring this country closer together in unity. I will be holding a press conference tomorrow where I will introduce my nominee to the country. I hope the Senate will move him through the process in a timely way and vote their consent for my nominee."

She then told them the name of her nominee. "I ask all of you to try your very best to keep his name confidential, until after my press conference tomorrow."

Senator Marino said, "Madam President, this decision took real courage. We were worried that another strong liberal on the high court would be hard for us to support, and a bitter fight might have occurred, splitting the country once again. You are one brave woman, Madam President."

"Thank you Senator Marino." Then she smiled and the mood relaxed again, and she added, "I promise you we will have some more disagreements in the future to fight about, but hopefully this nomination will not be one of those fights."

After the Judicial Committee hearings where the Senators questioned the nominee, his nomination went to the floor of the Senate where he was confirmed with a unanimous vote, the first time in recent history that had occurred.

Chapter 15

After a few weeks in Washington, Ahmed and Fahad had become bored with their work in the restaurants and spending all their free time in their apartment. One night when they were watching TV, Ahmed said, "We need to get out of here and go for a walk. Let's go to the convenience store for a couple drinks."

When they were on the street, Ahmed continued, "I know we are suppose to watch what we say in the apartment in case it is bugged, but seriously, I am going nuts. We have no idea how long we will wait for word to come. I can't just sit in the apartment all the time. Let's start looking around to get a better understanding of the city. Let's go buy some cameras tomorrow and start playing tourists. What do you say?"

"I agree," Fahad said. "The apartment is driving me crazy, too. We can't talk and there is nothing to do except watch TV. Let's start learning the Metro system and look for a place to do our work, if that remains the target. And let's just enjoy seeing the city. I think we should even go to some movies. We have plenty of money."

As the weather got warmer, their routine became work, sleep, and play tourist. Their standard uniform was jeans and a tee shirt, running shoes and a baseball cap, and they almost always wore their backpacks, with a windbreaker stuffed inside. They bought digital cameras and downloaded all the pictures onto their computer. They learned the Metro system and traveled all the lines just to become familiar with the whole network. They took lots of pictures on the trains, off the trains, inside the stations and outside the stations. They repeatedly walked around Union Station but were careful not to look too obvious with all the pictures they took.

They became fascinated with Washington. They visited all the Memorials and the White House and the Capital. Then they started visiting the museums. They kept going back to the Smithsonian Museum because it had so much to see.

One night when Ahmed and Fahad were walking back to their apartment from a movie, Ahmed asked, "Fahad, do you think we will be successful with our plan?"

Fahad replied, "I think about it a lot. If Allah wants us to succeed we will. All we can do is the best job possible. It is out of our hands regarding success. What I think about more is whether we will ever see our friends in Pakistan again. The chances of successfully placing the bombs, detonating them, getting away, and working our way back to Pakistan are not very high. I will tell you, I sometimes wish I had not been chosen for this job. I pray to Allah to give me the strength to be strong and to not doubt our leader."

Ahmed said, "I do the same thing. We are almost home so I guess we should watch what we say, just in case."

* * *

Faisal and Jamal were working on the delivery trucks delivering food supplies all over Washington. Sometimes they worked together on the same truck but most of the time they were on different trucks. The work wasn't difficult. They just had to do what they were told.

Their work clothes were jeans and a tee shirt. If it were cool they would add a sweatshirt and sometimes a light windbreaker.

They loaded supplies for a few locations on the truck, being sure to keep the orders separated. Then, when they arrived at the destination they would deliver all the food for that stop, and then drive to the next delivery. Each truck would usually make three or four stops before it headed back to the warehouse for the next load.

As long as they did their work and didn't work too slowly or mouth off, their bosses treated them ok. They saw other workers who would get hollered at when they said something to the boss, and if it happened more than once, the guy was gone. Faisal and Jamal kept quiet, worked hard, and paid attention to the routine and where the deliveries were made.

To their pleasant surprise they learned that their company delivered to the White House. They occasionally worked on the White House deliveries and learned the routine. All they had to do now was work hard and stay out of trouble.

Now that they had their student IDs and jobs, it was time to enjoy their free time in Washington. They had no idea when the call would come to activate the plan, but they had been warned it might take months to put all the pieces in place.

Faisal and Jamal began learning their way around Washington. They learned the Metro system, and the bus system, and even signed up for some of the tours of the city. They were fascinated with how modern and clean Washington was compared to Islamabad.

One day they were out for one of their walks near the Capital building. Suddenly, Faisal saw Ahmed and Fahad. "Jamal, look, isn't that Ahmed and Fahad? They don't see us yet. Do you think it is safe to say hello or should we avoid them?"

Jamal replied, "I think it is safe. I want to talk to them to see how they are doing."

As they walked closer, Ahmed saw them. He whispered to Fahad, "Faisal and Jamal are walking toward us. Don't show that you recognize them. Make it look like we just stopped to talk to some other men on the street."

They didn't embrace or do anything special to greet each other, but they all quietly said how good it was to see friends.

Ahmed said, "We now have new names. Mine is Jose and this is Carlos."

Jamal laughed, "You don't look like a Carlos."

Fahad laughed and replied, "I know, but I tell people my mother was from Pakistan and my father was Venezuelan. That seems to work."

They stood around talking, but watching carefully that someone wasn't watching them. They talked about how they had arrived in Washington, and found out that no one knew if Khalid and Masood had been successful getting in the country. They all wished they could contact the leader in the U.S., but they understood the need for caution. After standing near the Capital talking for almost twenty minutes, Faisal said, "There is a

Starbucks just a couple blocks away. Let's walk over and have a cup of coffee."

They spent another twenty minutes together in Starbucks and finally decided it was time to part. They agreed to meet outside the Starbucks again in a week. When they walked out of Starbucks they had no idea someone had just taken photos of each of them.

* * *

Ann already had the NSA monitoring Mohammad al Babar's phone and email messages. She added Waheed, Omar, and Mohammed to the list for electronic monitoring.

She also talked to her boss about physical surveillance of Waheed's sons, especially Mohammed. She was given permission to put an undercover agent on the campus of the University of Richmond as a transfer student studying physics, like Mohammed. Hopefully he could get close to Mohammed and build a friendship.

Another undercover agent tried to get a job in Omar's rug cleaning business, but he failed to get the job. Ann put Omar under surveillance to see where he might lead them.

FBI Agent, Roger Meyers called Ann and requested another meeting. He started the meeting by telling her he was under pressure to stop the surveillance of Jose and Carlos. "After the two got their jobs, they started venturing out of their apartment more often. Now, when they are not working they are playing tourist. They went to Best Buy and bought small digital cameras. Everywhere they go they take pictures.

"They've been spending a lot of time learning the Metro system. They seem to go there just to ride the trains. They travel all over the city, transfer from one line to another and ride and ride. They spend a lot of time at Union Station and have taken photos all over the station, inside and outside and on the platforms where the trains stop.

"They have also walked by the White House, visited the Capital, and visited every memorial and monument in Washington D.C. They are always together and they always wear backpacks. Interestingly, when they tried to visit the Capital, security stopped them to remove their backpacks. When they found out they couldn't enter the Capital, they left and came back a few days later, without their backpacks, and were able to go in the Capital on a tour.

"Finally, I kept the best for last. On one of their days of walking around, about a week ago, they talked to two other men, who looked like they might be Pakistanis. It was hard to tell if they knew them, but our judgment is they did. After standing and talking for about twenty minutes, the four of them walked to a Starbucks and sat inside drinking coffee and talking. When they came out Jose and Carlos went one way and the other two went the opposite. We couldn't tail both groups so we stayed with Jose and Carlos. However, Ann, how would you like some photos of our newly found friends?"

Roger took the photos out of a folder and slid them across the table to Ann. She smiled and almost exclaimed, "Well done, Roger. I was about to go to sleep listening to Jose and Carlos' activities, but it was worth the wait. I hope this means your boss will let us keep the surveillance going for a while longer?"

"He has agreed, but the guys doing the surveillance say they don't get paid enough to watch these guys. They are unbelievably boring."

Ann said, "Sometimes it takes time, but I am convinced these two are not good people. I'll take the photos and see if we can identify either of them. I assume your guys have no idea where they were headed when they left Starbucks?"

Roger said, "It could have been anywhere. Sorry."

Ann finished, "Thanks for your help, Roger. I'll let you know if we find anything on the two newcomers.

Ann ran the pictures through facial recognition and sent copies of the photos to the CIA station in Islamabad.

Several days later Ann received a message from Islamabad. The picture of one of the men identified Faisal Uzmani, a suspected terrorist in an Al Qaeda cell, believed to be working out of the northwest region of Pakistan. The leader of that Al Qaeda cell was believed to be Akbar Khan. They had been active in Afghanistan and Pakistan. No photos of Akbar Khan existed.

There was old information that at one time Akbar Khan was thought to be close to Zawahiri.

* * *

Khalid and Masood rested for a few days after they arrived in Richmond. The trip across the U.S. had been educational and fascinating, but it was stressful, especially for Khalid who had done all the driving.

They agreed their car needed to stay in the garage out of sight, so they began walking around the neighborhood. They found a small shopping center about four blocks away. There was a grocery store, a drug store and a few other stores that were of no interest to them. After a couple more days of walking in all directions, they concluded the shopping center was their only alternative within a six-block radius in any direction. They were in a quiet neighborhood of single-family houses. They saw children occasionally out on the street playing, and once in a while saw other adults walking, but it seemed that everybody drove when they needed to go somewhere.

Unless they wanted to risk being picked up without a driver's license, in a car with no registration documents, they were stuck just walking to the store.

Masood asked, "Do you think it is possible for one of us to get a driver's license in Virginia?"

Khalid responded, "I don't know, but we can look into it. Maybe we can find a way to call someone and ask questions over the phone."

Masood said, "The girl at the checkout counter in the drug store was nice and friendly. Maybe we can ask her how someone visiting the U.S. can get a driver's license. She might tell us what we can do."

"Great idea. Tomorrow you get to ask her. I'll go with you for moral support."

Khalid and Masood walked to the drug store and luckily the same girl was working the check out counter. Masood waited until she was not busy, walked up to her, and said, "Excuse me, can I ask you a question?"

She smiled at Masood and asked, "What can I do to help? By the way, my name is Sue, as you can see from my nametag. What's yours?"

"I am Masood. We are visiting the U.S. for the first time, and feel like we could see more of the country if we had a driver's license. Do you know where we can go to find out what we have to do to get one?"

"Sure, Masood. You need to go to the DMV. That stands for Department of Motor Vehicles. That's where we go to get our license renewed or to get a new one, and that is where to go if you have a car that needs to be registered. I don't have a clue what the rules are for getting a driver's license if you are a foreigner, but they will tell you at the DMV."

"Thanks Sue. Do you know where the DMV is located? How far is it from here?"

"You can get the address from the phone book. I think it is about two or three miles that way." She pointed out the front door to the left. Masood and Khalid's house was to the right.

Masood asked, "I am sorry, I just have one more question. Could we call a taxi to come get us here and take us to the DMV?"

"Sure. Do you want me to call now?"

Masood turned to Khalid to see what he thought, and Khalid said, "Why don't we come back tomorrow and try to call a cab then."

Masood turned back toward Sue and echoed what Khalid had said. As they were leaving, Masood sheepishly smiled and said, "Thank you Sue. We will see you tomorrow."

Sue said, "Okedoke."

Masood didn't understand that word. That was at least the second time he had heard it.

They talked again about the risks of getting a driver's license. They agreed they needed more freedom, and the inconvenience of being stuck in the house was too much for them to handle.

The next day they walked back to the drugstore. Sue was working the checkout counter and said, "Hi, welcome back. Going to the DMV today?"

Masood said, "Yes, we were wondering if you could call us a taxi?"

Masood decided that Khalid would be the one to try to get the license. At the information counter Khalid asked, "I am visiting the U.S. for a few months, and want to know if I can apply for a driver's license?"

A large black woman sitting behind the counter looked at him, and asked, "Do you have a driver's license from your home country?"

Khalid had to think fast. He had a license in Pakistan, but his passport said he was from Saudi Arabia. What should I do? He responded, "I have a driver's license in Saudi Arabia, but I did not bring it with me."

"The woman, appearing barely interested, asked, "How long will you be here?"

"I have a six month tourist visa."

"You can get one that is good as long as your visa is valid. But because you don't have your driver's license with you, you need to take a written test. Take this book and study the traffic rules and laws. Come back when you want to take the test."

"Thank you. I'll be back after I have studied."

When they walked out, their taxi was still waiting for a fare. He took them back to the drugstore. They didn't want him to take them to their house, for safety reasons.

The next day Khalid and Masood went back to the DMV. Khalid took the test and passed. The DMV took his photo and made him a driver's license that expired on the expiration date of his visa. Khalid now had a paper trail showing that he was in the U.S.

Chapter 16

Walter Bennett hit the ground running. His experience in business had developed his skills for multi-tasking. The job of Chief of Staff required someone who could efficiently watch over many priorities at the same time and appropriately filter and prioritize the time demands placed on the President. It required an understanding of all the issues facing the President and a general understanding of where she stood on the issues.

The President and Walter continued the tradition that she and Judy had started, having breakfast together. This time gave Walter the opportunity to become more familiar with Carolyn's positions on issues, and which issues were most important to her.

He chose to use dinners as a way to meet others in Washington. Whenever he was not needed at one of the President's dinner meetings, he would arrange one for himself. He started choosing one person at a time, but after a few one on ones, he decided to accelerate the process by inviting two or three people to join him for dinner. He had little or no previous working relationship with most of his invitees. Luckily, he genuinely enjoyed meeting people and getting to know them.

His wife, Sarah, decided to spend about half her time in Washington and the other half in San Francisco, closer to their children. She convinced Walter that he needed a suitable residence if he was going to be working for the President, so on her first trip to Washington she went house hunting. She quickly found a charming residence in Georgetown. They bought it, and she set about furnishing it. When she was in town, Walter included her in as many functions as possible. She was comfortable with Carolyn, and the President seemed to enjoy having her around.

The President was pleased with the start of the Immigration Reform process, but she was not pleased with the rate of movement through Congress. The congressional leaders had chosen to form a joint committee to address comprehensive immigration reform, but the committee had gotten bogged down in the details, and seemed to lose their sense of urgency.

The President and Walter talked about how to get Congress to accelerate their work on immigration reform, and agreed that another White House meeting with the leaders was in order.

They were already into November and the Thanksgiving break was only a few days away when Walter invited the four leaders to the White House for a "pre-Thanksgiving" meeting.

The President began, "Gentlemen, I know you are all busy trying to get things done before the Thanksgiving break, but we need to discuss the progress or lack of progress on immigration reform. I know the legislative process, on a complex issue like immigration, is complicated and time consuming. But I also know when we really want to get something done we can find ways to accelerate the process. So, here is my question. Why is the legislation bogged down? Are there specific issues that are standing in the way? Let's talk about what we need to do to get this reform passed through Congress and on my desk for signing before the Christmas break.

Senator Marino, as usual, went first. "Madam President, we are trying to craft legislation that will have bi-partisan support. As you know, we could pass a bill through both houses without a single Democrat vote, but we are committed to building a bi-partisan agreement on these big issues, especially on immigration reform. My general answer to you is there still remain significant differences in philosophy between the Republicans and Democrats. This may sound a bit strong, but it seems the Democrats in Congress would rather have the immigration issues unresolved, so they can use it as an issue against the Republicans in the upcoming mid-term elections. Every time we make a proposal, your side says no and proposes something that they know we will not support."

The President asked Senator Lehman if he had any comments he wanted to share.

Senator Lehman responded, "Madam President, I do agree with Senator Marino that there are wide differences in philosophy that have caused the progress to be slow. I still believe we can get to an acceptable compromise, but it isn't easy."

The President asked, "Can I expect legislation on my desk before Christmas? That question is for all four of the legislative leaders in this room."

"I am not sure, Madam President," replied Senator Lehman.

Senator Marino, the Speaker of the House, and the Minority Leader of the House all echoed Senator Lehman's response.

"Well gentlemen, that is unacceptable to me. I want us to start next year with immigration reform behind us. And I want to know what it is going to take to make that happen. I don't know who is to blame. I know we have differences in philosophy. Hell, that's nothing new. But what is new is a sincere desire to bring this country together. Immigration is an emotional issue, and there are differences in how people feel about it. We aren't going to make everyone happy regardless of what we do, but we are going to make most of the people unhappy if we do nothing.

"Here's my position. Senator Marino and Speaker Wolf, I want the legislation on my desk before the Christmas break. I want you to work with the Democrats and get as much support as you can, but in the end, I want something to sign this year. To help everyone, I'm asking Walter to meet with you to bring a fresh pair of eyes to the table. Maybe he will see solutions to some of the issues that are new.

"I was hoping for more optimism from everyone today. In spite of that, I wish all of you a Happy Thanksgiving. Enjoy your break, and come back with your batteries recharged and ready to solve immigration reform. Let's start the new year working on our next priority, tax reform."

Walter arranged private meetings with the four congressional leaders, all before the Thanksgiving break. He wanted to understand the specific issues that were standing in the way, and what both side's positions were on those roadblocks.

Walter met with the President just before Thanksgiving.

"Madam President, I think I can summarize both side's positions and how the differences can be solved. First, let's talk about the Democrats. They want to deal with the current illegal problem with a relatively clean, clear, short way to a legalized status, meaning citizenship for most. They don't really want to deal with the other part of the current situation, which is the people who came here legally, but are still here, long after their legal status expired. Many of these are students who came to study, and never went home. The other Democrat position is to generally ignore the legal enforcement of our immigration laws, current and future.

"The Republican position first and foremost is border security which you wisely dealt with and is no longer an issue. However, part of the border security issue was about trust, and even though you have dealt with the trust issue related to border security, there is still a major trust issue regarding enforcement of immigration laws, both existing and future. The Republicans want strong enforcement provisions in the immigration reform legislation, but they know the Democrats are not serious about enforcement. For example, how will we enforce the student visa provision in the future when we do not enforce it now? Republicans believe we need an ID for all people coming to the U.S. legally, and enforcement by tracking the ID for those who stay beyond their legal limit. Republican philosophy is to verify and enforce, Democrat philosophy is be compassionate and don't worry about enforcement, except for serious criminal activity.

"Republicans are willing to agree to a shorter route to legalized status because you agreed to strong measures for border security. But, they are not going to compromise on the enforcement needs in the future for people who start out legal and over stay their legal right and become illegals. They don't trust the Democrats when it comes to enforcement. They see it as the Democrats who let the problem get as large as it has become, and will do it again without strong enforcement wording in the legislation."

The President asked, "And what is your recommendation for the solution?"

Walter replied, "Give the Republicans what they want on border security, which you have already done, and give the Republicans what they want on enforcement. Get a shorter, cleaner path to legalization for the millions of illegals now here. It is a win-win. If you hold out for watered down enforcement provisions, like the Democrats in Congress want, you won't get comprehensive immigration reform this year and probably not next year."

The President asked, "Can you guide them to that solution after Thanksgiving?"

"I think so, Madam President."

"Good. Are you going to San Francisco to be with your kids for Thanksgiving?"

"Yes, I'm flying out late on Wednesday and I'll be back Saturday morning, if that is ok? Sarah will leave earlier and stay longer, but that is fine. Are you staying in town, or are you going somewhere?"

"I decided to stay here this first year. I'm going to visit some of our military men and women in the area on Thanksgiving Day. It should be fun. I hope you can enjoy a little break while you are out west."

Chapter 17

The physics students had a tradition to meet Friday nights for some fun and relaxation. Trying hard to fit in, Mohammed joined the group almost every Friday night. This Friday he walked around talking to a few of his friends. Someone new was talking to two of his friends, so he walked over and say hi. His friends introduced him to Phil, who was a new transfer student from the University of Virginia.

Mohammed asked, "Why did you transfer in the middle of the semester from Virginia, and why did you transfer at all? UVA is a great school."

Phil replied, "Well, I had a little problem, and they asked me to leave. My Dad knows some people here so they let me in mid-semester so I could stay on schedule."

Mohammed was curious, "What did you do to get kicked out?"

"I was screwing around and took a pistol on campus. I showed it to a girl that I thought would be impressed, but she freaked out and told security. Dumb bitch."

The next week Mohammed and Phil realized they were in a couple classes together. Cautiously, Mohammed started to build a friendship.

A couple weeks after they first met they were out together drinking and talking about their anger at 'the system'. Phil casually said, "You know, Mohammed, I think we should do something to make a name for ourselves. Maybe I should gun down some dumb students on campus. This whole education thing is driving me nuts. If it weren't for my Dad, I wouldn't even be going to college. I probably would have joined the Marines so I could go kill some people."

Mohammed thought he saw an opportunity. He said, "Phil, do you have any experience with explosives?"

"Well, not really, but I know where we could get some if we wanted."

"Where would that be?"

"I have a couple friends who are in the Marines at Quantico. They do all kinds of stuff with explosives. They learn how to disarm IED's and how to build IED's. They always need money, and I bet I could buy some from them."

Mohammed said, "Oh, I was just dreaming. I think I need to be heading home for the night. I'll see you in class Monday."

"See you, Mohammed."

One of Mohammed's responsibilities in the planned terrorist attacks was to get the necessary components to use with the uranium yellow cake to make the dirty bombs. The plan was two blocks of C4 explosive for each backpack, with two detonators wired to a cell phone.

Mohammed had been quietly searching for someone who could get him the C4 and detonators, but he had come up empty so far. He didn't know if Phil was all talk and no action, but he was the best lead he had found. He decided to sleep on it and think about whether he could trust some guy who was thinking about killing people on campus. He might really be off his rocker.

When Phil got back to his apartment he called Ann. "Mohammed and I are becoming buddies. He is definitely involved in the plot, I just don't know to what extent. Can you arrange for me to get my hands on some blocks of C4 and detonators? He asked me if I had any experience with explosives and I told him I didn't but I had friends in the Marines that do. He didn't ask me to get it, but he seemed desperate. I think he has been trying, unsuccessfully. It will be interesting to see if he brings it up again."

"Great job, Phil," replied Ann. "Be careful with him. You know he is the guy who ran me off the road and rolled my car with me in it. We don't know just how crazy he is."

"I'll watch my back. He just seems like a misguided college student. Any news from your end?"

Ann responded, "Not much. We just keep watching and listening, but every day that passes makes me more nervous. I take it as good news that maybe they haven't yet found the explosives they need. That tells me it may be the critical issue that is delaying their plan. Thanks for the call, Phil. Good night."

Mohammed had been thinking about the two Pakistanis living in the house he owned on the other side of Richmond. They had been there for quite a while, and maybe it was time to pay them a visit. He decided to drive over and introduce himself, even though he knew he was not suppose to have any contact with them.

It was a cool, fall night when he pulled in the driveway and turned off his engine. He rang the front door bell, but there was no answer. He wondered if they were afraid to answer the door, not knowing who he was. He rang the bell again, but still no answer. He took out his house key, and opened the door. Once inside, he said, "Anybody home? My name is Mohammed, and I am a friend." Still nothing. He walked in the bedroom, looked in the closet, walked back out to the kitchen and opened the door to the garage. The car was there, but nobody was around.

He wondered if they had walked to the store to get some food and things. He made sure the front door was locked, and then drove to the nearby shopping mall. He walked around the supermarket looking for two guys who looked Pakistani. The store was almost empty and clearly they were not there.

He was puzzled when he drove back to campus.

Mohammed and his brother, Omar, had dinner with their parents every Sunday. It had become a family tradition ever since the boys moved away and lived on their own. If they were not traveling, they always had a traditional family gathering. Mrs. Masori always looked forward to having her son's join them. She had a large mahogany dining room table that comfortably accommodated eight people. She always decorated the table with a fresh flower arrangement as the centerpiece.

Mohammed planned to mention the two missing men to his father, after Sunday dinner. His father would be upset that he had broken the rules by trying to contact the two men, but it was important to let his father know that something had happened to these men.

Omar was already there when Mohammed arrived. They greeted each other and then Mohammed gave his mother a warm hug and kiss, and did the same with his father. They talked casually before the meal, and continued during the meal. Waheed and his wife questioned Mohammed about school and whether he was dating any girls. Mohammed smiled, inwardly thinking, 'when will the routine ever stop?' Omar and Waheed discussed their business activities until Waheed's wife complained that they were always talking business.

After dinner, Omar was helping his mother clean up when Waheed and Mohammed walked into the study. Waheed asked, "Is there any progress on the supplies you are to acquire?"

Mohammed replied, "Father, I think I have finally found a source. You know I must be careful, but I think I will have the things we need in a few more weeks. I have another subject we need to discuss. I know you will be upset with me, but I must tell you anyway. I drove to my house in Richmond where our guests are staying, but they were not there. Their car was in the garage, and everything looked normal, but they were gone. I thought they might be at the grocery store so I went there, but could not find them. I worry that something has happened to them. Can you have your friend try to contact them to see if they are ok?"

Waheed said, "You know you were not to contact them and jeopardize our plans. I should be mad, but it is more important that we find out what happened to them. I'll check to see if they can be contacted. Please be careful, Mohammed. I don't want to lose another son."

After his sons left, Waheed placed a call to his long time friend, Mohammad al Babar. They were very careful with their phone conversations, assuming they were being monitored. They agreed to meet for lunch on Tuesday.

They met at their favorite restaurant in D.C. where they could talk privately and enjoy excellent Pakistan food. After the initial conversation about families and Waheed's business, Waheed told Mohammad that there might be a problem with the two men staying in Richmond. He explained that even though it was against the rules, Mohammed had driven to the house and found everything looking normal, except the two men were nowhere to be found.

Mohammad said, "We may be lucky that Mohammed broke the rules. I am very concerned about communicating by phone. I found a CIA analyst hacking into our computers, and I am almost positive she has the NSA listening to my phone calls. I am afraid if I call the men in Richmond it will alert the CIA to their location. We need to switch to a system of delivering messages verbally. Ask your son to drive to the house again, and see if the men are there now. If they are, have him find out where they were and if there is any trouble. If they are at the house, have him tell them that all future contact will come from him. He should tell them the phones may be compromised. Waheed, my friend, we must use Mohammed and Omar to contact the men when we are ready to implement the plan. I will get word to you, and you will pass messages to your sons during your Sunday family gatherings."

Mohammed drove to the house again. He rang the doorbell and after a short pause a man answered the door. Mohammed said he wanted to welcome them to America, and asked if he could come in. Khalid looked at the young man trying to decide what to do.

Khalid asked, "Are you from Pakistan?"

Mohammed answered, "No. My father was from Pakistan, but moved to the U.S. many years ago, and I was born here. I know you are wondering who I am. Let me explain. I own this house. The man, who is to contact you by phone, is concerned the phones have been compromised. He asked me to check on you and your friend to see if you are ok. Please, may I come in, instead of standing out here? We may be attracting too much attention."

Khalid relaxed and said, "Please come in. My name is Khalid."

"And I am Mohammed."

Masood stood up and said, "Hi, I am Masood."

Mohammed sat in one of the living room chairs, and the two men sat on the sofa. Mohammed asked, "First, I have a question. I came by several days ago, and you were both gone.

Your car was here, but you weren't. I checked the grocery store, near by, but you were nowhere to be found.

Khalid said, "We have been going crazy just sitting around with nothing to do and not knowing how long the wait would be. I got a driver's license and now we go for rides to see more of the area.

Mohammed asked, "But the car was in the garage. How do you drive around?"

"We rent a car. We have only done it a few times but it helps us to get out of the house. We always carry the phone with us in case we get the call. Now you say the phones won't be used?"

"That's right. I will be your contact. When I get a message I will drive here to give you the message personally."

"Do you know how much longer we will have to wait?"

"No. There are other details being arranged, especially the explosives and the other things that are needed. Everyone arrived safely and the others are waiting to be contacted. That is all I can tell you now. Before I leave, I must warn you to be very careful driving around. If something were to happen to you two, we would be in serious trouble. I understand your boredom, just be careful. If you are not here the next time I come, I will leave a note on the counter in the kitchen. I'll give you my phone number to call, but please only call if it is a real emergency."

Several days later, Mohammed and Phil were sitting outside one of the buildings on campus enjoying the cool evening. It had been a nice fall, but the temperature was beginning to drop a little every day. They were alone, and Mohammed asked Phil, "Were you serious the other night about being able to get explosives?"

"Yes," Phil said, and then continued, "I know my two buddies can get access to things the Marines have on base, and I know they would do it for me, if I asked. Of course, I'll need to offer them money. What kind of stuff are you looking for?"

"I would like to get my hands on several blocks of C4 and a similar number of detonators. Do you think that is possible?"

"Anything is possible with enough money. What are you going to do with that stuff? Blow up the university?"

Mohammed turned angry. He said, "You don't need to know. If you won't do it, I can get someone else."

"Relax, man. I was just curious. No big deal. Let me talk to my guys and find out if they can do it, and how much they want, ok?"

Mohammed replied, "Yea. Tell them I want six blocks of C4 and six detonators."

Later Phil called Ann again. "Mohammed asked me to get him six blocks of C4 and six detonators. That will make a lot of bombs, but maybe they are going to use a couple blocks in each bomb."

Ann said, "I wonder if they want that much so they can test some of it first, before they make the bombs?"

Phil replied, "That's a possibility, but that adds another risk for them. If someone sees them testing the C4 that could jeopardize their whole operation."

Ann added, "I'll make arrangements for six blocks of C4 and six detonators. They will all look like the real thing, but they will be fakes. They will also have tracking devices in them so we can follow their locations.

"Good job Phil. How is it, dealing with Mohammed?"

"He is naturally suspicious and cautious. He got a little pissed when I asked him what he was going to do with all the C4, but he settled down, and I didn't push him."

Mohammed and Phil were in their favorite bar just off campus talking about the test they had taken earlier that day. The bar was a favorite hangout for college students. It had several TVs showing live sports games, and had a pool table that was continuously occupied with students challenging each other.

Mohammed said, "That professor is a nut case. He tells us the test is going to be on the last three chapters we studied, and then he asks questions that are on an entirely different subject. What an asshole."

"Yea, I probably flunked it. My Dad is going to be so upset if I get bad grades this semester. He's already cut me off from the money he normally gives me, because of my antics at UVA. I might actually have to get a part time job."

Mohammed changed the subject. "Any news on that other thing we talked about a while ago? Did you talk to your friends?"

"Oh yea. They said it wouldn't be a problem. It will take a little time, probably about two weeks. Here's the deal. They only want to deal with me. They don't want anyone else to know who my source is for the stuff. And they want $10,000 each, or $20,000 total. And I want $2,000 for my role as the middle guy. Once I give them the go, they will get the stuff and then call me to arrange a place and time to make the swap. I bring the money to them and they give me the stuff."

Mohammed asked, "Let me get this straight. I give you $20,000 and trust that you will come back with the stuff. And what if you take the $20,000 and disappear, never to be seen again?"

"I am not going to disappear. I don't know any other way to make this work."

Mohammed said, "I do. I will loan you my old clunker. I'll keep your nice BMW. When you come back with the stuff, I give you back your BMW, plus your $2,000 middleman bonus. How's that sound?"

Phil responded, "Sounds like a plan. Do I tell them it is a go?"

"Yea."

A couple weeks later, Phil drove to the Quantico area and drove inside an empty building just off the highway. Ann Hunt and two of her associates met him.

One of the men with Ann walked over to the car Phil was driving and began to sweep it for bugs and GPS tracing devices. After a minute he turned to Ann and told her it was clean.

The other man took two boxes out of Ann's car trunk, carried them to Phil's car, and put them in his trunk.

Ann said, "That is the stuff you ordered, Phil. I just hope they don't test it ahead of time. You really need to watch yourself now. Once you deliver the explosives you are of no further use to him. We can only hope he doesn't want any bodies showing up that could jeopardize their plan, so he is safer leaving you alone. But you never know how these crazies think."

Phil said with a laugh, "Here's the $20,000. I assume you three will split it among yourselves?"

Ann smiled and said, "Yea, we each get $5,000 and we'll keep $5,000 for you. Good luck, Phil. Take care of yourself."

Phil drove back to Richmond with the explosives in the trunk. He drove to the agreed meeting place where Mohammed was waiting in Phil's BMW. Phil got out of the car and said to Mohammed, "I'll trade you this piece of junk for that BMW plus $2,000."

Mohammed asked, "Does that piece of junk have anything of value in the trunk?"

"See for yourself." Phil handed him the keys. Mohammed opened the trunk and looked at the two boxes. He opened both boxes and saw the C4 stacked in one of the boxes and the detonators in the other.

Mohammed looked at Phil and smirked while handing him the keys to the BMW. "You have a deal Phil. There is an envelope with your money on the front seat. Thanks. I thought I could depend on you, but one can never be sure."

"Will I see you in class tomorrow?"

"Yea, I'll just put this stuff away for a rainy day."

Both men got in their cars and drove away.

Phil called Ann to let her know the transfer had gone smoothly. He said, "I asked him if he would be in class tomorrow and he said yes. I couldn't tell if he was lying or not. If he disappears, I'll let you know. Hopefully, you will know before I do, if you are watching the GPS trackers."

* * *

Ann was having a team meeting. She said, "I think it's time to update our boss and the Director and finally the President's National Security Advisor. Let's review what we know. We have two suspects, Jose and Carlos, who continue to masquerade as tourists taking photos all over the city. They seem to be paying particular attention to the Metro system. We have another two suspects, an unknown and his partner, Faisal Uzmani, a suspected Al Qaeda operative out of a Pakistan cell lead by Akbar Khan. Khan is believed to have links to Zawahiri. Next we have Mohammad al Babar, the senior ISI official working out of the

Pakistan Embassy. And finally, we have the Masori family; the father, Waheed al Masori, and his two sons, Omar and Mohammed. Both sons are under surveillance, but there is no evidence to date that Omar is involved. Mohammed, on the other hand, purchased six blocks of C4 and six detonators with the help of our friend, Phil. The explosives are fakes and have tracking devices hidden in them. They are currently in the trunk of Mohammed's old car. Waheed's other son was killed in a drone strike on December 15th in Pakistan several years ago. And finally, we believe yellow cake was sold by the Iranian Republican Guard to the Pakistan Al Qaeda cell and was successfully smuggled into the U.S., but we don't know where it is. We also don't know if it is real yellow cake or fake. The FBI and NSA are actively involved, and Homeland Security has been briefed. What have I left out?"

George said, "How about other potential dates for the bombing?"

"Thanks George," Ann replied. "Osama bin Laden's birthday was March 10th, and he was killed on May 2nd. Both of those dates are too far in the future, in my judgment. If they are going to try to do it on an important date, I think December 15th is the most likely. And then, of course, December 25th would be a significant day to remember. Anything else?"

George had another question. "How will you answer the question, 'How many bombs do you think they are making, and what are the likely targets'?"

"George, you are thinking like the bosses. With six blocks of explosives we are looking at anywhere from one really big bomb to as many as six. Realistically, I think we are looking at two or probably three bombs, but that is only an educated guess. As to bomb targets, Union Station is a possibility and others could be the White House, the Capital, the Pentagon, the CIA headquarters, and other major government buildings. Also, Reagan and Dulles airports are potential targets. All of the targets are speculation and again, educated guesses."

They all agreed that those were all the important facts and assumptions at this time.

Ann briefed her boss and later they both visited Director Simpson and gave him the same briefing. The Director suggested

Ann give Rebecca Owens an update and find out if she wants to brief the President or if she wants us to brief her. It was a few days before Thanksgiving when Ann met with Rebecca in the White House.

Rebecca listened carefully to Ann's presentation.

"Ann, do you think Mohammed Masori could have the yellow cake? If he does, he could be assembling the bombs right now. Should we consider raiding his apartment to see if he has the yellow cake?"

Ann said, "It is certainly a possibility, but we have no evidence to confirm that. It is also a possibility that it is being held somewhere else. Our plan is to track the fake explosives when they are moved. We think it is better to wait for him to move the explosives and watch where he takes them."

Rebecca continued, "Ann, sounds to me like the evidence is mounting that we have a credible threat. I'll brief the President and call you with any feedback I get from her. She may decide to give your Director a call or may even want to talk to you. I will try to give you a heads up if I think she plans to call you, but I don't always know exactly what she will do."

"Thanks Rebecca. I'll let you know when anything changes."

* * *

The Masori family celebrated Thanksgiving like most American families, with a big turkey dinner. This year their special guests were Mohammad al Babar and his wife. Waheed's two sons joined their parents and the Babar's for the celebration.

After dinner the men adjourned to Waheed's study. It was a combination library and study, with bookshelves on two of the walls from floor to ceiling. Waheed had a large wooden desk in the room and a beautiful rug on the floor. Comfortable chairs and a brown leather sofa provided ample places for all to sit.

Al Babar began the meeting. "We are approaching the day we can celebrate punishing the United States for their action against Kareem. Our date for the attacks is the day they killed him, December 15th.

"I have a private house reserved for us to all meet on December 8th, one week before the attacks, to review with everyone all the specific plans and duties.

"The CIA and NSA are monitoring my activities and possibly yours. We need to be especially careful with our phone communications. From this point forward we should have no phone conversations with each other or any of the others involved with our plan. We must communicate verbally or with hand written notes, to be immediately destroyed after they are read.

"In addition to monitoring our phones and emails, the CIA often uses GPS tracking devices. These devices are very small and can be hidden and are almost impossible to find. I believe they have one on my car, and we should assume, for safety, that they are tracking each of you. Thankfully, we also now have very small devices that can be used to block their tracking signals. Before I leave today, I will give each of you one of these blocking devices. Just put it in your car so when we need to get a message to our operatives the CIA will not be able to track you.

"Mohammed, you especially are at risk. When you take the explosives to the operatives in Richmond, be sure to use the blocking device. I will give you extra blockers for Masood to put on each bomb, just for extra security.

"Even with their GPS tracking devices, they may also have us all under physical surveillance. Omar and Mohammed, when you drive to meet our operatives, pleases be sure to watch for someone tailing you and use evasive action to lose them.

"Mohammed, during the next few days, I want you to take the explosives to Khalid and Masood and leave the explosives with them. Tell them about our meeting on December 8th, and tell Masood he needs to have the bombs assembled before the meeting. You will pick up Khalid and Masood and bring them to the meeting, with the backpack bombs. Masood should leave his vest bomb at the Richmond house. You will take them back there after the meeting.

"Omar, you need to go visit the other four operatives in D.C. a few days before December 8th to arrange a time and place to pick them up on the 8th. It is unlikely, but still possible, that the CIA has them under surveillance. So arrange for them to meet you somewhere away from their apartments when you pick them up on the 8th.

"I have maps and directions to the house where we will meet, near Annapolis, on the 8th. We should all try to arrive between nine and ten in the morning. We will enjoy the day together, go over all the plans, and then take the six men back to their apartments and house.

"Any questions from anyone?"

Mohammed asked, "What if there is an emergency and one of us needs to contact you or some of the operatives, or what if an operative has an emergency? Can we use the phones if it is an emergency?"

Mohammad replied, "Sure, if there is no other way, then yes, use the phone. But just assume the CIA or NSA are listening to everything you say."

They spent a little while continuing their conversation until al Babar said he needed to take his wife home. He laughed and said, "Waheed, we have given the sisters enough time together to talk about us. We need to keep them apart so they don't have too much time to scheme against us."

The following weekend, Mohammed drove his old clunker to his Richmond house. He rang the doorbell and Khalid answered.

Mohammed said, "Khalid, please open the garage door so I can pull my car into the garage?" He parked his car and closed the garage door. He and Khalid walked in the house and joined Masood in the living room.

They chatted for a while about how they were doing, and finally Masood asked, "What can you tell us about the plan?"

Mohammad replied, "First, I have a present for you in the trunk of the car. There are six blocks of C4, six detonators, some wire, tools, tape, and several cell phones. I will take all the stuff out of my trunk before I leave.

"There is a meeting planned on December 8th, where everyone will attend and we will review all the plans. Our leader is very concerned about the CIA monitoring his phone and email communications, so he will not be calling you. I will drive here if there is any need for communications. He is also worried that the CIA has devices monitoring our travel so he has given us blocking devices to disrupt their GPS tracking devices. I have one on my car now, and he has given me three devices, one to be put on each bomb, just to be sure they can't track them.

"Masood, you need to have the two backpack bombs assembled and bring them with us when we drive to the meeting on December 8th. The other operatives will take them with them when they leave the meeting. You can leave your bomb here, because I'll be bringing you and Khalid back here after the meeting.

"The attack is planned for December 15th. Everything will be discussed on December 8th. Any questions?"

Khalid said, "No questions. We are ready. If we had to stay here much longer we would go crazy."

Masood added, "Let's get the things out of the car so I can have a look at everything before you go."

They walked into the garage and unloaded the trunk. Masood looked at everything and was satisfied he had what he needed. Mohammed handed Masood three small devices that were the GPS signal blockers. Masood put them in the box with the detonators, put everything in the corner of the garage and covered it with a blanket.

As Mohammed was leaving, he said, "I'll pick you up around eight am the morning of the 8th. See you then."

The same weekend, Omar visited the other four operatives. Before he left his home he made two hand-written notes, one for Ahmed and Fahad and the other one for Faisal and Jamal.

He waited until early evening, and when he left his home he drove around for a while until he was sure no one was following him. He then headed into D.C. and drove to the neighborhood where Ahmed and Fahad were staying. He parked a couple blocks away and walked to their apartment building.

After taking the elevator to the third floor, Omar knocked on their door and Ahmed opened it. Omar handed him the hand written note. It said, 'Please do not speak. Your apartment may be bugged. I am Omar, a friend. Will both of you please come with me for a walk outside so we can talk. Show this note to your friend.' Ahmed turned around and put his finger to his lips, signaling to Fahad not to talk. He walked to Fahad and showed him the note.

The three men walked out of the apartment building and headed down the sidewalk. Omar said, "Let's walk to the Starbucks a few blocks away and talk there."

They each bought coffee and found a quiet table where they could talk. Starbucks was not very busy at that time of night.

Omar started, "Welcome to America. I am Omar, and I am sorry it has been so long with no contact, but we can't be too careful. We are very concerned that the CIA has compromised our phones. All further communications will be verbal in face-to-face meetings, like this one. I am part of the small group of people who live here who will assist you. I am happy to report that all three teams arrived safely in the U.S. We now have all the items needed to follow through on the plan, and a date has been set.

"Our leader has scheduled a meeting on December 8th when everyone will be together, and the complete plan will be explained to all. I will pick you up in front of this Starbucks at approximately eight fifteen am on the 8th. I will be driving a black Mercedes. When you see me drive up and stop, please get in the car as quickly as possible. We think there is a chance you are being watched, and this will allow us to get away quickly and lose anyone tailing you. Have you noticed any men loitering around your apartment building, or have you seen anybody suspicious who might be following you?"

Ahmed said, "No, we are pretty careful."

Fahad added, "It is really great to finally hear from someone. We kept waiting for a call, and we were worried something had gone wrong."

Omar replied, "Nothing went wrong. It took a little longer to get all the supplies we need, but everything is ready. I think it is time for you guys to leave and walk back to your apartment. I will wait a few minutes and then walk to my car. See you here at eight fifteen on the eighth. Great to finally meet you guys."

When Omar walked out of Starbucks, an FBI agent sitting across the street took a picture of him.

Omar drove to American University and parked a few blocks from the apartment building where Faisal and Jamal lived. He walked to their apartment and went through the same procedure with them. They walked to a nearby café, and after they finished their conversation, Omar said, "It is great to finally meet you guys.

I will see you right here at about eight am on the eighth. See you then."

* * *

George was at work in his cubicle at the CIA on a Saturday morning when his cell phone rang. It was one of the tech guys monitoring the GPS tracking devices on the explosives. He said, "George, we have a problem. We just lost all the signals from the devices in the explosives. All the signals just went dead. Something must be blocking the signals. It's possible one of the devices may have malfunctioned, but not all six at the same time."

George said, "I'm in the office. Let me make a call and then I'll come down to see you."

George called Ann and told her the news.

Ann said, "Something is definitely going on. I just had a call from our agent who is watching Mohammed. He said Mohammed just drove off in his old clunker. The agent followed him, but lost him. Sounds like Mohammed is taking the explosives somewhere, and he must be using a blocking device to block our signals. I need to make a couple calls. Let me know if the signals come back on. I'll call you back after I make my calls."

Ann called her boss and gave him the news. He said he would call the Director and told Ann to call the National Security Advisor to give her the bad news. Ann gave the news to Rebecca. She said she would brief the President.

Ann thought about driving into her office, but decided there wasn't anything she could do there, so she called George.

"George, this is Ann. Any change in the status?"

George said, "I just got back to my desk from talking with the tech guys. The trackers are still not sending a signal. I can't think of anything we can do, so I guess we are just in a waiting mode."

"It won't help for me to come to the office so give me a call if anything changes. I told our boss and I called Rebecca. She is briefing the President.

Sunday morning Ann's cell phone rang again. This time it was Roger Meyers from the FBI. He said, "Hi Ann, enjoying your weekend?"

Ann replied, "Actually, no I am not. We just lost track of our explosives. Why are you calling me on a Sunday?"

Well your friends, Carlos and Jose, had a visitor last night. A Pakistani man walked into their apartment building and a few minutes later he came out with Carlos and Jose. They walked to a Starbucks and spent about a half hour inside. Carlos and Jose left together and a few minutes later the other man left. We managed to get a photo of him, but there wasn't much light when we took the photo. It is a little dark, but hopefully you can identify him. I'll send the image to your phone. Let me know if you want us to do anything."

"Thanks Roger. I'll let you know if we can identify him."

Less than a minute later a message arrived on Ann's phone. She looked at the photo and recognized Omar Masori.

First thing Monday morning Ann assembled her team. "Ok guys, we have a couple developments. Saturday we lost the GPS tracking signals on all the explosives. Mohammed drove his clunker somewhere and came back to his apartment a few hours later. Our guy tried to follow him, but he lost him. We don't know if the explosives are still in his trunk or not. Then I got a call from the FBI on Sunday. Saturday night, Omar visited Jose and Carlos at their apartment. He spent less than an hour and then left. I checked with our guy who has been watching Omar and he confirmed Omar left his house Saturday night and returned about three hours later. I have asked our guy who is sitting on Mohammed to wait until he goes to class, and then check his car trunk to see if the explosives are still there. Anybody have any ideas?"

They all agreed there wasn't anything they could do, but wait and continue watching the players. They also agreed that Omar's visit was curious. Why hadn't he just called Jose and Carlos? The conclusion was the suspects were being very careful and avoiding phone communications. They must believe the CIA and NSA are monitoring their phones.

Ann received a call from the agent watching Mohammed's apartment. Mohammed had gone to classes as usual. The agent checked Mohammed's car trunk and it was empty. Ann passed the news to her boss and called Rebecca once more to report the explosives were now officially missing. There were still no GPS tracking signals. The plan was to continue monitoring all the suspects to see what their next moves were.

Chapter 18

Walter Bennett returned to Washington after his short Thanksgiving vacation, and arranged meetings with the leaders of the Congress.

His first meeting was with the Democrats, Senator Lehman and Congressman Caldwell, in Lehman's office.

Walter began the meeting, "Gentlemen, the President asked me to bring some fresh eyes to the immigration impasse. I have done my analysis and I believe we can divide the issues into three major categories. First, there is border security. That issue has been solved, with your help, by going to a virtual fence. Thank you both for getting the Republicans to offer that solution, with your guidance.

"The second issue is enforcement. The Republicans are firm with their demand that the law define strong enforcement procedures for violations of our immigration laws. I know the Democrat's prefer the enforcement rules be left somewhat vague, but if we hold our ground on that issue the Republicans are not going to allow the reform to go forward.

"The third issue is the path to citizenship or some form of legal status for the millions of illegals who are currently in the country. The Democrats want a simple and relatively quick path to a legal status. The Republicans want a more complex and longer path to a legal status.

"To my fresh eyes, we need to find solutions to the second and third issues that both the Republicans and Democrats can accept. I think the solution is to compromise on the enforcement provisions, allowing the Republicans to get most of what they want, and convince the Republicans to accept most of what you want on the path to legalization.

"If I can get your support, I am planning to meet with the Republican leadership and outline the three issues like I have done with you. I am optimistic, with your support, I can convince the Republicans to compromise a little on the enforcement and the path to legalization. Now I would like your perspectives and thoughts on my suggestions."

Senator Lehman responded, "I think you have summarized the problems very well. I can get the Democrats in the Senate to go along with somewhat stronger enforcement provisions, if we can get a good, fair path to citizenship. The two sub-issues in the path to citizenship are the size of the fine for illegals already in the country, and the length of time to wait for full legal status or citizenship. If we can get the Republicans to be reasonable on the path to citizenship we should be able to reach a deal."

Walter asked, "I don't want to get into too many of the details, that is your job, but what are the differences in the fine being considered?"

Senator Lehman said, "We think a five hundred dollar fine is reasonable, but the Republicans think it should be at least one thousand dollars or even more, like fifteen hundred dollars."

"Congressman Caldwell, what are your thoughts?"

"I basically agree with Joe. Our people in the House really don't like the strong enforcement provisions the Republicans are demanding, and the fine is the big issue in the path to legalization. Fifteen hundred is quite onerous on many of the illegal immigrants, and it might result in many of them staying in the shadows."

Walter suggested, "You guys both know the enforcement provisions are somewhat of a blurry thing. We can put strong enforcement provisions in the legislation, but in reality, it still comes down to the way the justice department choses to interpret the law. But, I have to admit the enforcement issue is an important one. We have more than a million people in the country right now who came to the country legally, either on student visas or tourist visas who just stayed after their visas expired. We really need to find a way to deal with these people. With technology we should be able to develop a system to better track these people and reduce the numbers who over stay their visas.

Senator Lehman replied, "You are starting to sound like a Republican."

"Trust me, Senator, I am just trying to find a solution that the President can accept."

Congressman Caldwell said, "I support your plan to meet with the Republican leadership to see what their reactions are.

"Senator Lehman, how about you?"

"I am cautiously optimistic. The Republicans are playing hardball. They think if they stand their ground the President will go along with them. They are using this issue as a test. But, give it a try and see what reaction you get from them."

"Thanks. I have a tentative meeting scheduled with Marino and Wolf in two days. Let me meet with them and see how it goes. We may need to get the four of you together after I meet with them. I will let you know."

Two days later, Walter met with Senator Marino and Speaker Wolf. This time they met in the Speaker's office. Walter went through the analysis he used with the Democrats.

After Walter finished his comments, Speaker Wolf said, "Walter, you have taken a complex issue and distilled it into a pretty simple explanation. I think we can reach a compromise on the path to legalization, if the Democrats will let us put in the enforcement rules the way we want."

Senator Marino added, "I am not as optimistic as my friend from the House. The Democrats just don't want strong enforcement provisions, but we need to deal with the existing people who have overstayed their visas, and future people who come to the U.S. and stay longer than they are allowed. We must find a way to deal with that problem. As to the path to legalization, we are actually pretty close, but we are not quite there. The biggest hurdle is the fine an illegal will be forced to pay. The Democrats want it to be a token amount and we think it should be more significant."

Walter responded, "Thanks for sharing your thoughts. My understanding is the Democrats want a five hundred dollar fine and the Republicans want it to be at least one thousand dollars, or more. I am not here to actually negotiate any of these issues, but what if I can get the Democrats to agree to a seven hundred and fifty dollar fine? That seems like a reasonable compromise and isn't so onerous that it will keep people from coming forward and registering. Let me caution you, I don't have the Democrats support for this suggestion, nor do I have the President's support, but it sounds reasonable to me. The President really wants immigration reform to be completed before the Christmas holiday. She wants a fair and reasonable compromise that will be viewed as a bi-partisan solution to a problem that has plagued this country for too long."

The Speaker said, "Let me talk to our caucus and see if I can persuade them to accept the ideas you brought to us today."

Senator Marino said, "I'll do the same thing."

"That is all I request, gentlemen. Thanks for your time. It sounds to me like we are all close. Let's get the deal across the finish line."

Chapter 19

December 8th

Faisal and Jamal left their apartment a little before eight and walked to the designated meeting place. Omar arrived right on time. Faisal got in the front seat and Jamal climbed in the back. Omar said, "Good morning. Everything ok?"

Faisal said, "Everything is fine. I am really excited to see our friends from Pakistan."

Omar smiled and said, "Well you are going to meet Fahad and Ahmed in a few minutes. They will be riding to the meeting with us."

Fahad and Ahmed walked out of their apartment at eight and walked to Starbucks. They each bought coffee and sat outside at one of the tables on the sidewalk.

There were two FBI agents on duty outside the apartment building who followed Jose and Carlos on foot. When the two Pakistanis went into Starbucks, the agents crossed the street and sat at a table outside a small restaurant.

Omar arrived at Starbucks a few minutes early, but Fahad and Ahmed were already waiting for him. They saw his car pull to a stop, left their coffee cups, walked into the street, and got into the back seat. As soon as the door closed, Omar hit the accelerator and they were gone.

Across the street the FBI agents watched the action. One shot a quick photo of the car license plate and called Meyers.

"Roger, we have some movement. I think you need to call your CIA friend and tell her Jose and Carlos are on the move. They exited their building around eight this morning. They walked to Starbucks, bought coffee, sat outside Starbucks until a black

Mercedes drove up and stopped. Jose and Carlos jumped in the back seat, and the car drove away, quickly. I am sending you a photo of the license plate. The interesting thing is the driver was the guy who visited them a few days ago. I think you told us his name is Omar. I am pretty sure he was the driver today. There were also two other passengers in the car when it stopped in front of Starbucks. One more thing struck me as unusual. Jose and Carlos almost always wear their backpacks when they go out during the day, even when they go to work. But this morning they didn't have them any backpacks. Maybe it was nothing, but I thought I should mention it."

The agent watching Omar called Ann to tell her Omar had just left his house and eluded him when he tried to follow.

Roger called Ann to give her his news. He also sent her the photo of the license plate.

The minute after Ann hung up from Roger, her phone rang again. This time it was the CIA agent who was watching Mohammed, in Richmond. He told her Mohammed left his apartment in his black Lexus a little after eight o'clock. He tried to follow him, but lost him on the city streets. Ann thanked the agent for the news and said she needed to run.

Ann got her team together to brief them. "We have Mohammed and Omar leaving their residences early this morning for points unknown. Omar collected two men somewhere, drove into D.C., and picked up Jose and Carlos. Assuming the unknown men are also terrorists it looks like we have four terrorists plus the two Masori sons going somewhere, location unknown. Possible educated guess is that Mohammed will pick up others, and possibly the bombs, and rendezvous with Omar and the others."

Mohammed drove to his house where Khalid and Masood were staying. When he arrived Masood opened the garage door for Mohammed. Once inside, Masood closed the garage door and asked Mohammed to open the trunk of his car. He placed two backpacks and a small bag, holding two cell phones, in the trunk.

Masood said to Mohammed, "There is something I want to tell you about making the bombs. When I was examining the detonators prior to attaching them to the C4, I discovered very small tracking devices on each of the detonators. I have never seen such small trackers, but someone placed them on the detonators. I removed them and crushed them. They won't give us any more problems."

Mohammed asked, "Are the two backpacks ready to go?"

Masood replied, "They are armed. I have a cell phone for each one, in the bag, and all that is required is for someone to call the number written on the cell phone. That triggers the bomb."

"Great, let's get on the road," Mohammed instructed.

Masood opened the garage door, and Mohammed backed the car into the driveway. Masood closed the garage door, and then got in the front seat. Khalid sat in the back seat.

Mohammad al Babar drove to Waheed's house and left his wife to spend the day with her sister. Waheed rode with Mohammad to their meeting outside Annapolis. They arrived about nine thirty and by ten Omar and Mohammed had arrived with their six passengers. The six men from Pakistan were excited to see their friends and spent time talking among themselves about their adventures arriving in the U.S. and their activities since then.

The house al Babar had rented was a large two story stone house at the end of a long driveway. The closest house was more than a quarter mile away. It was a beautiful, secluded country setting with a gorgeous view of the Chesapeake Bay.

Mohammad let the men talk for a while, and then suggested they all congregate in the living room where he had arranged chairs for them to all sit in a large circle.

When everyone was seated, Mohammad began. First he introduced his dear friend Waheed and his two sons, Omar and Mohammed. He explained that Waheed's oldest son was killed a few years ago by a U.S. drone strike in Pakistan.

Mohammad said, "As you all know we are making this attack on the United States in retaliation for the killing our great leader, Osama bin Laden. We have chosen the date of Waheed's oldest son's death to launch our attack. That date is one week from today, December 15th.

"If Allah allows, we will coordinate all three bombs to explode at ten o'clock in the morning. That shouldn't be a problem for two of the sites, but the third site will depend on the timing of a delivery truck at the White House. It normally arrives around nine thirty, but there is always the possibility traffic could delay its arrival. Regardless, the planned timing for detonating all three bombs is ten o'clock.

"Let me go through the plan so everyone is informed. If any of you have any questions, ask them as we proceed with the briefing. Let's talk about anything that is unclear.

"First, Fahad will wear a backpack to Union Station, and Ahmed will travel separately to Union Station, but close enough to keep Fahad in sight. Ahmed will have the phone that will trigger the detonation. Once Fahad has placed the backpack at the agreed location in Union Station, he will casually walk toward Ahmed and they will exit together. When they are far enough away, Ahmed will trigger the bomb at precisely ten o'clock.

"The second team is Faisal and Jamal. They were able to get jobs delivering food supplies to various government buildings including the White House. Luckily, they have been excellent workers and their boss let's them chose which deliveries they want to make. They have made deliveries to the White House several times and are familiar with the procedures. Faisal will be responsible for the backpack and Jamal will have the cell phone. Once the backpack has been moved inside the White House, and Faisal and Jamal are outside, Jamal will detonate the bomb.

"The last team is Khalid and Masood. This one is a little different because of the security at the Capital building. Masood has fabricated a vest that carries the explosives, and will wear it as far into the Capital as he can go. Khalid will drive their car into D.C. and park it a few blocks from the Capital. As they walk to the Capital, Khalid will follow Masood at a safe distance, but close enough to not lose sight of him. Masood will enter the Capital and walk as far as possible until he is stopped by security. When Khalid sees that Masood has been stopped, Khalid will turn around and walk to the exit. When he is far enough away, he will trigger the bomb. Masood is willingly giving his life for our cause. Others of you may also be captured or killed, but if we execute well, everyone except Masood should get away.

"Are there any questions at this point?"

No one had any questions so Mohammad suggested they all take a break and have some lunch and refreshments. A caterer had previously brought sandwiches and assorted fruits and drinks, at Mohammad's request.

Mohammad and Waheed sat together and talked quietly while they enjoyed the lunch. The other six plus the two brothers sat in small groups and talked about their experiences in America.

Mohammad let them enjoy their time together. This would be the last time they were all together before their "day of destiny."

After lunch they assembled again in the living room, and Mohammad talked about the escape plans. Khalid would drive his car back to Richmond and wait for Mohammed who will pick up Fahad and Ahmed at their apartment and drive them to the house in Richmond. Faisal and Jamal were to return to their apartment and from there, go to the Baltimore airport (BWI) and get on a flight to Europe. From there they will buy tickets for a flight to Karachi.

Everyone else, Mohammed, Omar, and Waheed will return to their normal activities.

Al Babar asked Mohammed and Masood to bring in the supplies. They returned carrying the backpack bombs and the cell phones. Masood gave the backpacks to Faisal and Fahad and the cell phones to Ahmed and Jamal.

Mohammad gave them another break and again they talked among themselves and enjoyed the beautiful setting. Around three o'clock he suggested it was time to start leaving. Mohammed left first, and twenty minutes later Omar left, and finally Mohammad and Waheed drove away.

* * *

Ann was in her apartment fixing dinner for herself when her phone rang. Roger Meyers said, "Hi Ann, had your dinner yet?"

She replied, "I'm fixing it right now. Why, what's up?"

"Well, maybe nothing, but just maybe something important. Remember this morning when Jose and Carlos left their apartment, my guy noticed that neither of them were wearing their backpacks, which was unusual. Well, they just walked back to their apartment, and Carlos was wearing a backpack. How much would you like to bet that backpack has a bomb in it?"

Ann said, "I won't take that bet, because I think you may be right. I need to call my boss and recommend we take those two guys down. I don't like not knowing where the explosives went. These guys have had time since we lost the explosives to make the bombs. It is likely they all got together somewhere today, and the plan is about to happen.

"Is the FBI interested in participating in the capture of Jose and Carlos if I can get the approval from the bosses? What I am thinking is we take them from their apartment, collect the backpack and anything else that is relevant, and take them somewhere to interrogate them."

Roger replied, "Absolutely Ann, the FBI wants to be involved. Actually, you get the approval and we will do the work. The FBI should take the lead on capturing these two guys, but you are more than welcome to participate with us, if you want."

Ann responded, "Let me make a phone call and see if I have the support for action. How long will it take you to assemble a team to raid the apartment once we get the green light?"

"A couple hours, maybe three. I'll start getting them ready right away, and have them on standby when we need them."

"Talk to you later, Roger. Thanks for the call."

Ann called her boss, "Sir, sorry to bother you at home, but we have a situation. She briefed him on the day's activities and then said, "Jose and Carlos just returned to their apartment and one of them was carrying a backpack. They were not wearing backpacks when they left the apartment this morning. Roger Meyers, at the FBI, and I both think that backpack has one of the bombs in it. It is my recommendation we raid their apartment, take them into custody, and find out if one of the bombs and other evidence is in the apartment."

Ann's boss said, "I'll call the Director and see if he supports the raid. I'll call you back."

An hour later Ann's phone rang and it was the Director of the CIA.

"Hi Ann, sounds like things might be heating up. We have a meeting at the White House in an hour. Can you get yourself there? They will be expecting you. I'll see you there."

Ann replied, "Yes sir. I'll be at the White House in an hour."

* * *

December 9th

Fahad and Ahmed were sound asleep after a long, exciting day with their friends, when they heard the crash of their apartment door. A moment later, they were surrounded by men, dressed in black, aiming assault weapons at them, someone turned on the lights in the bedroom and the living room.

It was 4 o'clock in the morning. They were hoisted out of their beds and their hands were restrained behind their backs. Next they were blindfolded. Agent Roger Meyers, CIA agent Ann Hunt, and an FBI bomb specialist, Johnny, accompanied the six-man FBI assault team.

While the FBI team walked the suspects down the stairs and out to the two vans waiting at the curb, Meyers and Hunt began photographing everything in the apartment, and Johnny began looking for the backpack.

The two vans, with Jose and Carlos in custody, departed for Quantico.

Johnny found three backpacks in the bedroom closet, lying on the floor in plain sight. He cautiously examined the backpacks, and concluded two were empty and one appeared to be full of something fairly heavy. He very carefully picked up the heavy one, and carried it downstairs and out to another van, waiting at the curb. It was a special van used by the FBI bomb squads. He placed the backpack in a storage unit that had been specially built for transporting bombs.

Back upstairs Ann and Roger continued photographing and processing the rooms. They collected the passports, computer, and the envelop of money. In the bedroom they found three cell phones. One of the phones had a little piece of paper taped to it with a phone number written on it. Ann remembered the first time the FBI had searched the apartment there were no phones.

When Johnny returned to the apartment, they all looked at the other two backpacks. Johnny decided to carefully unzip them to see if they were totally empty. He found a light windbreaker in one and a baseball cap in the other. They decided to take them along as part of the evidence. The bomb expert told them he was leaving to take the suspected bomb to Quantico for analysis.

Roger said to Ann, "I'll have our crime scene investigators come over later this morning and go over the apartment with a fine tooth comb. When we leave, I think the door will still close, and I will put some of our yellow tape across the door.
I'll have someone contact the building manager and inform him that the door was slightly damaged, and that the two occupants were taken into custody for questioning. We will also ask him to contact the FBI if anyone comes looking for them."

Ann said, "Sounds good. Let's take the evidence down to your car and get on the road to Quantico. I want to know what the bomb guys find as soon as possible."

By the time Ann and Roger got to Quantico, the bomb guys were heavy into their work. They had x-rayed the backpack and determined there was something inside that was being shielded by lead, plus two blocks of explosive, a detonator, wiring, and a phone. They had checked the backpack for radiation, but found none above the normal level. They had also checked for booby traps, but were pretty sure there were none. Ann and Roger arrived just as they were beginning to open the backpack. The room where the men were working was sealed, but Ann and Roger were able to watch through a bombproof window and communicate with the workers on an intercom.

Johnny, who had accompanied Ann and Roger to the apartment, talked to them as the backpack was unzipped, "It looks like a pretty simple homemade device. There are two blocks of C4, hopefully not active, and a detonator attached to each block. The detonators are wired to the cell phone. All of what I just described is sitting on a lead container shielding something, possibly your yellow cake. We are going to disconnect the wires from the phone, take everything out of the backpack except the lead container, and then take the backpack to a different building where we will determine if the contents are radioactive. That will take a little while, probably an hour of more."

Ann said into the intercom, "Can you check the detonators to see if there is a GPS tracking device in each of them? We put a very small one in all the detonators, and it would help to know if they were removed or if they are still there, but just not transmitting."

"Hold on a minute and let me check." He examined both detonators thoroughly and came back on the intercom, "If there were tracking devices, they aren't there anymore."

Ann said, "Thanks. One more thing, can you check to determine if the C4 is active?"

"I'll have one of the guys check it for you and let you know after we complete the test."

Ann said, "We're going to talk to the suspects. We will be there when you have any answers on the yellow cake and C4."

The two suspects were sitting in separate rooms. Their blindfolds and hand restraints had been removed. When they were taken from their apartment they were only wearing their underwear. Once they arrived at Quantico, they were given plain orange jumpsuits and slippers to wear.

Ann picked one of the suspects to question, and Roger took the other one.
Ann started her interrogation, "Are you Jose or Carlos?"

He responded, "My name is Carlos."

"Carlos, we know your Venezuelan passport is a fake. Would you like to tell me your real name?"

There was no answer.

"Carlos, I was hoping we could have a friendly conversation and get acquainted. Would you be willing to do that?"

Again, there was no answer.

"Ok Carlos, I'm going to let you sit here for a while, and think about your situation. If you are willing to talk to us and help us, it can change the way you are treated, and can affect your future. I really don't care. It's your choice."

Ann stood and slowly walked to the door, and closed it behind her. A few minutes later, Roger came out of the other interrogation room with the same result.

It was about eight o'clock in the morning when Ann decided it was time to make a couple calls. First she called Rebecca.

Ann said, "Hi Rebecca, sorry to call you a little early, but I wanted you to have our current status. The raid went off without a hitch. Two suspects were taken into custody and are now at Quantico, but are not talking. The backpack was found in the bedroom closet, and was taken by the FBI bomb expert to Quantico for inspection. There was a bomb in the backpack. It was comprised of two blocks of C4, two detonators connected to a cell phone, and a lead package of, as yet, an unidentified substance. We should have an answer within an hour or two if it is yellow cake or something else. We have three cell phones, a computer, and assorted other evidence that we will study to see if we can learn any names, places, timing, etc. The tracking devices we put in the detonators had been removed, so we should assume someone, probably the bomb maker, found the tracking devices and destroyed them. We are also checking the C4 to be sure it is the inactive stuff we sold to Mohammed. I will give you a call as soon as we know more about the material in the lead shielded package."

Rebecca said, "Great job, Ann. Glad we listened to you. I will let the President know the status. Thanks."

Next Ann called the Director and her boss. Neither of them answered. She left a voice mail for each of them asking them to call her when they got her message. Then she called George.

He said, "Hi. You coming in today?"

Ann walked him through her last twelve hours, starting with the call from the Director asking her to meet him at the White House. After she got George up to date, she asked him to brief the team. Ann said, "One final thing. Based on this first bomb, if they are consistent, there will be two other bombs we need to find, and we aren't any closer to knowing the timing or targets of the attack. Tell everyone to keep at it. We need some more answers."

George said, "Ok boss. You probably should think about catching a catnap sometime. I think we are in for some more busy days."

Ann got a phone call from Johnny, the bomb expert.

"I have some good news and some bad news. Which do you want first?"

Ann said, "Get the bad news over first."

Johnny replied, "Ok, the lead shielded package contains uranium yellow cake. A little exposure wouldn't kill you, but it is definitely radioactive. It sure would cause panic if a bomb of that stuff were detonated in a metropolitan area. However, the good news is the C4 is inactive and the detonators are also inactive. So, if someone were to call the phone number of the phone we found in the backpack, nothing would happen. It will not explode."

Ann said, "Overall Johnny, that is great news. All we have to do now is find the other bombs before the terrorists figure out the C4 and detonators are fakes.

Ann called Rebecca again, and gave her the update on the yellow cake and the C4. Then she called her boss and the Director again, and this time she got both of them. She gave them a full briefing on the raid and what they had learned since getting to Quantico. She called George again and gave him the latest news on the yellow cake and C4.

* * *

Masood and Khalid got up the day after their meeting, glad to know their mission was only a few days away. They were sitting at the kitchen table having their breakfast when Khalid said, "Do you have anything special you want to do for the next few days?"

Masood replied, "You know something, Khalid? We are not too far from the Atlantic Ocean. It was so beautiful at the Chesapeake Bay, I was thinking we should rent a car for a couple days and drive to the coast so I can see the Atlantic Ocean. I would like to walk along the beach."

Khalid could tell Masood was feeling a little melancholy. He said, "Masood, if you want to see the Atlantic Ocean, I would be happy to drive you there."

Masood asked, "You don't think it is too much risk, do you?"

"No, I will be very careful driving and we shouldn't have any problems."

Faisal and Jamal awoke, feeling happy the waiting was almost over. Today was a workday so they ate a light breakfast, grabbed their backpacks, and took a taxi to work.

Mohammed and Omar went about their normal routine. Omar went to work and Mohammed went to class.

Ann spent the rest of the day going through all the evidence collected at Jose and Carlos' apartment. She found nothing that showed anything about the other terrorists or the targets. However, one of the cell phones showed one call had been made to a number she recognized as belonging to Mohammad al Babar. She counted over one thousand photos that had been downloaded to the computer. They had photos of everything all over Washington. The only thing curious was the large number of photos of the Metro system, especially Union Station. Her best guess was their target had been Union Station. The questions remained, are there one or two more bombs, what are the targets, and when will the attacks happen? Ann was convinced it would happen sometime in the next several days, but the most likely was December 15, because that was the anniversary of Kareem's death.

Late that afternoon Homeland Security issued a security alert to the greater Washington D.C. area, raising the threat level to the highest possible, meaning an attack was imminent. Ann had provided the photo of Faisal Uzmani, the only suspected terrorist who had been identified. Homeland Security included the photo of Uzmani with their security alert.

An FBI forensic team went to the apartment where Jose and Carlos were taken into custody, and went over every inch of the apartment. They found nothing of any value from their investigation. They removed the bugs the FBI had planted and the FBI surveillance team continued to watch the apartment building in case Omar or someone else came by.

Khalid rented a car and drove Masood on a quiet ride to Ocean City, Maryland. They spent two nights in Ocean City and then safely returned to their Richmond safe house. Ocean City had been cold and windy and nearly deserted, which was normal for the winter season. They had walked along the beach and spent time walking the boardwalk. Masood was lost in his own thoughts, realizing he was about to commit suicide for the greater good of Al Qaeda. He was prepared to make the sacrifice, but he had moments when he wondered if it would be worth it. After they returned to Richmond they spent most of their time in the house. On December 14th Masood decided he wanted to walk to the drugstore to see Sue one final time. Khalid said he would join him, and together they walked to the drugstore.

They wandered around the store looking at things on the shelves. Masood bought an ice cream bar and a bottle of water. He took them to the front counter where Sue was on duty, looking bored.

Masood put the items on the counter and said, "Hi Sue, how are you?"

Sue said, "Fine, it's a slow day. How are you guys doing?"

Masood responded, "We just got back from Ocean City. I had never seen the Atlantic Ocean, so we decided to take a trip for a couple days. It was really beautiful."

Sue said, "Wasn't it cold? Nobody goes to the beach in the winter."

"It was cold and windy, but we just wanted to see it, so we did."

Masood paid for his ice cream and water, and Sue said, "Thanks guys. It was good to see you." She looked at Masood and added, "Hope you enjoy the ice cream."

Masood replied, "Thank you Sue. Goodbye."

* * *

December 15th

      Masood and Khalid awoke early. Masood took a long shower and prepared himself for his mission. He had fabricated a vest that held the lead shielded container, the blocks of C4, the detonators and the phone. It was bulky, but when he wore the vest and covered it with a large coat he had bought for the occasion, he looked like a heavy man with a beer belly. Khalid backed the car out of the garage, closed the garage door, and waited for Masood to join him in the car. It was about an hour drive, but with the expected traffic delays, they left at eight o'clock, allowing plenty of time to be in place on time.

      Faisal and Jamal got up at their normal time and got ready to go to work. Faisal carried the backpack over one shoulder, and Jamal put the phone in his pocket. They walked onto the street and caught a taxi to work.
      When they arrived, they said hi to some of the other workers, and Faisal placed his backpack inside the warehouse along the wall where he had done the same thing each time he came to work. They had pre-arranged with their boss that they would work together today on the same truck. Their first stop on the schedule was the White House. Faisal and Jamal said hi to their boss and began loading all the boxes that were to go on their truck for the first run of deliveries. They packed the truck in reverse order, putting the boxes for the last stop on first and the boxes for the White House on last. When they were loading the White House boxes, Faisal casually picked up his backpack and put it into an empty food box and placed it on the truck. They pulled out headed for their first delivery scheduled at the White House at nine forty-five am.

      Ann sat at her desk feeling the tension. She knew today was the most likely day for the attack. Everything had been so quiet since the raid on the apartment. Mohammed had been going to classes every day, and Omar went to work cleaning rugs. Jose and Carlos remained uncooperative and refused to talk to the professional interrogators. With the restrictions on the interrogators, it was unlikely they were going to learn anything in time to be of any help.

Ann's phone rang and she grabbed for it, "Hello?"

"Hi Ann, it's Warren Simpson, anything happening?"

"No sir, not yet. It is a helpless feeling, but I still think today is the day. I'll give you a call if I hear anything, sir."

The Director added, "Sometimes, after we have done all we can, we just have to sit and wait, Ann."

The delivery truck arrived at the White House at nine fifty, a few minutes late. They were checked in by security and drove to the delivery area, like they had done dozens of times before. Faisal and Jamal began unloading the boxes and carrying them into the storage area. There were two security guards standing together chatting. As Faisal walked by carrying a box, the security guard recognized him from the Homeland Security alert. He casually walked away and spoke into his phone, "Red alert, suspected terrorist on the premises, unloading area." He walked back to the other security guard and just stood there observing the situation. Faisal and Jamal continued unloading the boxes from the truck.

Thirty seconds after the security alert a Secret Service Agent opened the door to the Oval Office and walked toward the President, who was in the middle of a meeting. He said, "Madam President, we have a security incident, please come with me, right now." He didn't wait for her to react. He walked up to her and grabbed her arm and escorted her out of the room. As he was escorting the President out, he said to the others in the room, "Another agents will be here in a moment to give you further instructions. Please stay seated until he arrives."

Within a minute of the first alert, six security personnel, with flak vests and assault weapons approached the delivery truck. Jamal saw them as he was coming out of the storage area. He immediately reached into his pocket for the phone. His hand was shaking when the security guard came up behind him and put a pistol to Jamal's head.

"Drop the phone NOW, or you are a dead man," demanded the security guard.

At the same time, the assault team put Faisal and the driver face down on the driveway as two team members stood over them with their rifles pointed at their backs.

An assault team member walked over to Jamal, who had dropped his phone, put his hands behind his back, in restraints, and walked him over to where Faisal and the driver were on the ground.

The leader of the assault team walked up to the security guard and said, "Show us the boxes they have just delivered. We are looking for a backpack or anything else that looks suspicious."

The security guard stooped down and picked up the phone Jamal had dropped. He said, "One of the delivery guys was trying to use this phone when I put my gun to his head. You might want to keep it, as evidence. The boxes they were delivering are all stacked over there." He pointed to where the boxes brought in this morning were sitting. "I think there are still other boxes in the truck that had not been unloaded yet."

By now additional security people had arrived to help. The commander instructed his men to carefully search all the boxes that had been delivered and all the boxes still on the truck. He told them they were looking for anything that looked suspicious, especially a backpack. A few minutes later they found the box containing the backpack.

Agent Meyers and an FBI team, including Johnny, the bomb expert, arrived at the White House scene just as the backpack was discovered.

Meyers debriefed the commander of the assault team while Johnny examined the backpack.

While Meyers was talking to the commander, he got a call that there had been an attempted terrorist attack at the Capital.

Khalid drove the Chevy Malibu they had used to travel across the United States. Masood sat quietly in the passenger seat, wearing the bomb vest covered by his winter coat. The traffic driving into Washington in the morning was bad and it took Khalid almost two hours for the trip. He drove to the Capital and found a parking place several blocks away. It was nine forty five when he parked the car.

Khalid said, "I think it is time to go."

Masood asked, "You have the phone, right?"

"Yes Masood, I have the phone, and I know what to do. Everything will be fine."

"Just remember, when you see a security person approach me, call the number. Don't wait."

"I will, I promise."

They walked toward the Capital building and arrived at the bottom of the steps leading up to the Capital at 9:55.

Masood turned to Khalid and said, "This is where we part, Khalid. Goodbye."

Masood started walking up the steps and Khalid waited before he began to follow. Masood was walking slowly when he reached the top step and the entrance to the Capital. He knew the security check point was just in front of him. There were about ten people waiting in line to go through the checkpoint.

Masood waited patiently, knowing that he only had minutes to live. As the line moved forward he was now second in line, then he was next. The security guard asked him if he had any metal objects in his pockets, and to remove them before he went through the screening machine.

Masood said he had no metal on him, and he expected the explosion any second. Nothing happened.

The guard asked him to step through the screener, and Masood stepped forward. The machine alarm went off. The guard asked him to step aside so he could check him.

Masood started screaming, "Allahu Akbar, Allahu Akbar". The guard drew his gun and called for assistance.

Khalid called the number he had been given, but nothing happened. He pushed 'end' on the phone and called the number again, still nothing. He tried a third time and then walked down the steps, away from the capital. The last thing he remembered was Masood standing with the security guard who was pointing his gun at Masood's head.

Khalid walked to his car, got in wondering what he should do. He was trembling and afraid. What had gone wrong? Why had the bomb not exploded? Why didn't the phone work? Why had he failed? He drove back to Richmond, got all his things including the envelop of money, and put everything in the car. He went back to be sure he had gotten everything, locked the door and drove away.

He had no idea where he was going, but he knew he had to get away.

Security people descended on the scene of Masood and the security guard. First they restrained his hands behind his back. Then they walked him to a room nearby they used for questioning people. When one of the officers started frisking him, he said, "He has something strapped to his stomach. It could be a bomb."

The officer in charge said, "Don't touch anything. I'll call the FBI and let them take him somewhere to disarm it.

The FBI got the call about the Capital bomb and sent a team with another bomb specialist. The team arrived, escorted the suspect to a waiting truck, and drove him to Quantico.

Ann got a call from Agent Meyers.

He said, "Thought you would like to know, we have Faisal Uzmani in custody plus one and possibly two other suspects. They were delivery guys on a truck that makes regular food deliveries to the White House. They got the backpack into the storage area in the White House, but thankfully it didn't explode. A White House security guard put a gun to the other guy's head, when he tried to use his phone. We are taking the three suspects and the backpack and phone to Quantico. Almost simultaneously, there was an attempted attack on the Capital. The guy was wearing the bomb. He has been taken into custody and is on the way to Quantico. I don't have all the details, but he was the only one taken into custody at the Capital. You are more than welcome to join us at Quantico if you want."

"Thanks Roger. Great job. I have a couple phone calls to make, and then I will see you in Quantico. Roger, one more thing. You should pick up Mohammed, Omar, and their father, Waheed, before they disappear."

"I'll make it happen. See you later."

Ann called her boss and gave him a briefing on the day's activities. Then she called the Director and told him the news. Next, she called Rebecca and gave her all the details. Ann asked, "How is the President."

Rebecca replied, "She is fine. The President told me, the first time the Secret Service barges in the Oval Office and drags you out, it is a little scary, but it is nice to know the system works. Do you think we got all the bombs?"

Ann said, "I can't be positive, but I think so. I will know more after I get to Quantico and see them first hand. We will be questioning the suspects and maybe we will get something from them, but don't hold your breath on that. I'll give you a call later today with another update for the President.

Ann got her team together for a quick update. She told them she would be at Quantico for the rest of the day, and probably night. She invited George to accompany her to Quantico and he gladly accepted the invitation.

The FBI arrested Mohammed, Omar, and Waheed, later in the afternoon, on charges of conspiracy to commit acts of terror against the United States.

When Ann and George arrived at Quantico, they went straight to the building where they examine, di-activate, and disassemble bombs. They learned that the bomb found at the White House was identical to the one they had found in Jose and Carlos' apartment. It had the lead shielded package of yellow cake, two blocks of C4, two detonators and a cell phone attached by wires to the detonators. The C4 and detonators were inactive, and the tracking devices, planted in the detonators, had been removed.

The FBI took longer with the bomb worn by the Capital bomber. After carefully checking for booby traps, they removed it from the carrier and examined it closely. They found it was essentially the same as the other two bombs. It included a yellow cake package, two blocks of C4, two detonators, and a cell phone. It was crude, like the others, but would have been very effective if successfully detonated.

Ann was now sure they had all the bombs. All the C4 and detonators were accounted for. She placed a call to Rebecca and told her things are never one hundred percent, but it was very unlikely that there were any more dirty bombs. She called her boss with the same news and asked him to call the Director.

Next, Ann went to find Roger.

Roger said, "Welcome, Ann. We have six suspects now. We are keeping them all separated, and we have not started interviewing them yet. Interesting, Faisal Uzmani, upon arrival, demanded to be allowed to call his Embassy. We have not honored that request yet. Thought you and I might want to talk to him first."

Ann said, "It is really important to keep them totally isolated from each other. I don't want them to know if the other bombers were successful. We need to keep them totally in the dark, figuratively, not necessarily literally. I agree, we should talk to Faisal first. Obviously, I don't want him talking to his Embassy. How long can we deny that request, before we get into hot water with "the law"?

Roger responded, "I think we can probably ignore his request for twenty four hours. It isn't like a citizen who asks for a lawyer, where we have to stop questioning him immediately. Assuming he is here legally with a valid visa, it is similar, but not exactly the same."

"Let's go talk to him," suggested Ann.

Ann and Roger walked in the room where Faisal was being held.

Roger started, "I am with the FBI, and my name is Roger Meyers. This is my associate, Ann. Will you please tell us your name."

Faisal looked directly at Roger and then looked at Ann. With a hard stare at Ann, he said, "My name is Faisal Uzmani. I am a Pakistani, in this country legally, and I demand to speak to my Embassy."

Roger responded, "Mr. Uzmani, I will assume, for now, that you are telling us the truth. Unfortunately, you do not have identification on you to confirm you are who you say you are. You should always have your passport with you. If you can tell me where your passport is, I will have someone retrieve it to confirm your information."

"You do not have the right to search my residence without my permission."

"Under most circumstances, you are correct. But you have just been involved in a terrorist act, and that changes the rules. If we suspect you have additional bombs, we can do pretty much whatever we want. In the spirit of cooperation, if you would simply give us permission to enter your residence to retrieve your passport, that could be a step toward confirming that you are who you say you are, and we can verify your legal status in this country."

"I demand my right to call my Embassy."

"Mr. Uzmani, unless we can verify who you are, you have no rights."

"I am Faisal Uzmani and I am a student studying at American University. The university helped me find a part time job delivering food supplies to buildings in Washington. I know nothing about any terrorist act, and I demand to speak to my Embassy."

"Mr. Uzmani, I am afraid we are at an impasse. Without proper documents, you have no rights. We will leave you to yourself for a while to reconsider our request to retrieve your documents for you."

Roger stood and Ann followed him out of the interrogation room.

Ann said, "Let's talk to the driver and the guy with the phone to see what they have to say. Then I can have someone talk to the food delivery company to see what we can learn there."

They talked to the driver first. He had his driver's license in his wallet and it showed his name was Jorge Gonzales. He was twenty-five years old, and lived in D.C. He was visibly nervous. He said he had been driving trucks for the company for about a year, and never had any problems. He said he hardly knew the two guys working on the truck, and didn't know anything about a terrorist act.

Ann asked George to make some calls to confirm the driver's story, and to have one of the other team members visit the company to find out how long Uzmani had worked for them, and any other details he could learn.

Roger and Ann entered the room where Jamal was waiting. Roger went through the same procedure with Jamal. Jamal said he was a student at American University and the university had helped him find a part time job, delivering food around D.C.

He told them his address and said they could retrieve his passport from his apartment. He even told them it was in the dresser drawer in the bedroom.

Roger asked him about the phone he had when he was arrested. Jamal said, "I was trying to call the company to tell them something bad was going on at the White House."

Roger sent a team to the address Jamal had given them. The team collected everything that might be useful, but other than confirming both Jamal and Faisal were legally in the U.S. on student visas, there wasn't anything of any value, except an envelope with a lot of cash. The FBI talked to the school administrator and confirmed both men had registered for two classes, but were not attending class on a regular basis.

Next, Roger and Ann paid a visit to Masood, the vest bomber. He was totally uncooperative. He appeared to be almost in a trance, like he was seriously depressed. He had no identification on him and would not tell them his name or anything else.

Roger and Ann were still at Quantico when Roger received a call advising him that the three Masori's were in custody.

Ann asked, "Can we question them tomorrow morning?"

"Sure, why don't we meet at nine at my office, and we can see what they have to say.

The next morning Ann drove to the FBI headquarters and asked for Roger Meyers. Roger met her in the lobby and said, "Let's use your car to go question the Masori's. I'll show you where to go."

On the way, Roger suggested they start with Mohammed and Omar, and save the father for last.

Mohammed was totally uncooperative and demanded to talk to his lawyer.

As they walked to the interrogation room where Omar was being held, Ann commented, "This may be a short visit if all three just ask for lawyers."

Roger said, "Maybe we'll get lucky with one of them."

They walked in the room where Omar was waiting, and Roger again introduced himself and Ann.

Omar let Roger talk for a while about the three attempted bombings, and the arrests of the suspected terrorists, and the charge of conspiracy to commit terrorist acts against the United States.

After listening for a while, Omar said, "I know I am going away for a long, long time. I have two ways to play this. I can ask for a lawyer and the interview will be over, or I can make a deal. I want a deal."

Roger said, "I am not sure you have anything to offer, but what kind of deal are you looking for?"

"This may surprise you but I don't want a deal for myself. I want one for my father. I will tell you everything you want to know, and I assure you I know everything. In return, I want a guarantee that you will not prosecute my father. He lost his first son to a drone attack in Pakistan. That attack essentially killed my mother and father. They will never recover from that tragedy. They left Pakistan when they were young, looking for a better life, and trying to get away from all the violence in Pakistan. Then, to have their first son go back to Pakistan, and get killed in a drone attack, was just too much for them to bear. Now, they are going to lose their other two sons. We will never see freedom again. I know this. I knew what Mohammed and I were doing was wrong, but I did it to honor my mother and my father. I am actually happy that the bombs did not kill anyone. So, you guarantee me you will not prosecute my father, and I will tell you whatever you want to know."

Roger and Ann were stunned. They had not seen this coming.

Ann asked, "Can you assure us that the three bombs that we have recovered are all the bombs?"

"Yes Ann, there were only three bombs."

Ann asked another question, "Do you know how and where the terrorists got the radioactive material, and how they got it into the United States?"

"Yes. I may not have all the details, but I know generally where they got it and how they smuggled it into the U.S. I will not reveal any of those details until I have your guarantee that my father will not be prosecuted. What is the need to prosecute him? With the loss of his three sons, what more can you do to him?"

Ann said, "Let us discuss your proposal, and we will get back to you. I am sure you are smart enough to know, we will only agree to your request on the condition that everything you tell us is true. If you mislead us with any information that is untrue, our agreement would then be null and void. Understand?"

"Yes Ann, I understand and I assure you everything I tell you will be truthful. By the way Ann, is your last name, by chance, Hunt? I will throw in a little extra about your unfortunate meeting with my brother on the Rock Creek Parkway."

Ann said, "Roger, let's leave Omar alone, for now."

They left the room and Ann said to Roger, "Let's go get a cup of coffee and talk about what just happened."

"Good idea. I'll buy."

They sat in an office Roger had taken over and discussed the proposal. They both agreed this was an opportunity they could not pass up.

Ann said, "You know what, Roger? I actually feel sorry for Omar. He knew what he was doing was wrong, but he did it to honor his family. We should be sending the father and Mohammed away for life and giving Omar the break. But we should take what we can get. We probably need to take this all the way to the President, assuming we can get our Directors on board."

"Yea, I am sure we need both Directors, the Attorney General, and the President to sign off on this one. I'll talk to my Director if you will talk to yours?"

Ann said, "Agreed. I think I should get back to the office and start this ball rolling. I don't think I need to talk to the father at this point."

"Fine. Can you drop me off on your way, or do you want me to catch another ride?"

"I will be your chauffer this time, " Ann smiled.

With the President's approval, the FBI agreed to the deal with Omar. Ann and Roger debriefed him for days, and learned the details on the purchase of the yellow cake, transporting it to Karachi and then to Mexico. They learned how the men got into the U.S., and learned the full names of the six Pakistani terrorists.

Omar also confirmed that Mohammad al Babar developed the plan and was the leader.

Ann and Roger confirmed that the delivery truck driver was not part of the team. And they learned that the terrorist who accompanied Masood to the Capital was named Khalid, and was still missing.

Chapter 20

One week after the attempted terrorist attacks, the President gave a televised speech to the nation.

"Ladies and gentlemen, I am speaking to you tonight about an attempt by terrorists to attack our great nation. They failed, and they will be dealt with appropriately. I obviously cannot discuss many of the details, but I want to share with you some important facts. We have remarkable people working for the American people. Without the relentless work by the CIA, the FBI, the NSA, and Homeland Security, this attack may have succeeded. I cannot thank them enough for their perseverance and determination to prevent attacks on our country. It was a great example of how far we have come since 9/11. The lesson learned from that dreadful attack was that our government was not sharing information among the various agencies. Today, that old culture is dead. The sharing that occurred was nothing short of amazing. I wish I could stand in front of the individuals involved and give them the personal recognition they deserve. Unfortunately, that is not possible, and actually, they don't expect the recognition. Their gratification comes when they are successful at what they do.

"When I became President, I had concerns that some of our intelligence methods and practices were infringing on our rights to privacy and maybe even some of our legal rights. I was even in the camp that believed more transparency was needed, and more open public debate. My first year in office has taught me a lot about many things, including our intelligence services and our security needs. My position is evolving on the balance between the need for intelligence and our needs for privacy and the legal rights of our citizens.

"When you are having a meeting in the Oval Office and a man barges in and says, 'Madam President, there is a threat, please come with me,' and then he grabs you by the arm and practically carries you to a safe place, that gives you a different perspective. Let me state my position as clearly as I can. Do we need independent bi-partisan government oversight of our agencies like the CIA and the NSA? Absolutely. Do we need transparency and an open dialogue about the methods and practices they employ to achieve their missions? No. This is a dangerous world. This recent attempt on our nations capital is a reminder that we must be vigilant twenty-four hours a day, three hundred and sixty five days a year. There are bad people in this world, and too often they want to hurt us. We must have the tools and be prepared to use those tools to keep America safe.

"Before you go to sleep tonight, say a little prayer of thanks to the men and women who serve our country. Thank you."

* * *

Five of the six Pakistani terrorists were sentenced to life in prison with no opportunity for parole. The sixth terrorist, Khalid, drove off in his Chevrolet, never to be seen again. There were a couple possible sightings in Texas of someone fitting his general description, but he was never found.

Mohammed Masori was sentenced to life without parole. Omar Masori was sentenced to 20 years and was paroled after ten years.

Waheed Masori and his wife retired to a quiet life in Georgetown, after selling their business, SPARS. Waheed spent most of his time doing charity work around the Washington D.C. area until his death a few years later.

Mohammad al Babar and his two assistants were expelled by the U.S. government and sent home to Pakistan. Before they left, Mohammad's personal bank account and his wife's personal bank account had all the money, except ten dollars, transferred out to an account in the Bahamas. One day later it was again transferred several times until it disappeared. Mohammad al Babar threatened to sue the bank, claiming he did not authorize the wire transfers. He never followed through on his threat. One month after his return to Pakistan, Mohammad was assassinated on his way to work. The assassin was never found.

Akbar Khan, the leader of the Al Qaeda cell responsible for the attempted terrorist attack on Washington, was killed in a drone attack on December 15th, one year after the attempted attack.

The President wrote a letter to the President of Iran. In the letter she stated that the United States had irrefutable evidence that the yellow cake used in the attempted terrorist attack on the United States was supplied by Iran. She stated that if the U.S. found any evidence in the future that Iran supplied any uranium product to another country, she would consider it an act of war, and would retaliate against Iran. Two weeks later three senior officials of the Republican Guard were arrested and executed.

Several days after the attempted terrorist attack, two million dollars disappeared from one of the Republican Guard bank accounts. There was no trace of where it went.

* * *

The Senate and the House passed the comprehensive immigration reform legislation and sent it to the President for signature. The legislation included the new concept of a virtual fence for border security, enforcement provisions including a new high tech visa tracking systems, and a path to legalized status with a seven hundred fifty dollar fine at time of registration. After registration, illegal immigrants in the country prior to the date of the legislation would be granted a new class of temporary visa, and become eligible to apply for citizenship, but would go to the back of the line of applicants who had already applied.

The President signed the legislation two days before Christmas.

* * *

The President was standing in the House of Representatives about to give her State of the Union speech, recapping her first year and talking about the future. It was little more than one year ago that she had been sworn in as the first woman President of the United States. She was wearing her charcoal grey suit with a white silk blouse. An American flag pin was on her left lapel.

The House Chamber was packed with Supreme Court Justices, the country's senior military officials, all of the cabinet members except one, and almost all of the Senators and Congressmen. The gallery upstairs was jammed with other dignitaries, officials, and special guests. Among those sitting anonymously in the gallery were Ann Hunt and Roger Meyers. Also, in another section sat Mike Sewell.

As the President stood in the House Chamber waiting for the applause to stop, she used the time to reflect. A lot had happened during her first year as President, and she looked forward to the challenges that awaited her. She thought about the changes that had occurred during her first year. Her best friend and loyal Chief of Staff had resigned when it was discovered she had been responsible for multiple murders, misguidedly thinking she was helping the President.

The country had lost the Chief Justice and another Justice of the Supreme Court and the Senate Minority Leader.

And a terrorist attack almost succeeded in exploding three dirty bombs in Washington; one at the White House, one at the Capital, and one at Union Station. The attack was unsuccessful only because of a brilliant and feisty young lady at the CIA.

The President thought about the speech she was about to give. She would talk about the strong economy. After almost a decade of slow or no growth, unemployment was finally down to almost 4%, and even those who had dropped out of the workforce were now coming back and finding jobs. The economy was growing at almost 4%, and the additional tax revenues created by the growing economy were allowing the country to begin to get its fiscal house in order.

She had managed to reach out to the Republicans who controlled both the Senate and the House of Representatives and reach a consensus on the priorities for the country. Together they had reached a budget deal, agreed to a multi-year debt ceiling increase, and passed major health care reform and immigration reform. They still had many other priorities to tackle in the years ahead, but after years of bitter gridlock, they had found a way to work together for the country. She was very proud that the data showed that consumer confidence was at an all time high, and generally the polls were showing that the vast majority of Americans felt the country was finally going in the right direction.

She was aware that the left wing of her base felt like she was compromising too often on her basic principles. She wasn't bothered by that knowledge. She had decided after the election that she had two choices: stand by her principles, fight the Republicans constantly, and live with gridlock for the four years of her presidency, or reach out to the Republican lead Congress, show leadership, and work to find solutions that were best for the country.

Then she thought back to the time just a couple months ago, when the U.S. was faced with a possible terrorist attack. She remembered how strongly she felt about the moral high ground of human rights, the rule of law, and protecting the individual freedoms of all Americans. Then she was confronted with the reality of terrorism and what is required to stop it. She struggled with this moral dilemma, but in the end reached peace with the knowledge that many things are necessary to prevent another terrorist attack on this great nation.

As the crowd finally settled and the clapping stopped she began her speech. She recognized all the appropriate dignitaries and then said, "My fellow Americans, it gives me great pleasure tonight to report that the State of our Union is STRONG!"

As everyone in the audience stood, cheers and applause erupted once again.

The End

Thank you for reading my book. If you enjoyed it, please recommend it to a friend. Also, please take a moment to leave a brief review at your favorite retailer.

About the author:

Kenneth J. Kerr is retired after a successful business career, which included extensive international travel and living overseas in Hong Kong and Japan for almost a decade. He now lives on Hilton Head Island, South Carolina, with his wife, Kryl, and their yellow lab, Etta. They spend the summers at their lake home on Lake Charlevoix, Michigan. Their daughter, Kathryn, lives and works in Washington, D.C.

After he retired, Mr. Kerr also lived in Krasnoyarsk, Russia for a year as a Peace Corps volunteer. That experience became the inspiration for his first novel, 'Life of a Double Agent', which he wrote and self published in 2013, at the age of sixty-nine.

'The First Madam President (and the dirty bombs)' is his second novel.

Discover another book by Kenneth J. Kerr

'Life of a Double Agent'

Connect with Kenneth J. Kerr:

Follow me on Twitter: http://twitter.com/kkerr19963
'Like' my Facebook Page:
http://facebook.com/thefirstmadampresident
Follow my blog: http://kkerr19963.wordpress.com
Visit my website: http://www.lifeofadoubleagent.com

32966983R00132

Made in the USA
Charleston, SC
31 August 2014